Chapter One

Maggie looked at the draped body on the stainless steel gurney. There was no point in waiting any longer. She took a breath and nodded at the medical examiner, who pulled back the cover to reveal the upper portion of the body. Maggie gagged at the stench and covered her mouth and nose with both hands.

She had been warned that after four days in the water there would be little to see in the way of identifiable features. Even so, Maggie realized she had been expecting to see her sister's face.

It was unrecognizable.

"*Mademoiselle?*"

Maggie tore her eyes from the amorphous, featureless face, cheeks bloated beyond anyone's ability to discern identity, only the drab brown hair looking remotely like Elise's. She looked helplessly at the medical examiner. He gave a loud, annoyed sigh, covered the body with a practiced flick of his wrist and turned to the counter behind him, where he picked up a small dish and presented it to her.

Nestled in the little laboratory dish was a charm bracelet, one of two she and Elise had been given by their grandmother when they turned sixteen.

Maggie's eyes filled with tears and she looked back at the form hidden under the laboratory drape. "It's her," she said, hardly recognizing her own voice, so raw and full of pain. "It's my sister, Elise Newberry."

A DNA test at a private lab back in the States would provide final confirmation of the news she and her family had been expecting to hear for three long years. As she turned away to exit the morgue's presentation room, eyes streaming, she realized that even though she and her family had been preparing for this moment for years she still wasn't ready for it.

Three hours later, Maggie sat in the terrace café of the Carlton Hotel and tried to process all that had happened in the few short days since her family had received the phone call informing them Elise was dead. Maggie had volunteered to identify the remains instead of her parents for several reasons, not the least of which was the fact there was now Elise's daughter to locate and bring home.

Elise's daughter, whom no one in the family had ever met or even seen a photo of. Whom, up until a year ago, no one even knew existed.

Maggie pulled out the card with Roger Bentley's name and number on it and reflected on the phone call her father had received from Bentley four days earlier. Although the details of how Bentley knew to contact John Newberry in the first place were unclear, he had told her father he was in possession of information that could help them locate Elise's missing child, Nicole. Before that phone call, the family hadn't even known Nicole existed, let alone was missing.

Now, part one was done. The worst part. The grisly part. Maggie had seen and confirmed the last of her dearest sister in a French morgue. She glanced at her purse, with the French certificate of death inside. She had spent the morning making the arrangements with the city morgue and the police department to have the body shipped back to Atlanta. *Surely that will give Mom and Dad some peace? Having her back—even this way—is having her home.*

Maggie took a deep breath.

Part two of her trip was still ahead of her. And for all her brave talk with her father before she left, she feared it nearly as much as looking down into the face of her dead sister.

She was going to kidnap her own niece, smuggle her onboard an international flight and bring her back to the States.

From the patio of the Carlton Hotel, Maggie could see the *Promenade de la Croisette*, its grand royal palms lining the broad boulevard like Titans shading the procession of a monarch. The air smelled sweet yet citrusy. If her reason for being there were different, the afternoon would have been magical. As it was, she felt as if she had been catapulted into a guest-starring role in somebody else's nightmare.

"Have you been waiting long?" He appeared from behind her and was suddenly seated next to her, breathless yet cool in all this heat. His accent was Oxbridge. "Snarl-up in Nice, sorry," he continued brightly. "You're Miss Newberry, right?"

Maggie nodded, a prick of relief coloring her face. He was tall, with a straight English nose and eyes that missed nothing.

"I thought so. Easy to spot from your father's description," he said pleasantly. "Roger Bentley."

Maggie shook his hand and felt relief sift through her. He looked competent. He looked like he knew what he was

9

doing. "I'm so glad you're here. I'm a little nervous about all this."

"Of course, you are. But don't you worry a tick. Do you have my package?"

Maggie reached into her bag and pulled out an envelope with thirty thousand *euros* in it and handed it across the table to him. His eyes never left hers and the smile never left his face as he tucked the envelope into his coat's breast pocket.

They would be spending several days together, she reasoned. He had plenty of time to count it at his leisure. It occurred to her that she should make him count it in front of her so he didn't accuse her later of shortchanging him, and she hated that the thought came into her head. She needed to trust this man.

He was the one who was going to find her niece and get them safely—and quietly—out of the country. Maggie wasn't absolutely sure why her father had paid for false papers instead of just attempting to go through the French system of getting custody of little Nicole, but she assumed much of his decision had to do with the advice he had received from Bentley.

A waiter came and set down a tray holding a china teapot, two cups and a plate of cookies. Bentley must have ordered it before joining her at the table. For some reason, the thought made her uncomfortable.

"Did you know my sister?"

"Met her once or twice. I'm sorry about your loss, by the way. You identified her this morning?" He took a sip from his teacup.

"I did. She'll be on the same flight with me and the little girl."

"Very nice." Bentley sugared his tea and picked up the teapot from the table. He poured Maggie's cup.

"My father said you told him Nicole had been taken from Elise months before she...before she died."

"That is correct."

"He said you told him that the girl was...*abducted*... from my sister's care."

"By the child's father. That is true.

Maggie pushed her teacup away and leaned in closer to the table. "I'm just trying to find out where you fit into all this, Mr. Bentley. I suppose my question is, if you didn't know my sister, what is your personal connection? Getting the license plate number of the car that snatched Nicole?"

"No, Miss Newberry. *Driving* the car that snatched Nicole."

An hour later, Maggie stood on the terrace of the *Gray d'Albion* Hotel and dialed her parents on her cell phone. It was half past eight in the evening back in Atlanta and she knew they would be waiting for her call.

"Hello?"

"Hey, Mom." Maggie watched the brilliant blue of the ocean in a constantly moving panorama of color. It hadn't taken her very long to realize why all the movie stars and the rich were partial to the Côte d'Azur. It was undeniably gorgeous in anybody's book.

"Darling, I'm so glad you called. Is everything all right?"

"Yes. I met the guy Dad talked to and he's going to help us find Nicole."

"Maggie, are you sure he's all right? This all seems so..."

"No, really, he's very nice. So, not to worry, okay?"

"Does he...did he know anything about Elise?"

Maggie could hear the hope in her mother's voice. "Not really, Mom."

"I see. And did that...did you..."

"It was her, Mom." Maggie wanted to get the words out as fast as she could so her mother could begin processing them, mourning them, getting over them—if that was at all possible. "But this Bentley guy knows where Nicole is," Maggie hurried on. "And he can help us get her."

"Maggie, just promise you're being careful,"

"Yes, I'm careful. Bentley thinks I'll have Nicole by tomorrow evening. I'm planning on being on a flight out of Nice to Atlanta either tomorrow night or first thing the next morning. But, I'll call you first to confirm."

"With...Elise."

Maggie hesitated. "Yes, Mom. And Nicole."

"Is...is the child's father there?"

"I don't think so. Bentley said Gerard left the area and left Nicole with some friends or something. That part's sort of hazy. I drove by Elise's apartment, though. It was tucked away off this little cobblestone walkway and there were big pots of geraniums and things all over the place. You would've loved it. It was really sort of beautiful."

It was a lie, and Maggie didn't know why she was telling it to her mother. She had no idea where Elise lived in Cannes, but every hint from Bentley indicated it was less than what most people would consider inhabitable.

Maggie heard unsteadiness in her mother's voice and didn't know whether to feel glad or guilty.

"Just be careful, darling." The loud-and-clear subtext Maggie heard was, *I've lost one daughter over there, I can't lose another.*

"I will, Mom." She glanced out to sea. "Kiss Dad for me. And don't worry, okay?"

Maggie disconnected and held the phone to her ear for another moment before dialing another number.

I wish I believed half of what I just told you, Mother. She rubbed her eyes and felt the exhaustion of the day descend on her as she waited for the call to connect.

"Selby & Parker's Advertising."

"Hi, Deirdre, it's Maggie. Is Gary there?"

"Hey, Maggie. How's Paris?"

"It's Nice, not Paris."

"Yeah, wow. Here's Gary."

"Maggie, you okay?"

"Hey, Gary. I'm fine. Just checking in."

"There's nothing going on here. Take us off your To-Do list. Attend to what you have to over there."

"It'll just be a few days. I'll be back at my desk at the latest by day after tomorrow—"

"Will you stop? Take care of your business."

"Okay, thanks, Gary. I'll see you when I'm back." Maggie disconnected and slumped one hip against the balustrade that contained the majestic stone terrace facing the sea. She had worked with Gary for five years, and recently she had begun to pick up on a restlessness in him that worried her.

It was hot out, even with the afternoon sun quickly dropping, and she needed a cool shower and a change of clothes before she met back up with Bentley. As she walked back to her hotel room, she ran her hands through her dark hair and tried to fluff it into some semblance of a casual, tousled look. When she caught a glimpse of herself in the elevator mirror, she looked like she'd been dragged down a staircase by her roots.

Her pale blue eyes were set in a heart-shaped face, lips full, chin strong and resolute. It was a pretty face, Maggie knew, but not like her older sister's. Elise had been the great beauty of the family. Everyone knew that.

At thirty-two, Maggie had never been married and was mildly embarrassed by the fact. She worked out three times a week, indulged in a facial at least once a month and had the dead ends trimmed off her straight dark hair every six weeks without fail. Now, standing in a foreign hotel and staring at her reflection in the mirror, waiting and wondering if she could really trust her new companion, Maggie found herself in a situation she couldn't control simply by picking up the phone or rearranging her schedule. She felt out of kilter with her body, her diet, and even the simplest attempts to communicate the most basic requests.

Before she left the elevator and its floor to ceiling mirror, she thought she saw a fleeting hologram of her sister Elise's face form and dissolve over her own. Maggie fought the feeling of melancholia that accompanied it, shaking herself out of the mood.

Missing her and getting sad helps no one, she reminded herself. *Combine it with jetlag and I'll only succeed in making myself useless in every way.*

Two hours later, after a quick shower and a nap, she pulled on a pair of slim white capris and a singlet she knew showed her figure off to full advantage. Although she wasn't one bit interested in Roger Bentley *in that way*, she still wanted to look good. If not for him, then for all the gorgeous people milling about this Mecca of beauty.

Besides, in her experience dealing with recalcitrant clients at the ad agency where she worked, the better she looked, the more pliable the client became—especially the male clients, of course, but she had seen it work across the board. She tucked her purse under her arm and hurried through the lobby of the *Gray d'Albion* Hotel. If there ever was a time she needed to be in control, or at least perceived to be, it was now.

One of five seafood restaurants studding the *Rue Felix-Faire, Petite Bouche* was tiny, frill-less, staffed with the prerequisite surly waiters and absolutely crammed with Mediterranean charm. Bentley had chosen for them to meet at the little restaurant, because it was so close to Maggie's hotel.

She saw him immediately in the outdoor dining section. A bottle of wine was already being opened as she approached.

"I took the liberty of ordering the wine," he said. She was impressed and surprised by the fact that he half stood as she neared.

She sat down and dropped her purse in the extra chair. "My mother doesn't know what to make of all this." She waved her hand at the dining room. "Me, here in Cannes, everything covert and under the table. You." She looked directly at him.

"I should think not." He poured Maggie a glass of wine. "Not the usual thing at all."

The hours that created the meal and their conversation—much of it talk that had nothing to do with her quest for her sister's child—flew away in a swirl of wonderful food, more wine than she ever drank in a week, let a lone a single meal, and the peaceful sounds of the ocean and the wandering guitar-playing minstrels.

At one point, Maggie stared at their dining table as if she'd never seen it before, let alone spent an unanticipated two and a half hours having dinner at it. A chipped crock of goose *paté*, a platter of half-eaten *pommes frites,* mushrooms *Provençal*, the ubiquitous Evian bottles (four of them), and the remains of two platefuls of veal and pasta.

Her eyes fell upon the pretty white saucers with the little primroses painted on them, each looking like an original, not part of a set. She pressed a finger to the crumbs, only a scattering of evidence to tell of the sticky-sweet strawberry tarts they'd both had.

"I hate to ruin the evening," Maggie said, accepting another glass of wine, "but can you tell me how you came to be driving the getaway car, and how you know Nicole's father...and where exactly the slimy bastard is now?"

"The *slimy bastard*, as you say, is no longer on the *Côte d'Azur*, I'm told." Roger took a savoring sip of his wine and Maggie half expected him to smack his lips in satisfaction.

"A friend of mine asked me to help him. Gerard Dubois—the child's father—is his cousin, and he had reason to believe that Gerard's child needed rescuing from the mother, who he said was unfit. I'm just repeating what he said, you understand."

"It's okay," Maggie said, feeling a wave of exhaustion. "Please, go on."

"Well, he said the mother was a drug addict. I was asked to give assistance in snatching the child so that she might live with her more responsible parent."

"Gerard."

"Right-e-ho." Roger squinted into the crowd, as if expecting to see someone he knew, then played with the stem of his wineglass. "In any case," he continued, "my participation in the kidnapping, as you call it, amounted to driving a car to an address."

"My sister's apartment here in Cannes."

"Hardly an apartment, but where she was living, yes. I waited with the motor running. My friend came out of the...dwelling, with the child in his arms. He deposited *l'enfant* in the car and I departed." He shrugged and took a sip of his wine.

"Where did you take her?"

"To an apartment near here. A jolly nice woman was waiting for us. She took the girl. That's it."

"Were you paid?"

"I told you. I was helping a friend."

"Will you take me to this address?"

"If you like, Miss Newberry, but I can tell you the child is no longer there."

"How do you know?"

Bentley sighed and motioned to the waiter hovering in the wings of the café. "I know, Miss Newberry, because I just do." He turned and spoke briefly to the waiter, his French competent but abrupt. The man disappeared into the restaurant. "Look, she's not there any longer but I believe I know where to find her, and isn't that the whole point?"

"I'd like to see this place that you took her. Is it a permanent address? Does the woman live there all the time or was it just a temporary thing?"

The waiter returned with another bottle of red wine and two chilled bottles of Evian. He deposited the mineral water, one at each of their elbows, and began to decant the wine. Bentley watched the man intently, as if ready to jump in and do the job himself if necessary. Bentley was handsome, Maggie decided, but his features were sharp, nearly hawk-like.

The waiter finished pouring the wine and left. Maggie reached out and touched Bentley's hand as he reached for his glass.

"You told my father Gerard was a very bad man."

Bentley looked at her sadly. "I did not know it at the time."

"But he is bad."

"Yes, Miss Newberry. The child is, in my opinion, in some danger by remaining with Dubois."

"He's had her for six months now."

"So I would say that time is probably critical, wouldn't you?"

Maggie looked around the restaurant, as if expecting to see Gerard and her niece seated nearby. "Is she in Cannes?"

"Oh, not Cannes. Surely you must be aware by now of the cost of a single room for one night in this town? I imagine, as Monsieur Dubois didn't have a *pied-a-terre* here himself—and probably wouldn't have been foolish enough to have taken the girl there even if he had—that she is somewhere in the country."

"And that's where she's been all this time?"

"Presumably."

"And you think you'll be able to find this place?"

"I believe so, yes."

"May I ask how?"

"Why don't we see how things go, shall we? I hate to tip my hand—and by doing so, get your hopes up in case things go awry. Let me try a few avenues, knock on a few doors, and see where it all leads."

"I'd like to be a part of this door knocking, if you don't mind."

"I'm afraid that is impossible, Miss Newberry." Bentley pushed aside their collection of dishes and glasses and drew an ashtray toward him. "I would suggest instead that you try to enjoy what the South of France has to offer. Why not hire a car and see the palace at Monaco tomorrow?" He lit his cigarette and exhaled a cloud of gray-blue smoke into the air above her head.

"There are some enchanting little villages along the way. I personally recommend *Villefranche*—a charming little place—or *Juan les Pins*. You remember the song? Do a little sightseeing and let me see what I can uncover. If it turns out we are successful, you will have to leave the country quickly, with a person who will possess false identification and a forged American passport. It would be best if you were as uninvolved as possible until that time."

Maggie nodded. She knew he was right.

"Just leave it to me, Miss Newberry. If all goes well, by this time tomorrow you will have your niece, her forged papers and two tickets back home to the U.S. Everything neat and tidy."

Maggie stared off into space, across the tables of diners and into the happy nighttime streets of Cannes. Dark gypsies, bejangled and braided, waved their wares of bracelets and bells, beaded necklaces and earrings from the sidewalk in hopes of attracting attention. Some accompanied their selling with soft crooning, which caught on the calm Mediterranean breeze and wafted back to Maggie at her table. The music of the night mingled with the scent of olives and lemons and dusky perfumes that pooled in the air over the little café.

The sensation of being slightly drunk seemed to muffle her hearing and her vision, and she found herself woozy and unclear. But Bentley was right about one thing;

she had come here for a single reason: to find Elise's lost daughter. Elise, herself, had been lost a long, long time ago.

Later that night, after she'd fallen into a fitful sleep that gave her no real rest, Maggie awoke, pushed back the duvet and scrambled out of bed. She flipped on the light in the bathroom and stood on the cool tile as she waited for her heart to stop pounding. She looked at her reflection in the warped mirror over the bathroom sink. *Oh, Elise.*

They hadn't heard from Elise in three years. At the age of thirty-two, she had dropped out of sight, with only the briefest, most painful glimpses of her filtering back to them in Georgia. *Elise had dropped out of her art classes. Elise had had a baby. Elise was arrested. Drugs? Prostitution? Assault?* The news was always vague, and always bad.

Maggie rubbed her hands over her eyes and turned out the bathroom light. She went back to bed, her head throbbing from the night's overindulgences.

As she tried again to drop off to sleep, her mind began to relentlessly review and catalog the day's events. She groaned and attempted to block out the image of Elise on the cold gurney, the puffed mass of tissue masquerading as a face unrecognizable and hideous. It was then, when she was trying *not* to remember the sights and odors of the experience, that a single memory shot through the rest and made her sit bolt upright in bed.

Too distracted by the horror of everything else at the time, Maggie only this minute registered what she had seen: a discolored puckering or dimple was half hidden by the stringy brown hair arranged around the body's shoulders.

Just above Elise's right ear was a bullet hole.

Chapter Two

Maggie jabbed a sliver of toast into the cracked and leaking soft-boiled egg in her eggcup. The morning had started off in a totally different vibe than last night had ended. As soon as she awakened—her head pounding in ways she didn't think people actually lived though—she remembered how Bentley had "handled" her.

Get her loaded and she'll be easy to manipulate. Put her on a sightseeing bus and get her out of your hair.

Well, if Roger Bentley thought he could cut her out of the face-to-face work necessary to get the job done, he could bloody well think again, she thought fiercely.

Especially for thirty thousand dollars!

"I can't say how long, exactly, negotiations will take." Bentley looked starched and smart in the late-morning swelter. He certainly didn't look like he'd matched Maggie glass for glass for over three bottles of high-octane rosé. He flapped his cotton napkin out across his lap and smiled across the breakfast table at her. He had again chosen their meeting place, the sunny and fairly private outdoor dining deck of yet another famous, old Cannes hotel, the Majestic.

"Might be a few days, actually. Need to be prepared to wait. All good things, and all that." He smiled at her and reached over to pour his coffee. "But I'm very happy with my plan—"

"Which you feel no need to share with me." Maggie stared at her speared eggcup, the toast point weakening at the base and beginning to collapse into the murky yellow.

"I hope you understand. I feel that I'm protecting you, Maggie."

On the face of it, she knew the service he was providing here was one she'd be hard-pressed to find someone else to do. If he hadn't called her father, they wouldn't even have gotten this far in their attempt to find Elise's daughter. In fact, up until that moment Maggie and her parents had chosen to believe that Nicole was happy in France—if not in Elise's custody, then with her father.

Roger Bentley had put an end to that little fantasy with one phone call. He convinced Maggie's father that Gerard, Elise's old boyfriend and Nicole's father, was a man who would eventually destroy the child. He insisted that he could locate the child for them and, in a single phone call, the Englishman had galvanized the Newberry clan into action.

That his call had come within minutes of the devastating one informing them of Elise's death by accidental mischance was unanimously viewed by all as enormously fortuitous.

Maggie watched the Englishman in the dining room of the shabby but still elegant Majestic Hotel and had to admit that if he hadn't called and offered to help them find the girl, they wouldn't even be this close.

Bentley attacked his breakfast with gusto, spreading the delicate French jellies onto his croissants with almost exaggerated hand movements, carving up his sausage and broiled tomatoes as if he didn't expect to eat this well again for a very long time.

"*Allo?* Roger? I am here, yes?"

The voice came from behind Maggie.

"Laurent! Wonderful! Come, sit down, Sit down," Bentley motioned to the empty chair next to Maggie. The man appeared to her right, and even without immediately looking up the impression Maggie got was that he was a very big man.

"Maggie Newberry, this is Laurent Dernier. Laurent, Mademoiselle Newberry. He's going to help us with our project. Coffee, Laurent?"

Maggie felt her irritation with Bentley ignite again. She did not turn to look at the newcomer, but tapped the side of her coffee cup gently with a silver butter knife.

"Look, Roger..." she began.

Bentley ignored her. "Been doing a bit of a brain tease on an engineering project in Algeria, Laurent has," Roger bubbled. "What's the name of it, old chap? Rather like that Super Collider thing you Yanks were putting together, I think." He turned to Maggie. "You know all about that, don't you?" He didn't wait for an answer, swiveling back to face the newcomer. "Sit down and tell us about it, Laurent. It's measuring or subdividing molecules or some such thing, isn't it? Terribly clever, our Laurent," he confided to Maggie.

"It was just a consulting job," Laurent said, still not seating himself.

"Of course it was! Couldn't afford the full bill of having you pull on rubber gloves and really going to it, I should say not." He turned back to Maggie. "Man's a mathematical genius."

"My family cannot afford any more money," she said curtly.

"I say, Maggie, who's talking about money? Laurent's here to help us get the job done. The price is the same, of course."

"You are unhappy about me, Mademoiselle?"

"No, no, no, Laurent. Mademoiselle Newberry just takes her time warming up to people, don't you, Maggie?" Bentley smiled, but Maggie detected the slightest edge beneath his tone.

"Look, I don't mean to be rude, really." She turned briefly to Monsieur Dernier without looking at him, then turned abruptly back to Bentley. "It's just that the nature of my business is rather delicate, and I would hope that you'd know the fewer people who know about it, the better. If you say you need this man to get my niece back, well, okay. Just understand my position, if you can."

"I should leave, Roger. She is not comfortable."

"No, hold on." Maggie turned to look at him fully for the first time. He was extraordinarily good-looking she noted, and forced her mouth not to fall open. Broad chested and large, he was easily six foot four. His face was calm, with a sweetness to it that almost seemed to belie his size. His eyes were piercing and dark, almost pupil-less. His light brown hair was thick and worn long to his shoulders.

He was looking at her with a kindness she had never felt from a total stranger before. It was a look between friends. *Good* friends. "I....well, you're already here, so let's just go on, okay?" she said, feeling a little flustered. "Forget it, all right? All right, Roger?"

"Of course, all right." Roger shrugged and reached for another roll. He winked at Laurent, making sure that Maggie noticed.

"If you are sure, Mademoiselle."

"Yes, yes. I'm just a little rattled is all. If you can help, well, then thanks. I appreciate any help anyone can give me." Annoyed and shaken by her reaction to Laurent's effect on her, Maggie pushed her breakfast plate aside and reached for the champagne bottle. Laurent leaned over and took the large flagon from her, and Maggie smiled her thanks as he poured the champagne into her orange juice tumbler.

"Right. Let's map out our day, shall we?" Bentley took a swig of his coffee and dropped his napkin onto the table. "First, I will begin with Step One of Plan A. Laurent, you will take Mademoiselle Newberry to Section Two of Plan A at the designated hour."

"Hold on, Roger," Maggie said, frowning. "Why do I have to go someplace special? Why can't I just hole up in my hotel room and wait for your call?"

"Anyone ever tell you that you have jolly little flair for adventure? It may not be a phone call, that's why."

"I don't understand—"

"*Must* you understand everything? You Americans —"

"And I'm officially sick of the *you Americans* shtick. I want to know—"

"You always want to know! Bloody hell! Can't you trust someone else to carry out the details without your having to know?"

"Roger! *Arretez!* Stop, now, both of you! You are causing a big performance, no?" Laurent leaned over and patted Maggie's hand in a gesture that was half consoling, half reprimand.

He wagged a finger at Roger. "*Mon vieux,* she is upset, no? Her sister is dead and she is....ahh, *triste*....very sad. The *responsabilité* is yours, Roger, *n'est-ce pas?*"

Roger placed his cup down. "I'm sorry, Maggie. I quite forgot myself and the situation. You must excuse me. I know things are very hard on you now."

Maggie knew she must look as tired as she felt. She nodded gratefully at Laurent and then looked into Bentley's canny green eyes. "Do what you have to do," she said.

He smiled at her and then at Laurent. "Good girl."

The street cleaners crept the early morning streets wielding their large garden hoses like weapons, rinsing away the rubbish and debris of last night's party. Maggie watched them from her hotel window. The early morning air was cool; the Mediterranean sun had not yet had the chance to perform its mellow alchemy on the coast. Maggie watched as two bedraggled partygoers picked their way across the rough stones of the *Rue des Etats Unis* back to their hotel. The woman wore a gold lamé gown with a pointy, cone-cupped brassiere over the top of it. Her hair looked like she'd gone swimming at some point in the evening. Her makeup looked it, too.

Maggie watched the man with her, his bowtie limp but still attached at the throat. He was handsome, but not young. She watched them until they disappeared around the corner. On their way back from somebody's yacht moored in the harbor, no doubt, she thought. Most of Cannes's parties happened on somebody's yacht, or so she'd been told.

She'd been in France for almost a week now. Each day Bentley either made an appearance at her hotel to assure her that the recovery of Nicole was imminent, or sent messages of similar content via Laurent. Laurent was a constant in her daily routine: escorting her around Cannes and *Cap d'Antibes*, climbing the hills with her in Monaco, which led to the Grimaldi palace, picking up the tab at frequent café stops, and always listening intently—

sympathetically—to her protestations that the search was taking too long.

She wasn't sure what to think of Laurent. He was kind, and in spite of his bad English she could tell he was intelligent, too. Perhaps too much so. Maggie got the impression Laurent held cards he wasn't showing. Nonetheless, she felt drawn to him. Among his many other talents touted by Bentley, Laurent obviously had a very special way with people.

Maggie forced herself not to think about the bullet hole she'd seen in the body's head—in *Elise's* head. She knew that if Elise *had* been murdered, the way she lived it couldn't come as a surprise to anyone. But whereas the matter of Elise was out of her hands, the case of her daughter, Nicole, was not. Maggie had booked two seats back to Atlanta for the next morning. The thought of returning to Atlanta without the little girl produced a hard knot in the pit of her stomach. *Elise's daughter, lost somewhere in France, in the custody of her brutish father.*

Maggie clenched her hands. She thought of the expression on her mother's face if she got off that airplane alone.

Downstairs, Laurent was waiting for her. He stood next to the *Gray d'Albion* check-in counter, flipping through a Paris *Express*. She hesitated a moment on the staircase when she saw him. His was a rough handsomeness, she decided. Weathered, been-there. She liked it, and she liked him. It was clear he'd begun to grow on her in a way that was pleasant, and slightly worrisome. And she was sorry about that because the timing was wrong, wrong, wrong.

Laurent looked up and caught her watching him from the top of the stairs. Tossing the magazine onto the counter, he bounded up the stairs to meet her, his bulk looking insubstantial and light when he did so. He gathered up her pullman and carry-on bag in one movement, and she thought for a moment that he would snatch her up as well.

She had long registered that Laurent had an unsettling effect on her, and felt flustered at his nearness.

"You had a good night?"

"Yes, thanks. So, now where?" she asked, a little breathlessly.

"*Allons y,* Maggie." He led the way down the stairs. "I have the automobile, this way, so." She kept her sights on Laurent's back as he pushed open the revolving door before her and led her to a waiting yellow Citroen. He opened the trunk and piled her luggage into the back, then looked up at her and smiled again.

"It is not far, okay?" he said as he handed her in, then squeezed himself into the driver's seat. The motor started with a jerk and the car pushed out into the early morning Cannes traffic. Maggie turned to watch his profile as he sped through the streets, whirling down alleyways, only to emerge unscathed (as did, miraculously, the pedestrians) on the other side.

"*La voiture, il est votre?*"

He turned his head to look at her, his eyes wide. "*Comment?*" He neatly avoided hitting a woman walking a French poodle by driving the car onto the sidewalk and then returned to the street.

"*La voiture, c'est voiture.*" She tapped the dashboard of the car. "*Il est votre voiture?*"

"Ahhhhh!" He closed his eyes and smiled. Maggie wished he would keep his eyes on the road. "*Mais, oui,* yes, *c'est ma voiture. Est-ce que tu aimes?*"

Now, that's more like it, Maggie thought, pleased with herself. He spoke quickly, beautifully. There was even a glimmer in his eyes that wasn't there during his labored English attempts. She blushed as she noted that he'd used the informal *"tu"* with her, something she knew isn't done until you've known each other much better.

"Oui," she said. *"C'est très belle."* She clutched the door handle as they revisited the sidewalk, this time to pass a little Renault Laurent obviously felt was going too slowly. *"Mais, vous...vous driv-ez très fou.."*

She edged closer to the window and watched the colored, striped awnings and tents of the city's marketplace spin by. Her eyes caught a crazy-quilt of color: tulips, asparagus, strawberries, bananas, hanging sausages, live chickens caught by their feet and twisting at the ends of long ropes, and all of it flying by in a hectic haze.

"Can we stop for breakfast?" she asked. *"Est-ce que nous arreton pour le petite dejeuner?"*

"Why you are speaking *le français?* It is because Laurent's English is very bad, *non?"*

"Je parle votre langue even worse and you know it." She turned to catch him looking at her curiously, a smile hidden behind his lips. "Breakfast, *oui or non?"*

"Ah, mais oui!" He turned the car abruptly into what looked like a brick wall but turned out to be a sort of bricked-up alcove serving as a parking lot. Laurent was out and helping her with her door before she had untangled her legs from the straps of her purse where it had been sitting on the floor of the car.

She could still see the gaily-colored tents of the early morning market and knew they were on the outskirts of Cannes. Laurent led her to a small café and ordered two coffees. They settled themselves at a rickety outdoor table with a view of the street and, surprisingly enough, the *Chateau des Abbes de Lerins*. Laurent pointed it out to her.

"You see *les Isles de Lerins? La?*" He pointed to the islands off the gulf and then turned and pointed to the hill overlooking the water where the castle sat, tall and ominous. "*Et le château?* Castle, yes?" He lit a cigarette, shaking an unfiltered one from his Mediterranean-blue packet of *Gaulouises,* offering it first to her. She shook her head.

Out of the corner of her eye, she saw their waiter leave the café and cross the street to a facing *boulangerie,* where he purchased one croissant from the baker. She watched him return to the café, place the roll on a small dish and then bring it to their table with their coffees.

Smiling hugely, Laurent took in a full breath while surveying the view they had of the Gulf of Napoule.

"Are we going someplace special today?" Maggie took a sip of her coffee.

"Ah, yes."

Do the French say "Ah" before every sentence they utter, Maggie wondered. It was almost as if even a comment must be savored like a piece of tender lamb smothered in rosemary.

"I will take you to a place. And then Roger will come with the little girl."

"And meantime? More sightseeing?"

"Not today." He paused to look at her, as if assessing how much she could handle hearing. *Or maybe that's just my imagination?*

"Roger will not come with the little girl until late. Your coffee is good?" He smiled at her and she felt a definite thrill filter through her, although whether from excitement or a tiny needle of fear, she wasn't sure. Did she imagine that his English seemed to be remarkably better today?

"So, we're still basically waiting for Roger, as usual. Is that it?"

"*Oui.* We are waiting again." Laurent finished his coffee and stared out at the Gulf, its startling blueness twinkling in the sunlight. His eyes suddenly looked hooded and careful to her. It occurred to Maggie that Laurent might have had other things he'd prefer to have done than shepherding her around the South of France for the last five days.

An hour later, Maggie stood with her back to the interior of a room and looked out over a little garden. A jumble of flowers and weeds, it looked as if it had been untended for years, yet was somehow more beautiful for its neglect. Geraniums exploded in uncontrollable bushes of rich reds and oranges to border all sides of the waist-high stonewalls which enveloped the tiny plot. Roses grew wild everywhere in snaking vines along the ground and up a rotted wooden trellis that reached toward the French doors and patio where Maggie now stood. Over the garden wall she could see the Mediterranean Sea—just a patch of it, but enough to fill her with delight. The air was fragrant with the scent of lemons and roses.

"*C'est magnifique, n'est-ce pas?*" Laurent stood to her left, a glass of white wine in each hand, his eyes squinting against the sunlight, his voice light and already familiar to her.

"It's beautiful." She turned and held her hand out for one of the wineglasses. "You know the people who live here?"

"No one could live here." He gestured at the ruin of the place: the garden a tangle of weeds and garbled, wayward shrubbery, the panes broken out of the French doors. There was a small wooden table in the one-room cottage, with two shaky benches propped up against it.

"But, a view of the sea? This property must cost a fortune. To just let it rot like this..." She walked out onto the patio with her wine.

Laurent followed her. "It is not a good house." Paint had peeled off in strips to lie in crinkled husks on the floor.

"I don't care if it's the local crack house, Laurent, location is everything. You could tear this place down and put a double wide here. I mean, look at that view!"

"*Incredible, non?*" Laurent said softly.

"It really is. The whole area is. I'd never been to the Riviera before. At least now I know what all the fuss is about. Mind you, the major fuss has to be the prices. A sandwich at the *Hotel Splendid* cost thirty euros! A bottle of Perrier there cost almost ten."

Maggie suddenly felt uncomfortable, as if Laurent's silence and the quiet beauty of the cottage were working together to unsettle her. "Um, when did you say Roger would be coming with Nicole?" She turned to face him, her back to the panoramic blue view.

"In a little while."

"What is a little while? Hours?"

"*Oui*, Maggie. Hours."

"And we're to stay here? But, there's nothing here for us to do. Couldn't we have waited in Monte Carlo? Or Antibes? I mean, it's pretty, but there's not even a decent table to sit at."

Laurent smiled. "We won't need a table. Come, bring your wine." He turned and scooped up a small backpack and moved out into the garden. Maggie followed him.

"Laurent?"

"*Oui?*" He took out a small tablecloth and spread it carefully, ceremoniously, across the weeds, buttercups and violets.

"Did you know my sister?" It had occurred to her on more than one occasion that Laurent might have been the friend who took Nicole from Elise for Gerard and, if not, then perhaps one of Elise's ex-boyfriends?

He began to unpack the small canvas bag of picnic supplies. "*Non,* Maggie, I met your sister only once. I am sorry." He took out a large jar of mushrooms swimming in olive oil, two long baguettes, fresh pears, strawberries, a small wheel each of Gouda and Edam cheeses, and a roasted chicken pricked with toothpicks of baby onions.

"So you're just doing all this to help out Roger?"

"He is a friend." He looked up at her again and smiled. "But perhaps I am doing *all this* for someone other than Roger."

Maggie started to feel that unsettled feeling in her stomach she sometimes felt when Laurent looked at her in a certain way. His eyes were so probing she knew he had probably already figured out exactly how she looked in her bra and panties—if not less. Just the thought made her blush, and work to change the subject.

"But Roger told you about Elise?"

"He said she was a girl who had trouble."

"That's true." Maggie sat down next to Laurent and picked up a pear. It felt fat and juicy in her hand. "When did you buy all this stuff? I never saw you do it."

"Ahhh, we French, we are clever, *non?*"

"Roger never really knew her either." She put a hand on Laurent's sleeve and he seemed to freeze under her touch. "But you've heard stuff. You heard about her, didn't you, Laurent?"

He sighed and finished emptying his knapsack: napkins, forks, another bottle of wine. "What you hear in a town like Cannes is..." He shrugged.

"Look, Laurent, I know my sister did drugs. I don't think you can tell me anything that is going to surprise me. But if you know anything about her..."

Laurent turned without speaking and put a large hand on top of Maggie's slim one. When he did, she felt an electric shock build in her chest and begin to hum down her arm to where it connected with his. His eyes were dark and unreadable. "You would not be shocked," he said, "*mais non*, and in my country, to have the *bèbè* with no father is...not so terrible." He shrugged.

"Please, tell me what you've heard."

"Nothing very bad. Perhaps she smoked cannabis and she was *toujours* a part of the *folie à deux*, you *comprends? Always she was choosing the wrong man.*"

Maggie moved her hand from his and picked up the jar of mushrooms. She watched them bob and float in their oily mire. "I imagine you're right about the men she chose. She was an artist. Did you know that? She came to Paris six years ago." Maggie put down the mushrooms and stared out to the Mediterranean.

"You were close with her, yes?" Laurent tore off a piece of bread, dipped it in a saucer of olive oil and offered it to her. She took it absently.

"When we were kids. After we got older, we weren't. She dressed odd and hung around weirdoes and she wasn't interested in college or anything." She looked at Laurent and suddenly wondered what it would be like to kiss those full lips. She turned away.

"Nothing like me. I always knew what I wanted to do. I liked college and I liked outfits that, you know, matched. She scared me a little, and that's funny because that just now occurred to me. And if you knew her, you'd think I was crazy because she was totally unintimidating. Sweet and maybe a little goofy, but not formidable at all.

"Anyway, she came over here to go to school. Our folks said they thought it would be good for her. Or maybe she was just this major embarrassment to them back home and it was easier if she did her aimless mayhem from a few thousand miles away. That's an awful thing to say." She looked at Laurent and found him watching her intently. "I loved her."

"Bien sûr."

"And I still can't believe she wanted the life she wanted."

"It was not a life you would have chosen."

"Smoking and shooting dope?"

Laurent made no response.

"And having babies out of wedlock? Maybe y'all do that sort of thing over here and it's no big deal, but it's a definite *faux pas* where I come from."

"Perhaps that is why your sister came to France, *non?* It is, for her, a world that understands her better."

"I just couldn't believe she could live the childhood we both had—going to the beach and the mountains, with our own ponies and private schools and stuff—and after all that she could say, 'Naaahhh, not for me.'"

Laurent poured her a glass of wine.

"At first, she wrote home, but soon she stopped going to classes and then she stopped writing or calling. Turns out she'd gotten pregnant, *had* the child, and never mentioned it to us. Never called to tell us. Can you believe that?"

"Your mother and father were angry?"

"They were worried. But I have to admit, I don't know why more wasn't done." Maggie pushed her thick, dark hair from her eyes. "I hate myself for thinking they didn't go looking for her because they were afraid they might have found her. Like maybe she'd want to come home and be the crazy artist in their neighborhood and around their country club and stuff." She looked into Laurent's eyes, her own misting. "Why am I thinking that? My parents adored Elise. They did."

"But they did not look for her?"

"It was about three years ago and I was all caught up in my job and stuff. I mean, I knew it was all going on, but I was super busy at the office. I'm in advertising."

"Ahhh." He nodded and smiled politely and Maggie found herself feeling stupid again.

"It's a really great job. I write the words, you see, for the ads. You know? Television commercials and stuff?"

Laurent nodded while he unscrewed a jar of fragrant *tapenade* and rummaged in the basket for a knife with which to spread the olive mixture.

"Anyway, it's a great job," Maggie repeated, her eyes watching the blue horizon of the Mediterranean as it merged with the blue southern sky. "Very fast-paced and exciting. You meet a lot of interesting people, too. Plus, it gives me a creative outlet. I think that's important."

Laurent lit a cigarette and exhaled a puff of blue smoke between them.

"I've wanted to be a copywriter ever since I saw the early Heineken ads...you remember the ones?"

"I don't watch much television," Laurent said.

"They were print ads."

From across the courtyard and down the vineyard-studded hills, she noticed a colorful, flapping line of laundered clothes starkly visible against the landscape of browns and muted greens. The clothesline bucked and twisted in the bright sky like the gay signal flags she'd seen on the yachts moored in the harbor at Monte Carlo.

Maggie brushed a dusting of pollen from her cotton dress and Laurent reached over and took her hand in his. She looked at him, her heart pounding with the thrill of what she knew was coming as the big Frenchman leaned over and kissed her gently on the mouth. She felt the coarseness of his rough face against her cheek.

Slowly, she moved toward him, folding herself against his broad chest, smelling the soap and sunshine in his blue cotton pullover. A moment passed and he lifted her chin with his fingers and looked into her eyes. He kissed her again. His tongue pushed gently past her lips into her mouth and his arms tightened around her.

Maggie was vaguely aware of the Mediterranean sun caressing her bare arms and legs, and of her cotton sundress pulled high across her thighs. She could smell the redolent mixture of olives and lemons and sun-sweetened grass and roses. And when she felt him kiss her, she felt nothing else about Elise or Nicole or Atlanta, or her own fears of failure.

Murder in the South of France

Chapter Three

Maggie had seven hours to roll the thought over and over in her mind: *an indescribably sexy Frenchman brought her to a magic place by the sea and then made her his own in every sense of the word.*

Twice.

Every time she thought of it—thought of him, his large warm hands on her skin, his full lips nibbling at her ear lobe, his husky, whispered voice against her throat—she began to tingle and blush in a way that made it impossible to sit still.

And then she had gotten on a plane and left.

Even now, Maggie found it difficult to believe she could have gone where he took her, emotionally and physically, only to walk away for good. Had she really not expected something like this to happen with him? With *Laurent*, whose every smile, every gesture was so damn sexy she nearly had to fan herself just sipping an espresso with him in broad daylight on the rue Meynardiers. Had he *really* taken her by surprise? Or hadn't she been longing for it, *for him,* ever since she looked up to see him standing next to her at the breakfast terrace of the Hotel d'Albion that very first day?

From the warmth and exhilaration of their sweet union late that afternoon until this moment, where she sat on a Boeing 747 revving its engines for takeoff, it was clear that a very right thing had developed between them. A very right, but very fleeting thing. Her heart stuttered at the thought of not seeing Laurent again, and she cursed the fact she couldn't just enjoy the moment—and the adventure—for what it was. She glanced over at the child siting next to her and reminded herself that it had been a very successful adventure on all counts.

Bentley brought Nicole to the little house not an hour after she and Laurent had made love on the grass by the sea. One brief hour to lay in each other's arms and talk—or not—and feed each other the picnic feast…and make love again.

One hour before the whole adventure successful concluded with the sound of Bentley rapping on the door in the early evening and placing Nicole in her arms.

When the flight attendant walked by to double-check everyone's seatback tray compliance, Maggie glanced down at the blank-eyed child sitting next to her. Elise's baby, her own niece, flesh of her flesh. Maggie spoke softly, gently to the girl. "Nicole? *Ça va*, Nicole?"

The child lifted her head and looked at Maggie, but her eyes held no expression. In spite of the seatbelt sign and the imminent departure, Maggie had an impulse to gather the girl up into her arms and hold her, as if by doing so she could make it all right again.

Bentley had very little to say about the details of where he had found Nicole. He gave Maggie the forged passport—well paid for by her father—and after dropping her and Nicole off at her hotel, he and Laurent disappeared into the night. Maggie had been so busy with the overnight care of the little waif she barely had time to process what had happened between her and Laurent.

Or the realization that he was gone.

Nicole hadn't spoken a word all night, but Maggie wasn't worried. She assumed the poor thing was frightened, and she had every confidence that her mother would bring Nicole around—with love and chocolate chip cookies and unfailing doting.

Nicole was small—smaller at five years than Maggie had imagined she'd be. All the Newberry women were leggy creatures—lanky girls and tall women. All except Maggie, who was the recipient of the family's good-natured teasing for her sole petiteness.

Sole until now, it seemed.

The girl's hair was dark, unlike Elise's. Her eyes were wide and fringed with thick lashes. Her full bottom lip quivered slightly.

Now, as Maggie watched her, it occurred to her that Nicole wasn't really frightened so much as she was... nothing. She didn't flinch or cry or recoil at Maggie's touch or words. She simply stared, her face a blank mask, her eyes dry.

Maggie tried to imagine Nicole as a part of their family, with a place at the Thanksgiving Day table, her own stocking at the hearth, and knowing her grandfather's jokes and feeble puns as well as the rest of them did.

Was it possible this little collection of bones and tremors would someday be a laughing, happy, integral part of the Newberry clan in Atlanta? Maggie stroked the little girl's hair. Nicole did not flinch.

Maggie gazed out the airplane window and felt a needle of fear war with the excitement and warmth of the memory of his arms around her, his kisses on her.

Would she ever see him again?

Eight hours later, Maggie scanned the crowd at Hartsfield International Airport for her parents, Big John and diminutive, auburn-haired Southern beauty queen Elspeth, the Newberry matriarch.

She glanced down at her charge, who huddled by her side. Nicole looked even less like a blood relation this morning, Maggie thought. She was so dark—more like Maggie—but unlike Maggie, Nicole's features were blunt and full. Her eyes were round as an owl's and dark, like unfathomable, bottomless pools.

The child had spoken not a word the whole trip. She'd given no indication that she needed to go to the lavatory, wanted water, was hungry, was fatigued, or even fearful. Nothing. She had sat in her seat, her new, airport-bought outfit making her look like a refugee from Disneyland, and stared out the window of the airplane. Maggie spoke to her in French and then English. No response.

Maggie saw her parents waiting for her at the top of the escalator. They looked fretful as their eyes searched the crowd for her. She watched them, her waving hand faltering a bit. In a flash, she realized they were not really looking for Nicole. She could see the look in their eyes. In a strange, inexplicable way, they were looking for Elise.

Maggie's hand dropped to her side and she felt sick with the intensity of her parents' longing. She looked down at Nicole, who stood motionless beside her. They would not find their Elise here, Maggie thought sadly.

"Maggie! Darling! John, she's over here." Maggie looked up and smiled at them. She propelled the girl forward and Nicole walked robot-like into the arms of her maternal grandparents.

"Darling, you're here!" Maggie felt her mother's hug, and the light, familiar scent of Chanel No. 5.

Maggie watched her mother greet Nicole. Elspeth touched the child without hesitation, ignoring Nicole's blank expression. Elspeth smiled at Nicole with true joy and hugged her to her. Maggie could see Nicole stiffen, but she did not resist.

"Long flight, darling?" Maggie's father leaned over and gave her a squeeze.

"Not too bad. She doesn't speak any English. Nicole? *Ceci ton grandmère et grandpère, comprends-toi?"* Maggie straightened up and shook her head. "She's been through a lot."

"Of course she has." If Elspeth Newberry was less than impressed with her brand-new and only granddaughter, she did not show it. The girl stood quietly among them. "It's just going to take a little time," Elspeth said as she knelt beside the child, the silken hem of her designer dress dusting the airport tile. "And we've got lots of that, don't we, *ma petite?"* She touched the girl's face with her hand and looked into her dark, expressionless eyes.

Maggie's father shifted uncomfortably from one foot to the other. "The casket?"

"Yeah, about that," Maggie said. "There was a miscommunication or something. When I went to get the paperwork at the airport yesterday morning, they said there wasn't to be a casket."

"You didn't bring Elise home?" Maggie saw her father's face contort into a grimace and he quickly looked at her mother.

"No, I did, Dad," Maggie said. She tapped the hard leather box strapped to her luggage. "They cremated her.

I'm sorry. They were apologetic about the misunderstanding."

Her father stared at the leather box and then gently put a hand on it. "Pretty big misunderstanding," he said.

"We can still run DNA tests on it. You know, to be sure."

"Let's just get your niece and your mother home in one piece," her father said. Maggie could tell he was barely holding it together, and that it wasn't easy. "Brownie came with us," he said. "He's out by the car."

"Brownie?" Maggie looked at her mother, who had stopped walking and was waiting for Maggie and her father to catch up. Brownie and Maggie had dated in high school —seriously enough for Brownie to achieve the coveted title of *honorary family member* with Maggie's parents. The two had eventually decided to be just friends. At least, Maggie had.

"He didn't want to come in, dear." Maggie's mother stood and shifted her purse to her shoulder. "He thought it should just be the family when we all met. Although, I told him he was certainly family as far as we were concerned."

Maggie's heart twisted at the memory of Laurent standing at the Nice Airport departure lounge, his big hands shoved in his pockets, his feet planted solidly. He had surprised her by coming to see her off. While she had to admit their goodbye at the house had been heartbreakingly lacking as far as she was concerned, she had tried to force herself to accept that he probably viewed the liaison for what it was: two convenient ships connecting in the night.

I mean, he's French after all.

She was still amazed that every moment of that magical afternoon at the abandoned house by the sea seemed to have been completely untouched for her by the notion that they would, of course, part. It simply hadn't occurred to her. Remembering him now, as he stood watching her walk away down the long corridor to Security and the flight gates beyond, little Nicole shuffling along beside her, she just wanted to break down and cry.

When they pulled into the long drive of her parents' home, Maggie couldn't help but look at Nicole for her reaction to the estate. She had guessed correctly there would be little visible effect, but it was hard to resist looking. As for herself, she felt the same happiness and belonging she always did when she came home. Not too large, certainly not by the standards of the neighborhood which showcased the biggest and the best in Atlanta homes, the Newberry homestead was covered in a tangle of magnolias, weeping willows and oak trees that gave the mansion a feeling of intrigue, even masquerade.

That night, as she lay in her bed unable to sleep, she turned to catch a whiff of her mother's roses. They grew in profusion right outside her window, and her mother had gathered several in a crystal vase on Maggie's bedside table. Maggie watched the sheers on her window puff toward the bed and then go slack as the gentle Georgia night breeze cooled the house. It seemed to waft the lovely rose scent right into the bed with her.

She closed her eyes and remembered so many under-the-cover giggles with her sister in this house, teasing and conspiring together. As sleep began to claim her, Maggie found herself wondering if Elise's little foreign-born daughter—sleeping now in Elise's old room—had ever heard her mother laugh.

It occurred to her that she had never heard Laurent laugh.

*****

"You did well, me bucko, quite well. I'm impressed." Roger leaned back in the chair and finished off his Campari and soda.

"It is not like that, Roger."

"Well, whatever it's like, old boy, I'm impressed. She was a handful right from the start and I couldn't have done it without your running interference for me. Although, I must say, to get paid on top of your *rapports sexuels* seems a bit much under the circumstances, don't you think?"

"I think life is good, Roger.. Give me my half of the money."

"Yes, well, next time, you go out and get muck up your pant legs and *I'll* stay back to comfort the dove, eh?"

"Where did you find the girl?"

"You know where. Does it matter?"

Laurent shrugged and counted his euros.

"Don't trust me, Laurent?"

"Anyone can make a miscalculation, Roger. Do not be offended." He looked at his friend and held up his own drink. "And I think I have miscalculated how long this business will take."

"What do you mean?"

"I need to go to the US to finish the job."

"Oh, really? Well, that's up to you, of course." Bentley stood and dropped a few coins onto the table. "But I'd be careful, old son. They do things quite differently in America. Take it from me." He clapped the big Frenchman on the shoulder. "Quite bloody differently."

Chapter Four

The parking ticket dispenser stuttered abruptly then stopped, without the tongue-like flick proffering the needed ticket to park for the day. The machine simply burped to a halt. Gary leaned out his BMW and smacked the machine with his hand. It whirred and spat out several tickets at once. He grabbed one while the orange-striped arm at the entrance barricade lifted to allow his car into the garage.

Gary parked his car, hopped out and wriggled into the coat jacket he'd tossed onto the back seat. It was a fine day. Last night's pitch to Huffy Tractor Lites had gone well. He'd been in good form, anticipating questions, offering suggestions in an "even-if-you-don't-hire-us-as-your-agency" manner—ingratiating and fluid. He felt only a little nauseated in retrospect.

It used to help that Darla didn't take his business seriously, even if he had to. Darla was a light touch in a feverish world. She used to tease him about the amount of "servicing" his clients required. Lately, however, it seemed her teasing was laced with less humor and more irony.

He marched off the elevator and nodded to the receptionist positioned like a marine in her guard box just inside the foyer of Selby and Parker's Advertising. "Maggie in yet?" he called out as he thundered down the hall to his office.

"Yes, Gary," the receptionist chirped. "She signed in an hour ago."

He stopped at one of the offices, his briefcase dangling from one hand and pushed open the door.

"So, you're back?"

Maggie turned in her chair and swiveled away from her computer screen. She was wearing a deep, emerald green suit that dramatically accentuated her coal-colored hair. He was surprised to see her looking so pretty. Usually, as fond of her as he was, he neglected to notice her in the physical sense. Today, she seemed to radiate allure. He found it unsettling.

She smiled at him. "Clearly."

"You look good. What's the deal?"

"What do you mean *what's the deal*?"

"No kidding, you look good. Did something happen?"

"Will you stop being so offensive. Nothing happened. There is no *deal*."

"You met somebody over there."

"Are you kidding me?"

"I'm right, aren't I?"

"You're incredible."

"So, what did you do, meet some frog, boff him, have his child, win over a small village and then think you could just show up for work like I wouldn't notice or something?" He moved into her office to get a better look at her. "Who is he?"

"He's a Frenchman."

"No shit. You went to *France*."

"Do you want to hear about him?"

"Of course. Lunch? You can tell me everything. Just remember, nothing gross or anything that involves swapping body fluids while I'm eating, okay?" Gary smacked a rolled-up sheath of papers against his thigh.

"Meanwhile, let's do traffic. Would you get Deirdre to call the meeting over the PA? I haven't had coffee yet." He hurried down the corridor to his office.

Maggie's cellphone sat on her desk seeming to mock her. She couldn't help checking it every fifteen minutes to see if Laurent had called. He hadn't. In spite of that, she was aware that she was at least trying to put him and their week together out of her mind—something that would've been unthinkable at any time yesterday. Today, she let open a small window of possibility she might never hear from him again.

"Traffic meeting in the conference room," the public address system announced in wall-rattling tones. Their receptionist was new.

Maggie gathered up her work diary of the week's schedule of jobs in-house and her laptop and proceeded to the conference room.

Selby & Parker, once Selby and Associates, was a friendly little ad shop of ten employees and 1.2 million dollars in billings. None of them were going to retire any time soon on the fees of their clients, but they were comfortable for the moment. Up until last year, Gary had been just another copywriter, like Maggie. But the death of their then president, a nefarious wheeler-dealer, had left a clear path for someone with guts and initiative to take over the helm. So, with the bulk of his life savings and the support of his wife, Gary had stepped in to fill the void.

Maggie took her place at Gary's right hand at the small conference room table. Joining them was the agency art director, Bob Mason, the senior art director, Pokey Lane, the media buyer, Dr. Patricia Stump, and the traffic manager, Deirdre Potts.

Gary began the meeting by indicating that he wanted the meeting short, to the point, and everyone back at work racking up those billable hours as soon as possible.

"All right, Deirdre," he said briskly. "What have we got?"

Before Deirdre could speak, the media director, Patti Stump, who was seated on the other side of Gary, tapped the table with her pen to get Gary's attention.

"You said you'd make a decision on my office, Gary." Her blonde hair was teased into a frizzier version of what Gary was sure was popular these days. Her makeup was a little toned down today, though, and she looked, if not pretty, at least not awful.

He took a long breath to bear what was to come, but he was fast tiring of all the petty squabbles and imbecilic demands from his employees—most of who reminded him of so many bratty children. *If this is the life of a CEO, you can have it.*

"Is this something we should be discussing in a traffic meeting?"

"I can't get you alone outside meetings and you're not returning any of my emails or texts."

"I'm not?" Gary looked at his cellphone, as if the problem must be with his equipment.

"You said I could have Pokey's corner office as soon as he bumped up to Nigel's old office."

Gary sighed with exaggeration and looked at Pokey. "Are you out?"

"Yes, boss," Pokey said with a slow drawl. "Ages ago."

Gary looked back at Patti. "I really do not want to waste billable time talking about this crap."

"The *problem*, Gary," Patti said breathily, "is about the chair you said I could have. It's expensive and Jenny, the new girl, won't order it unless you—"

"No. No chair. Deirdre? May we continue?" Gary looked at the traffic manager, who in turn looked at Patti, who clearly was not done.

"But you said I could have it!" Patti said, raising her voice and tossing down her pen.

"I can't imagine in what universe I would have said you can have an expensive chair, Patti," Gary said, tossing down his own pen onto the table. "Move into Pokey's office. In fact, Pokey, help her do that, please, right after this meeting."

"I don't need or want his help!"

He turned to her and put his hand out as if to prevent her from standing. "We're done talking about the chair. Anything more you want to say, text me."

"So you can just ignore me better?" Patti said, her face flushed with her frustration.

Gary turned away. "Let's go, Deirdre," he said firmly.

*****

"I'm afraid it's going to take awhile." Elspeth Newberry spoke quietly into the phone. "She's very unresponsive. Mostly just sits by herself and stares. She doesn't even seem to want a toy or a stuffed animal to cling to."

"What did the doctor say?" Maggie shifted the phone receiver to her other ear and absently pushed the shift key to bring the document she was working on back to the computer screen.

"He said she's a little undernourished—"

"I meant her mental state."

"He recommended she be seen by someone. But I'd like to wait and see what a stable home life and love will do first."

Maggie turned away from her computer terminal and glanced out her office window. The sky was a hard wash of blue-gray with a battalion of puffed-wheat clouds moving quickly across it, their edges heavy with the promise of rain. "Do you see any sense of Elise in her?"

"Well, of course I do. Will you be coming for dinner tonight, dear?"

"No, I'm seeing Brownie, but maybe tomorrow."

"Tomorrow will be fine. Oh! We want to talk with you about adding a security system on your apartment too, Maggie."

"I don't need it, Mom."

"It's not for you, sweetheart. It's for your father and me. We have trouble sleeping knowing you're in mortal danger."

Maggie laughed and so did Elspeth.

"Come over tomorrow if you can. And don't worry about Nicole. These things have a way of working themselves out."

Maggie hung up and turned back to her document on the screen, but she couldn't seem to focus on the work. She rested her fingers on the keyboard.

What had Gerard done to the poor kid?

Come to that, what had Elise done to her?

Between thoughts of poor little Nicole and what was obviously a Franco one-night stand, Maggie felt the beginnings of a bone-wracking fatigue wash over her. Would raising an emotionally-handicapped child in their twilight years serve to assuage the guilt her parents felt about their older daughter? Would it help them pay enough dues for a good night's sleep? Maggie rubbed her eyes.

"Ready to talk about Hi-Jinks Kiddee Wear?" Gary poked his head in her office, a disposable diaper pulled down over his face.

Maggie smiled and gathered up her notebook. "Product testing?" she said as she followed him into the conference room.

*****

Gerard Dubois slammed the car into gear and accelerated loudly up the steep incline. *So, Elise's sister has been and gone, has she?* He sped up the rough-stoned pavement that lined the little village of *Mandelieu*, narrowly missing an old woman and her flower cart.

He would kill that bastard Englishman for his part in this. Shake every *euro* he earned in the deal out of his hide and then cut his stinking English heart out of his chest with his own penknife.

She's taken her precious niece and vanished. Skulked off like the thief she is, thinking she fooled Gerard Dubois. Thinking she had cheated me of my own daughter. The arrogance of the bitch! To believe that her American dollars could buy her anything she wants. She will think again—and through her tears—to have tried to trick Gerard Dubois.

Murder in the South of France

54

Chapter Five

The summer passed in Atlanta in a steamy swelter of wilted magnolias and scorched traffic knots. Polo ponies fainted from the heat in Alpharetta, church picnics never began before sundown, and hundreds of the city's children found themselves in emergency rooms suffering from dehydration or heatstroke.

The humidity was an amazing eighty percent nearly every day, and this without a single drop of rainfall. Roses shriveled up like insect husks draped on a fence, and the Georgia Power electric company became richer still as air conditioning units operated at full bore all over the city.

Darla watched a lycra-clad group of women go through their paces. The music the women were dancing to in the large gymnasium was loud and the words unintelligible to Darla. Their leader, a trim young woman with hair pulled into a ponytail on the top of her head like Pebbles Flintstone, bounced and kicked and squealed her encouragement to the crowd. Her large breasts were just barely restrained in her bright orange bra top. They were the only part of her that jiggled, Darla noted.

"Sorry I'm late. Been waiting long?"

Although she'd been expecting her, Darla jumped at the sound of Maggie's voice.

"God, you're edgy." Maggie and Darla hugged quickly. "I thought in-town living was supposed to be chill."

"It is," Darla agreed, hefting her gym bag to her other shoulder. "It's coming into Buckhead I find unnerving."

"Oh." Maggie made a face of understanding. "Gary give you a hard time about meeting me here?"

"Define hard time."

"I'm surprised he let you come." Maggie led the way to a set of empty lockers and tossed down her gym bag. "He's so paranoid about the crime in town these days."

"We had words about it," Darla admitted. "Maybe it'd be best for my marriage if you and I do lunch in Roswell or Smyrna next time."

Maggie sat down on the bench in front of the lockers and looked up at Darla. "Is that all that's bothering you, Darl?"

"It's nothing." Darla set her bag down and began rummaging around inside it, extricating gym clothes, deodorant, aerobic shoes and socks. "I'll tell you about it sometime when we're both too bored with talking about everything else first."

Maggie continued to watch her friend. "Really?"

Darla stopped digging in her bag and looked at Maggie. "Really," she emphasized. "Besides, it's you I want to hear about. What happened in France? Gary said you met someone."

"I did but it turned out to be nothing." Maggie pulled off her slacks and folded them loosely before placing them at the bottom of one of the lockers.

"How nothing? Come on, Maggie, spill it."

Maggie held her biking shorts in one hand and looked at them as if doubting the chances of squeezing into them.

"He was one of the guys who helped us get Nicole back. He and I had a thing." She shrugged. "I really fell for him, Darla," she said, tossing the shorts down and sitting on the little metal bench. "I wish I could describe how he made me feel. He was so caring, but also really exciting. I can't stop thinking of him."

"And you haven't heard from him."

"It's been four months."

"You didn't know him very long."

"True."

"Was his English very good?"

"Better than my French."

"But y'all were able to communicate okay?"

"We managed, I'd say, wouldn't you, Darla?"

"Oh, dear. Gary didn't mention this part. You slept with him?"

"God, Gary is such a prude. I guess he thought he was protecting my reputation or something by not telling his own wife?"

"You know Gary."

"Yes, I slept with him. It felt right at the time."

"I'm sorry, Maggie."

"Me, too. You know, Darla, I hate to forever destroy the sophisticated image you probably have of me as a single-gal-about-town, but I haven't slept with a lot of guys, and none that I didn't know really well."

"I understand, Maggie. I don't think the man who preaches the Baptist service at our church would, but..."

"Why can't I shake it off?" Maggie pulled off her blouse and slipped a tee shirt on. "I mean, I work ten hours a day, I work out at the gym—for what, I might ask? So I can continue to look good in my off-the-rack nearly-designer dresses to impress *clients*?" Maggie pulled on her socks and athletic shoes and began lacing them up. Darla sat down next to her on the bench and pulled out a water bottle.

"Well, you do look good."

"I want stuff that I don't have, Darla. Stuff I don't even see on the horizon, you know? Husband stuff, children stuff, sharing my life with organisms other than a cat kind of stuff." She paused. "I don't even have a cat."

"Sweetie, you're just lonely."

"How long were you single before you met Gary?"

"Me?"

"Yeah. How long were you on your own?"

"I didn't get a chance to be on my own. I envy you that, Maggie. I really do. I mean, you know for sure that you can take care of yourself."

Maggie shook her head and resumed lacing her sneakers. "I appreciate the effort, Darla, but it's not all that tricky to buy your own groceries or pay the rent online. So what other reasons can you think of to envy me?"

Darla leaned over and gave Maggie an unexpected hug. "Something good is going to happen to you, Maggie. I can just feel it. Maybe not this hunky French guy you met over there, but somebody else, and soon. I know it."

"Thanks, Darla. I sure hope you're right."

Later that night, Maggie returned to her darkened apartment on Peachtree Road. She flipped on the lights, made herself an iced tea, kicked off her espadrilles and heaved herself onto the couch. The air conditioner in her apartment hummed loudly, reassuringly, but she felt the weariness of the hot day settle onto her shoulders. She glanced up at the stark, high-tech wrought-iron clock on the living room wall. A little after seven.

She glanced at the coffee table where she'd dumped the mail without looking at it. She picked it up now. A bill from Macy's, the electric bill, and a postcard from Cyprus. Her throat closing up with excitement, she dropped the rest of the mail to read the card.

Dear Maggie Hope this finds you well. Having a bit of a holiday in Cyprus. How is little Nicole? Doing well, I trust? Take care of yourself. Cheers, Roger Bentley.

Maggie turned over the postcard. An artist's pretty blue and white rendition of the city of Paphos in watercolor on the picture side.

Even Roger felt pity enough to drop me a line.

Her cellphone rang, and when she glanced at the screen she saw it was a blocked call. "Yes?" she said sharply into the receiver.

"*Mademoiselle* Newberry?"

Maggie held her breath and then let it out in a rush. "Laurent?"

"*Comment?*"

"Who...who is this?"

She sat up on the couch, the postcard fluttering from her fingers to the floor.

"I am Gerard Dubois. You are knowing me, yes? I am your sister Elise's boyfriend?"

Maggie stood slowly, her heart pounding furiously in her chest. The hand holding the phone was immediately clammy. "What do you want?" she asked, wondering how she was able to sound to calm.

"What do you think I want?" The voice was high and nasty. Maggie detected a fuzziness to it too, as if alcohol had been the *aperitif* to the call. "I want my daughter that you and your family stealed from me. You are surprised, yes?"

Maggie felt the panic creep over her like a spreading acid. *This cannot be happening,* she thought with horror. "I am talking to *Monsieur* Roger Bentley, yes? You are familiar, yes? *Monsieur* Bentley?" Maggie's eyes flicked automatically to the postcard on the floor. "He is telling me that you have Nicole. Is true, *n'est-ce pas?*"

From the barely restrained glee in the man's voice, Maggie suddenly understood why he was calling her. This call had nothing to do with getting Nicole back—it had to do with how much the Newberrys wanted to keep her.

"How much?"

"And Elise said you were so stuupeeed."

"Shut up about my sister, you filth!" Maggie was trembling with rage and almost didn't hear the click as the man disconnected the line. "Hello?" Shaken, she dropped the phone on the couch sat down hard next to it.

Oh, God, *now* what was she going to do? He was going to try to take Nicole away and she couldn't even go to the police. (*"Exactly how did the child come into the United States, Miss Newberry?"*) She covered her eyes with her hands and hunched over her knees.

The phone rang again and she snatched it up.

"You will not speak to me like that. You are a pig, *comprends?* That you steal *mon enfant.* You will give me five thousand dollars. Immediately! You are understanding me?"

Maggie's mind raced. The banks wouldn't open until nine tomorrow. Her father would still be at the club. *Did he have that kind of cash lying around?*

"Where?" She watched the hands on her living room clock spasmodically twitch off the seconds across its face. It looked vaguely malevolent to her now.

A high-pitched giggle assaulted her from the other end. "You will come with the money to the car park at the Lenox Mall, you understand? *Les grandes magazins?* The shopping stores?"

"How will I—?"

"Park your automobile. Gerard will find you. Perhaps when I find you, I will screw you first, eh? And then you give me the money. Ha! Ha! You will pay Gerard to be screwed!"

Maggie felt perspiration form on her face. The man might be insane, she thought. *Could he have gotten into the country with a gun? Could he have gotten one since arriving?*

"What time?" she asked, her stomach twisting in nausea.

"Three hours. *Exactement.*"

Maggie looked at the clock again. "Midnight."

He hung up. Maggie took a deep breath, then dialed the number of her father's club. *Would he have the money? Should she call Brownie? How can our customs and immigration people let such scum into the country? Don't they have eyes?* Does this Gerard person look *normal*? Should *she* bring a gun? Her dad would have one. God! She suddenly realized she couldn't tell her father the full story behind why she needed the money. He'd never let her meet this creep alone in a darkened mall parking lot.

"Hello? Cherokee Country Club."

"Yes, could you please see if my father is there tonight? John Newberry?"

"Yes, of course, Mr. Newberry is upstairs. On moment and I'll connect you."

"Thanks." How were they going to make sure Gerard Dubois didn't bother them again? How were they going to get him out of their lives permanently?

Then, her dad's strong, gentle voice was on the line. "Hello, sweetheart? What's up?"

The towers surrounding Lenox Square, the Southeast's once super-eminent shopping mall, loomed over all avenues leading to the retail complex. Mingling with the massive, full-leafed trees that lined nearly every street in Atlanta were the me-too office structures, strange testimony to an architectural confusion the city seemed intent to promote. The combination of trees and towers gave the part of Peachtree Road that led directly to the front of Lenox Square a feeling of secrecy, as if anything could be hiding behind them, from an upscale bookstore to a fast food restaurant…to a maniac with a hunger for killing.

Maggie left the lights and late-night traffic of Piedmont Avenue and, turning right, drove slowly down the subdued stretch of Peachtree Road in front of the Financial Center and the Swissotel.

She glanced briefly at her purse in the seat next to her. Five thousand dollars in hundred-dollar bills, almost like her father expected to need it handy one day.

"Are you sure this will be enough to help your friend, Maggie?"

"Yes, Dad. I'll be able to give you full details later."

"I understand."

"It has to do with Elise, Dad," she'd blurted.

"I understand, Maggie. I trust you that you, personally, are in no danger?"

"Of course not."

"Very well. Call me when it's done."

Maggie shivered. A part of her was sorry that he hadn't wanted to know it all. That he hadn't demanded the truth. But he just wanted to throw money at the problem and to trust Maggie that this would be the end of it. Did she really believe that about her own father? She stared at the road ahead. Elise would have believed it.

Maggie waited at the light and glanced at the Swissotel, which ascended to the west of the shopping complex, and wondered if Gerard Dubois was registered there. More likely, he was settled in at one of the pimp-cribs downtown where shootings and drug overdoses were as prevalent as clean towels. Probably more so.

Sitting at the traffic light, a movement caught her eye like shifting vapors behind the trees, whose unruly branches were so long they reached out and nearly touched her car. *Would Gerard come on foot?* She stared into the somber web of trees and thought she could make out the form of someone standing there, watching her. Then the light changed and the half-seen figure dissolved into the deepest shadows, until she wasn't sure she'd seen anything at all. She turned into the nearest parking area of Lenox Square.

Her eyes darted the full width of the parking lot as she drove cautiously to the building entrance. The mall had closed two hours earlier and there were only a few other cars in the lot.

She decided she was too nervous to park very far away from the mall itself. Even as a darkened, largely vacant hulk, it felt like a source of security to her, probably from years of mindless, depression-solving shopping junkets there. She peered at the nearest car—about a hundred yards away—as she parked her Honda. There didn't appear to be anyone in it, but of course he could be hiding, crouched down on the floorboards.

A cold wave of fear fluttered over her. Her fingers fumbled for the small leather-encased tube of mace she kept at the end of her key chain. A faint hum of traffic from Piedmont came filtering down to her in the little cement valley.

Don't these places have security? But there seemed to be no activity, no movement anywhere, as if, when the doors had closed at ten and the last shopper had finally been expelled, the whole shopping arcade had been vacated by managers, restaurant workers, maintenance, clerks and security guards, too.

She called Brownie earlier but he didn't pick up. She was sorry now she hadn't left a message. She gripped the steering wheel and felt the knots in her stomach clench and unclench, then clench again.

Would this be the end of it? Would he just take the money and go away? Was Roger okay? What about Laurent? Does Gerard know Laurent, too? Her stomach tightened again.

She heard the car before she saw it. Her shoulders rigid, clutching her mace, she held her breath as the car crept slowly toward her, its headlights turned off. Inside, Maggie could see two people. One head—considerably lower than the driver's—looked like it belonged to a small child. For one irrational moment she thought, *My God, he's taken Nicole!* The car pulled up next to her and stopped.

Maggie gaped at the car's driver. His face was illuminated by one foggy streetlight overhead and Maggie saw, with surprise, that Gerard was handsome. She was stunned that the man who could destroy her sister, torment her niece, and blackmail her entire family could be something other than physically repulsive. He drove until their drivers' windows were next to each other.

"*Mademoiselle?*" His voice broke the silence. High and ugly, it distorted his pleasant face and created a leering visage of wickedness. "Gerard is here, *n'est-ce pas?* You have the money?"

Afraid to take her eyes off him, Maggie fumbled for the packet of bills in her purse and tossed it through her window into his hands. She immediately started her car and pushed the gear into place, ready to peel out and away from this man.

"*Attendez!*" he shouted at her, and she thought for a moment he was going to get out of his car. The form next to him, huddled in the shadows, hadn't moved.

"You don't have to count it," she said breathlessly. "Now, leave us alone." Maggie knew her voice sounded frail and she hated herself for it.

He laughed, a shiny web of spittle forming on his lips. *How could Elise have loved this? Slept with this?* Maggie shivered, the hand on her stick shift still holding her tube of mace.

"I give you a little something too, eh?" He pushed his face through his window, so close that Maggie could smell the wine on his breath. She was suddenly angry to think he had been out having dinner somewhere, enjoying a glass of wine or two, while she'd been scraping up five thousand dollars and worrying her father.

"Don't contact us again. Do you understand? We'll call the police next time."

He spat at her, a fleck of the spume grazing her cheek as it splattered against her car door. Her foot slipped from the clutch and her car stalled. Before she could re-start it, Gerard leaned over the form seated next to him in the car, jerked open the passenger side door and pushed the person out onto the parking lot tarmac.

"A little something I don't want anymore. Compliments of Gerard Dubois!" He slammed the door shut and drove off with a squeal of tires. Maggie watched, shocked and aghast as he drove away, leaving the lumpish bundle of clothes, arms and legs in a heap on the ground. She stared at the body. It twitched slightly and then moaned.

Maggie jumped out of the car and ran to the body of what turned out to be a woman on the ground—it was clear it was not a child after all.

"Hello, can I help you?" Maggie knelt next to the woman and touched her shoulder gently.

The woman groaned and struggled to rise up on one elbow. Maggie could see she'd scraped her arm in her exit from Gerard's car, but her hair hung in tangled sheets of brown snarls, obscuring her face.

"*Parlez-vous anglais?*"   Maggie scanned the darkened parking lot for any sign of another person, or a car.

"I am American." The woman croaked out the words as if unused to speaking. "Where...where am I?"

Maggie grabbed the woman's arms and pulled them away from her face, the woman weakly resisting her as she did so. Maggie touched the ravaged face, pulling it toward her, her fingers pressing into the woman's skin. Their eyes met, one pair haunted and cloudy, the other wide and disbelieving.

It was Elise.

PART II

"Rose-Lipped Maids Are Sleeping..."

Chapter Six

Maggie knelt beside her sister and put her hand to her face, pulling back the hair that fell in filthy dreadlocks around it.

Dear God. Elise. Alive!

She gripped her sister's shoulders and the face—the haggard and lined face puckered into a cowering visage of pain—cried out. Maggie released her. "Elise," she whispered. "It's me, Maggie."

She watched as her sister struggled to recognize her.

"Maggie?"

Maggie gently touched her shoulder again. She looked closely into her face. The resemblance was so strong. The voice was right. But her face...her face looked like a police artist's rendition of what Elise might look like at fifty. It was lined and haggard, as if it had formed every exaggerated expression of woe and mirth and had no elasticity left. But her eyes were the worst. Protruding in their sockets, they looked at Maggie with hunger and despair.

"Is it really you?" Elise asked, a shaking, withered hand reaching up as if to touch Maggie's face.

Maggie took her hand and felt its warmth, felt it trembling. A surge of joy hit her as she began to slowly pull Elise to a sitting position on the pavement and the reality of her new world began to sink in.

Elise was alive! She was home!

"I'm taking you home, Elise," Maggie said, her voice full of emotion to hear the words come out of her mouth, to imagine the miracle that could allow the words to be true. She envisioned her mother's bliss to see Elise back from the dead, saw little Nicole running to Elise with happy shrieks of "Maman! Maman!" Thought of her father weeping with joy and gratitude for the gift of second chances.

She helped her sister to her feet and moved her to the passenger side of her car. Elise was so thin. She walked like an old woman. Her clothes smelled as if she lived in them.

Maggie had so many questions for her but she forced herself to hold back.

How did you get here? Are you still with Gerard? Why did the Cannes police think you were dead? Who was that woman in the morgue?

Maggie bit back her questions and focused on getting Elise safely to her apartment—concentrated instead on the ecstatic videos playing in her head of the tearful, joyful reunions to come.

Maggie pulled the seatbelt around Elise as if she were a child. Her sister slumped against the door and quickly fell to sleep. Worried that she should take her straight to an emergency room—*no telling what the bastard Gerard has drugged her with!*—Maggie decided that what Elise needed first was rest and a bath and to be safe. She looked around the parking lot to confirm they were alone and that Gerard wasn't watching them, ready to pounce and snatch Elise away. She started the car and drove slowly back to her apartment building, her hand on Elise the whole way there. As she drove, with Elise softly snoring in the passenger's seat, Maggie's mind was awhirl with feelings of joy and worry. She touched Elise's hand, limp in her lap, and knew that whatever was wrong with her, she and her family would fix it.

Elise awakened long enough to shuffle down the hallway of Maggie's apartment building and collapse onto her couch. Maggie's plans of helping her with a bath and a decent meal evaporated when it became clear that Elise was semi-comatose on the couch and likely to remain so for several hours. Maggie covered her with a blanket, made herself a cup of coffee, and sat in the armchair in the living room to wait.

Maggie sat in her living room, a bulky cardigan pulled around her. The heat of the Southern night had given way to a chilled moistness. Her mind struggled with conflicting ideas and urges. Twice she'd nearly picked up the phone to call her parents, and twice, for reasons she couldn't name, she'd stopped herself. She rubbed her arms in agitation, as if to bring a surge of warmth back to them, and looked at her sister on the couch, sleeping peacefully.

Now that she'd had a good couple of hours to process the sheer magic of having her sister back from the dead, Maggie found herself questioning how it had happened. *Are she and Gerard back together? Did they travel here together? Is she here for Nicole, or for money from the family? Was she a part of Gerard's ploy to get the five thousand tonight?*

Maggie felt a surge of annoyance at herself for that last thought, but it had to be considered.

No one in the family had heard from Elise in three years. Who knew what she was capable of now?

A sound from the couch snapped Maggie's attention back to the present. Elise struggled to sit up. Maggie watched her look around the room in confusion and then croak out the word "water."

Maggie jumped up and grabbed two bottles of water from the fridge. She set one down on the coffee table in front of Elise and handed her the other one.

"Hey, sis," she said softly. "Remember me?"

Elise glanced at Maggie as if not at all surprised to see her. She took the water. Her lips were cracked and she drank as if she'd not quite mastered the skill. Water trickled out of her mouth and down onto her shirtfront. When she finished, she looked at Maggie, her eyes filled with such pain that Maggie's throat closed and she worked to control her emotion.

Oh, Elise, what happened to you?

"Little sis," Elise said as she leaned back into the couch. She looked around the apartment but said nothing more.

"How do you feel, Elise?" Maggie didn't know what else to say. It seemed too early to ask the one million questions she had buzzing around her brain.

Elise spoke carefully, as if unused to talking in English. "I'm a junkie. I don't feel too good."

The words stabbed at Maggie's heart. *Other people, Elise. God, other people.*

Elise rubbed her hands across her face then looked around the room again. "You've got a knack for color, Maggie. I'm surprised."

"Elise, can you tell me what happened? You were out of touch for so long. And God, please explain to me about Gerard. I guess you know Nicole is with us?"

Elise continued to stare at the room as if she hadn't heard Maggie. "Your bedroom at home was always so...orderly. Everything in its place." She shrugged sleepily and reached for the other water bottle. Maggie picked it up and handed it to her.

"But no style. No color or flair or...life."

Maggie wondered if Elise was really aware that they were in the present, not back in their teen years. "And *your* room was always a shambles," she said.

"Full of life."

"Yeah, teeming with it." Maggie smiled nervously at her and Elise smiled back.

Elise, back from the grave. Maggie suddenly realized she had spent a good deal of the past month mourning the loss of her sister. Her tears over losing Laurent had become indistinguishable with her grief over losing Elise, too. Seeing now how the reason for that grief was never true made her feel off-balance—as if anything were possible.

If Elise can be alive when we all knew she was long gone, anything can happen.

"I loved him," Elise said, and Maggie realized she was answering one of her questions. Elise sat with the bottle of water in one hand and gazed out into the night through the French doors that faced Peachtree Street. Maggie knew she was seeing Gerard in her mind's eye, and she was seeing the girl she was when she met him.

"From the moment I laid eyes on him, I needed him."

Elise dragged her eyes back to Maggie's face. "All you see is the monster who could dump me out of a car." She shrugged. "He was a loving father, too, in the beginning. Nicole was born with a heroin addiction. I can still hear her screaming, not for food or to be changed..." She looked at Maggie and smiled weakly, sheepishly. "But because she needed a fix." She sipped her water.

Who are you? Suddenly, Maggie wanted to leave, not to have to hear everything she knew Elise would eventually tell her. Not to have to keep it all from her mother through the happy times, warm times, close moments that she was sure were still ahead of them. To listen to Elise—and she had to listen to her—was to help her keep her awful secrets.

"How did you get here? Did you come with Gerard? I thought you two were finished."

"Is anybody ever really finished?" Elise shrugged. "I scored the money for the tickets. But he didn't have to come with me. I think he was delivering me back to my family. To your care."

"Maybe he thought he could humiliate you this way. Or us."

Elise just smiled as if she hadn't heard Maggie.

"How did you score the money?" Visions of Elise wheeling and dealing with nefarious underworld characters on Mediterranean piers and ports for the price of cocaine and smack sprang into Maggie's head.

"I may not look like much to you now, Maggie, I know."

My God, she sold herself. Maggie nodded to indicate she understood.

"You really don't want to hear where I've been, do you, little sister?"

The tears formed at the rim of Maggie's lashes. "I do, Elise," she said. But her heart whispered, *no.*

"When I first met Gerard," Elise said, burrowing into a little nest of cotton throws and satin pillows that studded Maggie's couch, "it was on the *Rue de la Paix.* Can you believe that? You know, the café where they say if you sit there long enough you'll see someone you know? Well, I saw him and I *knew.*"

Maggie settled back into her chair. *Let her talk. Let her tell.*

They met on the last day of summer the year she turned twenty-nine. They fell into bed that same afternoon, and before long their world became a spin of activities belonging to the province of lovers. They visited the flea markets on Saturday mornings, fingers intertwined tightly, huddled in their greatcoats against the drizzle of winter days. They claimed quiet, early-afternoon cafés as their special snuggeries, slept late every morning in Elise's tiny one-bedroom flat on the Left Bank near Notre-Dame, and before the gold had left the autumn skies to reflect the famous green-gray ceiling of Paris in winter, Elise had stopped attending classes at *L'Ecole des Beaux Arts*...and had stopped writing or answering letters from home.

Elise had found a world, finally, that understood her. A world she had defined but never knew existed. Her new world accepted that grime and the absence of care gave her wardrobe the desired patina that all her painstaking fashion planning could not. She learned to let go. The people in her new society used needles—sliver-thin, beautiful spines that pierced her unpocked flesh in an experience that made her high school pot smoking look sophomoric and ridiculous.

Because Elise was an artist she saw the world differently, and she was finally living in a world that understood her, encouraged her and inspired her. And Gerard applauded louder than anyone. Gerard, with the doe-brown eyes that spoke love even in the throes of a crack-induced half-coma, even when he was hurting her. Because that was a part of her new world too. To be truly wretched, to be honestly and completely in despair, was a feeling of pleasure to Elise that she found nearly unbearable. And she sought this drug, the singular intensity of this high, more earnestly than any other. And Gerard, beautiful, sensitive, loving Gerard was the only pusher in town for this particular brand of agony.

She used to believe, long after she stopped painting and all her brushes and canvasses and oils were gone, that if she had never gone to Paris, never met Gerard, she would simply have walked through her life in America, in Atlanta, like some servomechanism or automaton going through the motions of eating, and painting and loving and dreaming...with some essential core inside her faulty or nonoperable. When she thought of how closely she'd come to living a pedestrian life of appointments and movie dates and Sunday dinners—a life like Maggie's—she trembled.

"I'm sorry about Mom and Dad." Elise picked at the cheese sandwich Maggie placed before her on the coffee table. "I thought I was doing them a favor by dropping out. I had this idea that now they could just mourn me and get on with their lives." She made a gesture in the air of wrapping up a box. "All the embarrassing questions and stuff, just tidy it up, cry some, and make it go away."

Maggie looked at her and licked her lips. *Your little experiment in pain management just about killed Mother.*

"You don't remember them very well, I guess."

"Ah, that must be it. Very good sandwich, little sis. I don't usually have much of an appetite. Perhaps you'll change me in that way."

"Why did stop writing or calling?"

"I don't know. Just didn't think of it, I guess."

Maggie felt a flash of anger at Elise's titanic selfishness. She caught a glimpse of Elise, not caring, wrecking everyone's lives that she came into contact with —a glimpse of the Elise they all knew so well.

"How about Nicole?" Maggie said evenly. "Did you ever think about what was good for *her*? The kid's a basket case. She doesn't even speak."

"She doesn't speak English, I'm afraid, darling."

She doesn't speak *anything*, Elise. Not English, not French, not baby-talk."

"That's not true. Nicole is a normal child—"

"She was born a dope addict!"

"That was years ago. She's a normal little girl now. She talks as much as—"

Maggie leaned forward toward her sister. "Elise, I know you love Nicole, but she is *not* normal. You'll see for yourself soon."

Elise didn't answer, her Mona Lisa smile firmly back in place.

Maggie cleared away the sandwich dishes and carried them into the kitchen. She caught a glimpse of herself in the hall mirror as she returned to the living room and was surprised to see how fresh and relaxed she looked. She didn't feel that way at all.

"The woman whose body I identified in the Cannes morgue," Maggie said, "she was found wearing your charm bracelet."

"Oh, really? Did you get it back? That's worth money. The bracelet is eighteen-carat gold."

"No. They said I would—just like they said I'd get the body to bring home. I'm not even sure whose ashes they gave me."

"Oh, well."

Maggie decided not to mention the fact that the woman everyone thought was Elise had been murdered. "My question, Elise, is how did she get your bracelet? Did you know her?"

Elsie seemed to concentrate in thought for a moment. "It might have been Delia. I think I might have sold her the bracelet last year some time."

"You sold your bracelet?"

"How nice it must be to never feel hunger or have to think about selling your precious memories to feed your child."

"Please don't give me that shit, Elise. You chose to walk away from this family and the constant stream of funding you know Mom and Dad would've shot your way so that you could instead sell a sentimental charm bracelet for peanuts."

"Oh, I see you haven't been keeping up with our story and how the world turns, darling." Elise rearranged the blankets around her knees and Maggie could see the rest and the food had strengthened her. "Dad cut me off three years ago. Goodness. Now I see why you're so annoyed with me. Are you sure he really wants me back? Be kind of hard to align his version of the truth with mine, don't you think?"

"Dad cut you off?"

"It was a very dramatic my-way-or-the-highway kind of speech as I recall."

"I didn't know," Maggie said. She sank down on the couch next to Elise.

"It doesn't matter now, darling," Elise said with a heavy sigh. "I'm here to get my baby back. And that will make everything all better for everyone." Her eyes looked clear and focused, and within seconds the two sisters were in each other's arms.

"I missed you so much," Maggie said into Elise's shoulder.

"I know. I missed you, too." Elise held her tightly. They sat that way and rocked for a few moments before Maggie pulled back.

"When do you want to go over there? I can't wait for them to see you."

Elise shook her head. "Let me get myself cleaned up first." She gestured to her clothes. "I want to present myself to them, you know? Not like this."

Maggie nodded uncertainly.

"And Maggie, darling, I'll need to score some stuff, sweetheart. I'll need you to help with that." Then, seeing the expression on Maggie's face, "Just enough to get through seeing them again. After that, I'm kicking it, okay? I promise. But I can't see them while I'm messed up, right?"

"Nicole will be so happy to see you," Maggie said.

"I expect she's changed a lot since I saw her last. It's been nearly a year, you know."

"Mother's been working with her."

"I can't imagine a better person to be mothering her. Meanwhile, I'm exhausted." She rubbed her scraped elbow from Gerard's dumping and grimaced. "Body-worn, jet-lagged and ready to sleep."

"Will you be ready to see Mother and Dad by this weekend, do you think?"

"That should be fine." Elise yawned and stood up from the couch. "You really don't have to give up your bed to me, Maggie. The couch would be fine. God knows, I've slept on worst."

"Don't be silly," Maggie said, as she stood up, brushing her trembling hands against her jeans. "I'll get an extra blanket for you." Elise shuffled across the floor to the bedroom door and then turned.

"Find me something pretty to wear and I'll get my hair cut or something..."

"Combed?"

Elise laughed. "It's a thought, anyway. "

Maggie snapped off the living room lamp and went to the hall closet for extra blankets.

"Oh, Maggie?"

"Yes, Elise?"

"See if you could find something with some color to it, would you? Maybe pink? I'm so sick of black I could die."

Chapter Seven

The headline across the front page read: *Intruder Robs and Rapes 2nd Victim.* Deirdre smoothed the page flat with her hands. *When are they going to get this guy?* She moved her mug of decaffeinated coffee closer to her and started to read the story.

"Maggie in yet?"

She looked up and nodded to Gary as he was coming in the door. "Are you on the front desk today?" he asked. "Where's Jenny?"

"Sick, I guess." Deirdre shrugged and managed a smile for Gary's scowl.

"Again?" He snapped his daily paper against his thigh. "What's the deal here? She's always sick. What's the point of having a receptionist if she's never here to receive? Oh, never mind." He turned on his heel and stomped into the recesses of the office, presumably to wind his way down the corridor to the kitchen where Deirdre had a fresh pot of coffee perking away.

She looked back down at the newspaper article. *"An unidentified woman at the Claymore Apartments was awakened in the middle of the night by an intruder, who told her to put a pillowcase over her head..."*

"Hey, Dierds, is Gary in yet?"

Maggie leaned over the receptionist's desk to sign the agency attendance sheet.

Deirdre nodded. "He just got here."

"Where's Jenny? That girl is hopeless. What is it this time?"

"I don't know. Just sick."

"Gary's in, did you say?" Maggie hurried down the corridor not waiting for a reply.

Deirdre sighed and straightened the newspaper. *"...after which she was sexually assaulted by the man, said to be in his early thirties. Detective Lieutenant John Burton revealed that the woman was forced to..."*

The phone rang and Deirdre gave another sigh, pushed the paper away and picked up the receiver before it could ring again.

"Selby & Parkers Advertising. Good morning," she said, wondering if this day was going to be as long as it felt.

***

"Have I got news for you." Maggie pulled a chair up to Gary's desk and settled her briefcase on the floor.

"I hate it when people tell me that."

"Guess what."

"I don't like guessing. Just tell me."

"Elise is back."

"What are you talking about? Your *sister*? What do you mean 'back'?"

"I mean, she's here. In my apartment. Gary, she's alive!"

"Maggie, that's wonderful!" Gary stood up and squeezed her arm. "But how? How is she—"

"It's a long story. She was trying to protect my parents by dropping out, I guess because some of the things she was involved in at the time. She thought it was for the best. Can you believe it?"

Gary shook his head slowly. "Wow," he said. "But then who was the woman in France you said was her?"

"I don't know. I think my father was planning on running a DNA test on the ashes, so we would've found out soon enough that she wasn't Elise."

Maggie looked so happy, so beamingly, foolishly happy, that Gary could only sit and smile at her. "Man, that's great, Maggie. Your parents must've flipped."

Maggie hesitated. "I haven't told them yet."

"You haven't?"

"Gary, she looks like hell right now. She looks like a junkie, okay?"

"Sure, Maggie. It's just that, I don't know, your parents are thinking she's still dead when she's sitting in your apartment drinking Perrier and making tuna salad sandwiches just feels wrong to me."

"It's just until the weekend. I'll call them Friday and tell them the news and then we'll both go over on Saturday. If I was to call them now, they'd be over at my place and, I don't know, Elise can be sort of funny. I want things to go as well as they possibly can."

"I'm sure you know what you're doing. That's great news that she's back. How is she at answering phones? We need a new receptionist." Gary began shuffling through the papers on his desk.

"I'm not finished. I also met the famous Gerard last night."

"You're kidding."

"That's how I got Elise. Gerard called and demanded five thousand dollars or else he'd cause trouble with Nicole —"

"He called to blackmail you?" Gary was incredulous.

"Well, I guess he *did* blackmail me, because I got a hold of my Dad and he scraped up the money—"

"You paid him blackmail money?"

"Gary, he was going to cause a stink about Nicole. I brought her into the country illegally, you know."

"You did?" Gary stared at Maggie as if he were seeing her for the first time.

"I told you all this!"

"You most certainly did not."

"Well, that confirms that you don't listen to me. Anyway, I handed over the money to him—"

"When?"

"Last night, Gary. All this happened last night."

"When last night?"

"Around midnight in the parking lot at Lenox Square."

"I cannot believe you were running around after midnight. I won't even let Darla take the garbage out because of all the crime in this town!" He tossed a newspaper in her lap. "Read any headline. Read the funny pages. Nothing but murder and rape in lovely ATL."

Media director, Patti Stump, stuck her head in Gary's office doorway. "Are we still meeting on Hi-Jinks, Gary?"

Gary ran a hand through his hair in exasperation. "Oh, God, I don't know. I don't really want to."

"But we need to."

"I know. Okay, five minutes in the conference room. Maggie, you need to be a part of this too. That is, if you're not busy committing any felonies between now and then."

"What is your problem, Gary?"

"My problem, Maggie, my problem is..." He looked at Patti, still hovering in the doorway and smiled artificially at her. "Why don't you go on ahead, Patti, and we'll be right there." She shrugged and left. "My *problem* is that I worry about you and you don't have the sense God gave lettuce."

"Thank you for that vote of—"

"Here I am worried sick about Darla and Haley, and I have to worry about you too because you haven't got brains enough to stay inside behind locked doors when the city's crawling with maniacs and psychos. I swear, I feel like the whole world is squatting right on my shoulders."

"Gary, I'm sorry—"

"Don't be sorry. Be smarter. Please. I worry about everything, you know? I mean, give me a break, Maggie. I would greatly appreciate it."

She stood up to leave. "Gary, are you sure you can handle all this?" She waved her hand to take in the office. "I mean, it's not worth having a stroke over."

"Five minutes. The conference room. And...I am glad your sister's back."

She picked up her briefcase and walked to his doorway. She turned to look at him but he wouldn't meet her eyes. She made a mental note to call Darla later. Maybe Darla could give her a better idea of what was going on with him. She walked down the corridor to her office, where she was startled to find Patti sitting at her desk.

"Hello. This is a surprise." Maggie forced a smile. She wanted to oust the woman from her swivel chair and spend her five-minute grace period getting a mug of coffee. That didn't seem likely now.

"Hey, Maggie, I wondered if you have a minute."

"The same as you." Maggie dumped her briefcase on the desk. "Five of them."

"Oh, yeah, right. Well, I wondered if you might have some time to talk with me about a situation I've got. Maybe you could give me some advice on how to handle it."

"Well, sure, what can I do for you, Patti?" She perched on the edge of her desk, hoping it was hint enough to the media director to relinquish Maggie's chair.

"It's a guy." Patti blushed and smiled.

Maggie was surprised. Before this minute it hadn't occurred to her that Dr. Stump might have a softer side to her.

"He's very special and I'm hoping he will become a more permanent fixture in my life."

Maggie should have guessed Stump wouldn't have a normal affair of the heart. It already sounded less like a love affair and more like she was shopping for a towel rack. "That's great, Patti. So what seems to be the problem?"

"How do I get him out of neutral gear? I mean, he seems content to keep things as they are. That is unacceptable to me." She shrugged. "I want more from him."

Maggie shifted uncomfortably on the desk edge. "How long have you known this guy?"

"About six months. We've gotten pretty close."

"Are you thinking marriage at some point? Is that what we're talking about here?"

"Marriage would be very agreeable," Patti said, smiling almost shyly.

"Well, in that case, I'd just tell him what you want." Maggie hopped down from the desk corner and began to pick out the materials she would need for the meeting. "I mean, just say, 'I'm hoping this leads to marriage. That's what I'm looking for with you.' Be direct and then see how he reacts."

Patti stood up slowly. "Right. Well, thanks, Maggie," she said coldly.

"Does that help?" *Why does she always make me feel so uncomfortable?*

"What do *you* think, Maggie? A man is acting reluctant to advance a stagnant relationship and you suggest I torch the whole project by pushing him to the point where he has no alternative but to reject me? What sort of help do you think that qualifies as?"

Maggie reddened and gathered up her notebook and schedules. "Well, look, I'm sorry you don't like my advice. But that's what I'd do," she said defensively, although a little voice in her knew it wasn't at all.

"Sure you would, Maggie." The smile had returned to Patti's lips, but it was not a nice one.

The day was dragging on interminably. After a long and essentially unproductive product meeting with Gary and Patti—where Patti refused to look at or speak to her for most of the meeting—Maggie came back to her desk to find the cellphone she'd left in the drawer full of urgent text messages and voice mails from Brownie.

Crap. She'd forgotten she'd called him last night.

She dumped her notebook on the desk and dialed him. "Hey, Brownie."

"I cannot believe you went out last night!"

Maggie closed her eyes and rested her chin on her hand on the desk. "Funnily enough, I've already been yelled at today for this infraction, Brownie."

"Not by me, you haven't! I could throttle you, Maggie. Do you have any idea—"

"I called you at eleven-thirty last night and *you* weren't home. I mean, unless you were screening my call?"

"I left my phone in the car."

"All night?"

"Goddamn it, Maggie—"

"Oh, well, I'm sure it's none of my business *where* you spent the night with your phone sitting out in your car."

"Will you just tell me what the hell happened last night? I talked to your dad and he said he gave you five thousand dollars and never heard back from you."

Shit. She'd forgotten to call her dad back, too.

"Well, if you'd calm down for a minute, I'll tell you."

"There was a rape committed yesterday! *In your neighborhood.* Are you totally insane? Should I talk to your father about the wisdom of letting you have responsibility for yourself? Are you not old enough to have your own apartment?"

"I'm hanging up now."

"No, don't! Just...look, just tell me what happened, okay?"

"If you'll shut up for five minutes, I will."

"I'll shut up. Talk."

"Okay. Gerard Dubois called last night around ten o'clock—"

"Oh my God..."

"He said I had to come up with five thousand dollars immediately or he'd make trouble about Nicole. I couldn't have him going to the police, Brownie!"

"Are you crazy? He's probably a convicted felon back in France! He'd no sooner go to the police over here than—"

"Well, then he might call up my mother or something. He could harass us, Brownie. Do you want to hear my story or not?"

"Go on."

"So I got the money from my dad."

"Did you tell your father?"

"No, but I think he had an idea of what I wanted the money for."

"Jesus! And he didn't stop you?"

"Well, maybe he's just not as good a father as you'd be, Brownie."

"I apologize for that remark. Please, go on."

"So I met Gerard at the parking lot over at Lenox Square. And don't tell me the woman was raped right across the road from there because I already read all about it. I gave him the money and he gave me Elise."

"He gave you Elise? As in your sister Elise? She's alive?"

"I know, isn't it great?"

"And you haven't told your parents?"

"She asked me not to. She looks pretty rough."

"Well you could at least tell them she's alive, Maggie. You don't have to—"

"Brownie, I promised Elise I wouldn't call them."

"Okay. Can I come over?"

"I think that'd be great, Brownie. But can you make it nine? I'm clothes shopping for Elise right after work."

"Fine. Nine, then."

"Sorry about the squabble."

"Yeah, me too."

Maggie hung up and stood and stretched, working the knots out of her neck by rolling it from side to side and letting it flop--chin down onto her chest—as she'd done hundreds of times before during the cool-down segment of her gym workouts. She had been trying to get Elspeth to try aerobics for the benefits of stress relief.

She hated not telling her parents about Elise. It felt wrong on every level. But she had promised Elise she would wait. On the other hand, it might well be an awful shock to both her parents just springing Elise on them out of the blue. Perhaps Elise could at least talk with them on the phone.

Satisfied with this plan, Maggie called her apartment. She waited for ten rings before hanging up. She had talked with Elise two hours ago and knew she was spending most of the day sleeping. She looked at her watch. It was two thirty. Rest was probably the best remedy for Elise right now. She imagined her mother's face animated by rapture at reclaiming her daughter. She saw her father, with tears of unrestrained joy as he embraced his oldest child. Maggie felt a thrill run through her.

How many times in your life can you actually anticipate the happiest of all moments to be lived? For, surely, that is what Saturday will be for her unsuspecting mother and father, Maggie thought.

As she was toying with idea of running downstairs to the lobby delicatessen for a sandwich she could eat at her desk, Deirdre came into her office and dumped a pile of mail on her desk. "Merry Christmas," she said grumpily. "It's come."

Assuming Deirdre was getting tired of taking on the roles of both the receptionist and the traffic manager, Maggie didn't process the meaning of her words until she'd sorted through the pile of industry magazines, artist portfolio postcards, a computer software catalog, and one small aqua-blue airmail envelope.

Maggie hesitated as she looked at the letter, then picked it up as she registered that the slick magazines were tumbling to the floor. Deirdre had already opened it for her.

Her fingers were trembling as she extricated the tissue-thin wafer of paper with her name written at the top.

Maggie,
I miss you very much and think of you. I will see you
in a little time.
Very soon, ma chérie.
Laurent Dernier

If Elise's reappearance hadn't officially made today the happiest day of her life, then Deirdre just had by delivering the few brief words that Maggie had hungered to hear, to read, to see, for nearly five months now. She sat holding the small page and memorized the words, ran her finger over the ink and committed the artwork of his cursive hand to her heart.

Was she really going to let him just waltz back into her life after five months of no word?

She closed her eyes and clasped the now mangled note to her breast and let the joy radiate through her.

*****

Gary gazed out his office window into the late afternoon pollution-dimmed haze. "And that kind of frequency looks good to you?"

"It looks excellent to me, Gary." Patti sat opposite Gary in his office. "This buy will guarantee saturation, practically."

"Practically." The voice came from the doorway.

Gary looked up at Pokey Lane standing in the hall, smirking. "Ah, Pokey. Leaving for the night?"

"What do you mean, 'practically'?" Patti swung her bony legs into a crossed ankle position, as if aiming them at the art director in the doorway. "What do *you* know about frequency? Give me a break."

"Hey, come on, Patti..." Gary made a *calm-down* gesture with his hands. *It was too late in the day for this shit.*

"I know as much as any first-year assistant buyer would know, darling—that if you spend a fortune on drive-time and every other kinda prime air time that you can saturate just about anything. 'Practically,'" he added sarcastically.

"How much *are* we spending, Patti?" Gary looked up from his hands.

"I don't believe this!" Patti huffed. "I have a budget. Does anybody remember the budget?"

"Yeah, that's what the client is gonna wanna know." Pokey said.

"I don't know what your problem is, asshole," Patti snarled at Pokey. "But I—"

"Hey! That's not necessary, Patti," Gary said. "Come on, let's pack it up for today, what do you say?"

"We definitely *should* pack it up when a little monkey-faced layout artist can tell me how to buy time—"

Gary wanted to reach over and wrap her red floral scarf around her flapping mouth. "Please, stop it, both of you. Pokey, go ahead and knock off for the day." Pokey shrugged and gestured to Gary in a catch-ya-later-buddy motion that served to further infuriate Patti in its attempt at male confederacy. She folded her arms and glared at the retreating art director.

"God, Patti, why do you let him get to you?" Gary rubbed his eyes and leaned back into his chair. "I mean, what is it between you two? Are you, like, ex-lovers or something?"

"Don't be revolting. The man's an ape."

"Well, stranger things have happened in my experience."

Patti paused dramatically as she stood up from the swivel chair that faced Gary's desk. Her face was flushed, her eyes wide and fixed on Gary. Her long fingers groped unconsciously at the loose cotton belt that hung from her waist.

He found himself bracing against her words.

"Gary, I would like to talk with you about something that's personal."

"Patti, did you talk to Maggie? You know I have all the women in the office talk to her."

"I know you do, and I did. She was useless."

"I see. Well, can it wait?" In his present state, he'd probably give her a thirty percent salary increase just to be able to be in his car and on his way home within the next fifteen minutes.

"I don't feel it can, no."

"All right." He stood up and began packing up his briefcase, hoping this would at least be moving them both in the right direction: out the door.

"There is someone in the office who is making it difficult for me to perform my job."

"Do you mean Pokey?"

She made a face. "No, I mean difficult in that I find myself distracted as a result of our close working relationship."

Gary snapped shut his briefcase and looked up at the woman. She was dressed in some awful polyester double knit skirt suit. A tall woman, she nonetheless looked like she was swimming in the bulky material, and Gary was struck by how warm she must be in it. "Let's continue this in the elevator, shall we?" He nodded toward the door.

She picked up her briefcase at the foot of her chair.

"You know, Patti, these things happen all the time." He knew he sounded idiotic. "But we're expected to behave professionally in any case, you know? We need to transcend our feelings and get the job done. I mean, what would the industry be like if we all just behaved according to how we felt at the time? Like, if I hated a particular voice talent but he was the best one for the job, I'd be shooting myself in the foot, right?" *I'm blathering*, he thought as he jabbed his finger at the down arrow button on the elevator. "So, we all have to, you know, do things and work with people we don't—"

"Why do you keep implying that I'm having trouble getting along with someone?" Patti's brittle voice stabbed at the airspace between them with no air conditioner's hum to buffer its abrasiveness. "I am *attracted* to someone in our office. I think they may be *attracted* to me too."

"Well? What's the problem?" Gary punched the down button again.

Stupid elevators! Has the building turned off the damn electricity or what?

"The problem, Gary, as I'm sure you know only too well, is that I'm in love with you."

As Maggie drove down Peachtree Road toward her apartment, she leaned over her Macy's department store purchases to reach for the letter again.

I think that I will see you in a little time. Did that mean he's coming to Atlanta? Perhaps he was going to suggest she come back to Cannes? She tucked the letter into her handbag on the passenger seat. Why does he say *and think of you? Is that just bad English, or is he some place special that's made him think of me?* She rubbed her eyes tiredly. It didn't matter. He'd written her. Finally. He'd reached out.

And that was all that mattered.

She pulled into the back parking area of her building and looked up at the darkened structure. Smack in the middle of fashionable, trendy Buckhead, The Parthenon was a throwback to another era. A huge, looming edifice, it looked more like a castle than a honeycomb of modern apartment units. Somber and out of step with its surroundings, it had been an area landmark for over one hundred years. The Parthenon was that curious mix of something so wrong for its eco-climate and cultural setting that it was perversely viewed as a resounding success.

She glanced up at her apartment window and was glad to see the living room light was on. That meant Elise was awake, she thought, and immediately was struck by the pleasant anticipation she realized she'd been feeling all day long. Elise hadn't answered the apartment phone all afternoon, and Maggie realized how much she was looking forward to telling Elise about Laurent. Maggie couldn't wait to tell Elise how mysterious and sweet and sensual Laurent was. From his heavy, expressive eyebrows to the subtle twitch of his full French lips.

Maggie unlocked the heavy back door to the building and shifted her parcels in her arms. She'd stopped for Chinese food on the way back and now the aroma of steamed dumplings and moo shu pork rose deliciously in the air. She hurried down the narrow carpeted hall to her apartment. As soon as she'd entered the building, she heard a rumbling hum of voices coming from the hallway.

Something was wrong.

Later, she would say it was the noise, the sounds of burping police walkie talkies, the velvet mumblings of a gathering crowd that stood on both sides of her apartment door attempting to peer past the lone policeman standing outside.

When she saw the policeman she found herself groping for the least painful option available to her. She had talked with Elise shortly after eleven this morning and then not again the rest of the day. If Elise had reconnected with Gerard, if she had somehow gotten more drugs, if she had…it was hard to think, impossible to imagine why the police would be in her apartment unless…

Before she could push her way to the front of the scrum of bodies, she saw the gurney begin to make its slow exit across her apartment threshold.

It wasn't until the policeman snapped his head in her direction and the rubberneckers who surrounded her began to inch away that she realized she had screamed.

Maggie stumbled to the head of the crowd and felt the hands of the policeman come down hard and unrelenting on her arms. But all she could see was the black body bag on the gurney. She twisted out of the policeman's grasp. "That's my sister!" she said, hoping it wasn't true, praying there was some way it wasn't true.

"Do you live here, Miss?"

Maggie still gripped the handles of her shopping bags as the gurney stopped in front of her. She nodded.

"Detective! This woman lives here."

Maggie felt the policeman's hands on her relax into a guiding pressure as she was pulled away from the gurney and into her apartment.

Two men not in uniforms stood in her living room. At least four other police officers were in the dining room.

Maggie saw that a lamp had been knocked over and a candy dish lay upside down on the carpet. Aside from that, the living room was tidy, each cushion in its place, the smell of Chinese pancakes and plum sauce slowly beginning to mix with the scent of lavender potpourri on the coffee table.

This can't be happening.

Maggie looked into the faces of the two detectives and she could see by their mouths that they were speaking to her, but the volume seemed to have gone down on her world. She staggered to the couch and sank onto it, her heart a heavy weight of emotion. She turned to stare blindly out the narrow French doors that led to the small stone balcony overlooking Peachtree Road. She could see the tips of the lone mimosa tree just outside her apartment, its stubborn, flamboyant blooms unfurled amongst a stand of the ubiquitous Georgia pine, a radiant reminder of nature's individuality, its irony.

Her eyes, dry and wide, lowered to fall on the Macy's bag at her feet—her sister's triumphant homecoming gown. A pretty fuchsia dress with lace tatting at the collar that Elise could now, finally, be buried in.

Chapter Eight

Maggie sat in her living room, her hands folded in her lap. The small travel alarm clock she kept perched on a shelf in the living room bookcase blinked out the digitized time: 9:47. Brownie had shown up thirty minutes earlier.

Elise had been found strangled in Maggie's bedroom.

Maggie watched the older of the two detectives. He was big, like Laurent, a little stoop-shouldered, and she thought he had a kind face. The other one, in the kitchen talking to Brownie, just looked unhappy.

"Miss Newberry?" Chief Detective Jack Burton sat down in a tub chair facing her. "I need to ask you a few questions."

Maggie looked up and knew her eyes must look like two ragged, red holes.

"Miss Newberry?"

"Yes?" She could hear the murmur of voices from the kitchen and wondered if they thought Brownie was a suspect.

"I need to ask you now while everything's still fresh, and I know it's hard."

Even though it was well over an hour ago, Maggie could still hear the squeaking sound of the gurney as it began its heavy journey across the worn hall carpet to the front door. The coroner had finished his preliminary, on-site inspection. The rest of his invasions of Elise would be done in the privacy of a sterile laboratory.

"...what time, exactly, would that be?"

She shook her head, bringing her fist to her mouth.

"It's all right, Miss Newberry. I know how hard this is. Take your time."

"Could you...could you repeat the question?" she managed.

"The first time you called your sister. When was that?"

"Eleven, or so. Maybe a little earlier. I had a late morning meeting." *A million years ago, a late morning meeting where we all sat around laughing and joking.*

"And she was home?"

"Yes." Maggie looked up at the detective. "I assumed she was home the other times I called too. I figured she didn't answer the phone because she was resting. She'd been sick."

"You say she hadn't been in town very long?"

"That's right."

"And she was staying with you until...?" He left the sentence unfinished.

"Until..." Maggie searched for an answer.

"Miss Newberry, the point of my question is to ascertain whether this was going to be a long visit or just a passing through visit."

"She was back for good." It occurred to Maggie that she didn't know if that was true.

"And she flew here from France?" Again, the kind face, the gentle voice. Maggie noticed a slight tic in his lip as he spoke.

"That's right." Maggie's eyes rested on the Macy's shopping bag still at her feet. *Oh, Elise, how could you be gone? We were going to be a family again.* She looked into his eyes and found herself thinking: *He's seen this sort of thing a thousand times before. Seen someone, just like me, feel and act just like this. A thousand times over.*

"When you came home tonight did you notice anything different or strange at any time? In the parking lot? Walking up to your door? Inside your apartment?"

Maggie shook her head as he spoke. "No. What am I going to tell my mother and father?"

Burton grimaced in an expression of sympathy. "I'm sorry, Miss Newberry."

Maggie smoothed her damp palms against the cotton fabric of her skirt.

"The coroner will give his report after the autopsy. There'll be an inquest. Probably next week. Once all the evidence is in."

"Was this random, do you think?"

"Too early to say."

Burton signaled to his partner to check on Brownie in the back room. "I'm afraid we'll need to ask you to vacate your apartment for the next three or four days while we take fiber and hair samples."

Maggie turned away from him. She needed to cry very hard for a very long time.

An hour later, sitting in Brownie's car as they drove along the immaculate, sycamore-lined road to her parents' home, Maggie held Brownie's free hand, her lips pressed together in a grim line. She tried to tell herself that for her parents to have seen Elise in the state she had been in would have been tantamount to a visitation of the horror tale *The Monkey's Paw*, where a grief-stricken mother wished her recently dead son back with her again and got her wish only to have something monstrous return to her from the grave.

That would have been Elise, Maggie told herself. With her ruined face and arms, pocked by blunt, used needles, her clothes and skin smelling of sweat and urine, her hair a matted mess of gnarly dreadlocks.

Maggie's vision blurred as she watched the passing neighborhoods, where houses went for nothing less than four million. Mostly a lot more. The top tier of Atlanta real estate.

Her throat closed, because she knew that even if Elise had been presented to them mad as a hatter, screaming and naked, filthy and profane, her parents still would have wept tears of joy to have her back.

She looked at Brownie and tried to take strength from his solid grip on her hand. Tried to tap into his stoic front, his resiliency. And all she could think as he drove her closer and closer to her mother and father was: *if by some miracle, some fantastic cosmic piece of magic, you got the chance to have five minutes with a departed loved one, just five minutes to say I love you, I miss you...*

And Maggie knew she had cheated them out of that forever.

Darla Parker picked up the teapot, with its imprint of faded roses, and held it over her husband's teacup. Her eyes watched him, not her aim, as he sat, face buried in the newspaper. She spilled hot tea onto his sleeve.

"Damn it, Darla!" Gary snatched his soiled cuff away. "What is your problem this morning?"

Darla replaced the teapot and sighed. She folded her hands in her lap.

"First you practically kill me with that stupid whatever it is you left on the stairs—"

"Vacuum cleaner."

"Look, Darla, don't start with me today, okay? I've got this *one* day in the week to relax and forget the office and I don't mean to spend it at war with you." Gary flapped the newspaper out and returned to the article he was reading.

Darla took a small sip from her own cup and then cleared her throat. Gary threw the newspaper onto the table and covered his face with his hands.

"God, am I having a nervous breakdown, or what?" His voice sounded strained.

"Quit your job, sweetheart."

He groaned. "Who am I gonna quit to? Myself? I'm the boss, remember?"

"It's making you miserable, Gary. It's bad for all of us. I can see it even if you can't. Quit the job."

"Stop saying that!" Gary stood, picked up the newspaper then slapped it back down on the breakfast table. "I can't quit the job! Why not just say move to Alaska? Or get a lobotomy? Or become a priest? I can't! I can't do it! God! Can nobody hear me?" He was turning to leave the room when the kitchen phone rang. Enjoying the dramatic punctuation of its timing, he snatched it up and barked, "Yes?"

Darla slowly got up from the table and began to clear the dishes.

"Hey, Maggie, what's up? Everything okay?" He turned to catch a glimpse of Darla, but she stood at the sink with her back to him, rinsing cereal bowls and listening.

Gary heard Maggie's voice catch and he stiffened. *God, now what?* "What's happened?"

Darla turned to face him.

"Good God!"

"Gary, what is it?" Darla was at his side now, tugging on his sleeve. "What's happened? Is she okay?"

"Her sister was killed last night in her apartment."

"Oh, my God." Darla's hand flew to her mouth, her eyes wide with horror. She studied Gary's shocked face, as if she might somehow be able to hear the story just by watching his face.

"Maggie, how?" Gary asked, his voice tense. Darla could hear the kitchen clock ticking as Gary listened and Darla waited. "Are you kidding? She *let* him in?" Gary's eyes flicked to Darla's and she shook her head in disbelief.

"Maggie, it could've been you. He could've gotten you. God, your poor parents. How are they?"

Darla watched her husband frown as he listened.

"Well, *don't*. It doesn't do anybody any good beating yourself up for it. Do you want some company? Do you want me and Darla to come by?"

Darla nodded vigorously at him.

"Okay, well, you know we're here if you need us. I'm so sorry, Maggie. So sorry for you and your parents." He returned the receiver to its cradle and stood staring out the breakfast room's large bay window. From it he could see their eight-year old daughter, Haley, playing with some neighbor children.

"Oh, Gary. Poor Maggie. How awful."

Gary tore his gaze away from his daughter and looked at his wife. "Maybe you were right, Darla. Maybe this job isn't such a good thing."

Darla searched his face and tried to smile encouragingly.

Maggie lay on the guest bed in her parents' house and stared up at the white ceiling. Tiny, fluorescent stars blinked back in a faint constellation painted on the ceiling. Maggie had never noticed them before.

She had looked into her parents' eyes as they tried to understand when she told them of Elise's murder earlier that day. She held her father's hand and watched him nod as if she were warning him that the Dow Jones might plummet soon. She watched her mother weep, and, impossibly, nod understandingly as to why Maggie hadn't called when Elise showed up.

After all the talking, Maggie had cried. She cried for the daughter who had finally come home, for the impetuous artist, the hopeless romantic, the recalcitrant single mother. But most of all, she cried for the sister she'd known so little.

The next day, Maggie sat in the gathering room with Nicole. The room was a light and cheery place, which captured the sun's needles of light and spun them into prisms and rectangles of luminescence.

Nicole's face, as usual, gave nothing away. Her eyes, large and implacable, met Maggie's gaze easily.

"*Grandmère* is very unhappy right now," Maggie said. "And it's me who's done it, you see." Maggie reached over to pat out a wrinkle in Nicole's cotton corduroy jumper.

Will she never come out of the warm little burrow in her mind and join the rest of us? Is wherever she is so nice and safe that we will never know her?

Maggie leaned over and touched Nicole's baby-soft cheek and thought, for an instant, that her eyes flickered in response.

Are you all we have left of her now?

"Darling?"

Maggie turned to see her mother enter the room and her heart ripped at the sight. Elspeth had obviously had a hard night. Her beautiful face was weary and lined.

"Did Brownie leave?" Elspeth asked.

"He had to get back. He said he'll call later."

"I'm sorry I missed him this morning."

"Are you going to come in?"

Elspeth shook her head and tried to smile. "I think I'll read in my room today, darling, if you don't mind. Annie will be here shortly to look after Nicole. How are you, *ma petite*?"

The girl looked blankly at her grandmother.

"What are your plans for the day, Margaret?"

Maggie shrugged. "I might go back to my apartment and pick up a few things. Detective Burton said I could. They've got some people there, I guess, to help me. Then, I don't know."

There was a brief silence before Elspeth turned to leave.

"Mom, I'm so sorry I didn't tell you about Elise."

"I know, darling. But it doesn't matter."

"I don't know how I can live with myself."

"Don't be silly, Maggie. It's in the past." Her mother's back seemed to stiffen during the exchange, as if her body couldn't lie as easily as her voice could. "Let's not talk about it in front of Nicole."

"She doesn't know?"

"There doesn't seem much point. I'm off now. Dinner is at six, as usual."

"Okay."

Maggie watched her mother's retreating back and felt worse than before Elspeth had come downstairs. She looked back over at Nicole, who was watching Elspeth's departure.

"She's really sad right now, Nicole."

The little girl blinked once and looked at Maggie.

Did Nicole somehow know Maggie had cheated her out of her one last chance to see her mother? Did she, unencumbered by the love that bound Maggie's parents, feel free to hate her aunt for her stupidity and selfishness? For surely selfishness had been a major part of it, Maggie thought. The notion of presenting Elise to her parents as if she were a beribboned parcel had loomed dominant in Maggie's daydreams.

When the doorbell sounded, it was so gentle and musical that, for a moment, Maggie thought it was one of the many house clocks unobtrusively heralding the hour. Elspeth had a passion for clocks of all kinds and collected them to the point where her husband had finally forced her to weed them out of the house. It was true, Maggie thought as she got up from the heavy Queen Anne armchair to answer the door, the house had begun to resemble a large and noisy clockmaker's shop a few years ago. All the ticking and chiming and onerous hourly and quarter hourly booming had nearly driven her poor father mad, and served as the starting point for hours of family jokes.

Maggie walked to the end of the sitting room, where two pairs of French doors led out to the garden. Although not the main entrance, the garden portal was the closest to the driveway and so the one most commonly used. Besides, Elspeth said she liked the idea of visitors enjoying her garden as they walked to the door. She thought it much friendlier than the tedious, precision-manicured box hedges and bricked path that led to the front, with its massive columns and imposing porticoes.

"A little bit of Tara goes a long way," she liked to tell her daughters. "The point is not to intimidate people."

"Just to have more money than them, that's all," Elise had quipped in return.

Elise had never given her mother much quarter.

Maggie peered through the panel sheers in the door and, seeing nothing, pulled open the doors and stepped outside. The warmth and humidity of the morning struck her. The air conditioning had prompted goose bumps on her arms and legs, but they dissolved upon contact with the moist Southern air.

She stepped out onto the flagstone patio that curved away from the double doors. A small stone bench sat nearly hidden among a cluster of spirea, forsythia and camellia. Vines of thick, glossy ivy snaked along the ground and up and over the dry stone wall that contained the whole garden. The fragrance from the rose bushes—lurching their way up a rickety trellis—was light and sweet on the heavy Georgia air.

A blooming bush of American Beauty roses shook slightly in the corner of her vision making her turn, hands still on the door handles, to see a tall man standing next to the bush of blood-red roses.

It was Laurent.

Chapter Nine

Maggie stood quietly, her breath sucked out of her. He was wearing jeans and a blue jersey tee shirt. His eyes smiled sadly at her.

"*So,*" he said softly. "I am here."

She released the door handles and moved out onto the bricked, terrace steps. Laurent caught her in his arms and lifted her off the ground. She wrapped her arms around his thick, sunburned neck and laid her cheek against his chest. For this perfect moment, she didn't care to see his face, examine his eyes, hear his story, or mark his changes. It was just enough that he'd finally come.

"*Mon amour,*" he murmured. He held her for several moments and then set her down and looked into her eyes. "I know it is bad for you now, *chérie.*" He leaned down and kissed her. "But it will be all right now, *comprends?* Laurent is here."

Maggie kept her hands firmly on his arms, as if afraid to let him go a second time. He was so looming she had the odd sensation that he blotted out the morning sun, at the same time he brought light into the garden. "I can't believe you're here," she said. "After nearly six months of no word, no letter." She felt her heart crumble into his hands as she looked at his handsome face, so longed for, so well remembered. And loved.

"I told you I would come," he said, his eyes probing hers.

"I just can't believe I'm seeing you again, that it's really you." She knew she should let go of him, but she couldn't bring herself to. "Where are you staying?"

"With you, *bien sûr!*" Laurent smiled and she felt her heart expand in her chest in an attempt to encompass her joy. *Bien sûr.*

"How in the world did you find me? How did you know I'd be here?"

Laurent waved away the question as if it were a fly droning about his head. He nodded toward the interior of the house. "Come, I think I am meeting *la mère?*"

"Margaret? Is everything all right, darling?"

Maggie turned to see her mother standing in the French doors, Nicole positioned at her side like a miniature sentinel.

"Mother." Maggie dropped her hands from Laurent's arms and turned to face her mother. "This is a good friend of mine. I...we met in France. He helped us get Nicole back. Laurent Dernier, this is my mother, Elspeth Newberry. Mom, this is Laurent."

Elspeth Newberry stepped forward onto the flagstone pathway and offered Laurent her hand. He took it in his large sunburnt hand and murmured, "*Enchanté, Madame.*"

Elspeth's eyes darted to Maggie, but her smile stayed intact. "I am pleased to meet you, Laurent."

"I am so sorry about your daughter. *Je regrette, Madame.*"

Elspeth's eyes filled. "*Merci,*" she said, turning to lead the way into the house.

Laurent looked at Maggie. *Ca va?* She nodded and reached out to take his arm again. *Oh, baby, ça va,* she thought.

That night at dinner Maggie couldn't help feel as if he had always been with them. As foreign as he was—from his size to his accent to his very maleness in what had become an increasingly feminine household—Laurent just seemed to belong at the Newberry family dinner table. Maggie was pleased to notice her mother had seen to it that the big Frenchman would not be homesick or hungry his first night in Atlanta. She had Becka, their cook, prepare a rabbit smothered in rosemary, followed by mini crock-pots of honey and saffron *crèmes*.

Nicole sat between Maggie and Laurent, her brown hair gathered in a French braid with gold velvet ribbons interlacing the plaiting. She wore a simple chocolate-brown shift. Its floppy Peter Pan collar displayed Nicole's small head like a cabbage on a platter.

At several points in the evening, Maggie saw Laurent watching Nicole closely, and once or twice he attempted to engage her. Nicole sat at the dinner table quiet and seemingly unseeing, her only movements the slow, robotic ones that carried her spoon from her plate to her mouth.

Laurent's meeting with Maggie's father was a warm and friendly one. John Newberry was good-humored, if a little wounded in general, and he welcomed Laurent wholeheartedly into his home. Watching the two of them talk at dinner made Maggie wonder if Laurent and her father might become friends someday.

After dinner, her parents and Nicole retired to the gathering room to read or watch TV, leaving the deserted dinner table to Maggie and Laurent.

"Becka will bring coffee in a bit," Maggie said, as she leaned back into her chair. She had almost gotten her fill of looking at him and reassuring herself that he had, indeed, not forgotten her.

"I like your *maman* and *papa* very much. They are good people."

"They are."

"They love that little girl, too. Such a sad one. *Tch-zut!*" Laurent sucked his teeth and shook his head.

"I'm not sure she's really Elise's."

A thin veil seemed to come down between them and Laurent suddenly looked guarded. "Of course she is your sister's daughter. Roger took her from Gerard's house."

"I know, Laurent. It's just that she's nothing like any of us, you know?"

"Give her time, Maggie. You are so impatient, I think." He smiled at her.

"Why did you come, Laurent?" Maggie leaned across the starched white tablecloth toward him. He pulled out a blue packet of *Gitanes* and lit one from a box of matches. He held the smoking match between his fingers and looked at her inquiringly. She got up and walked to the large walnut hutch in the dining room and began rummaging around for an ashtray. "Do you have business in town or something?"

Becka, a middle-aged black woman with shiny, dark skin nearly the color of the hutch, entered the room carrying a silver tray with a coffee pot and creamer. The sugar bowl was delicate light-blue china, with two matching cups and saucers.

"Hey, Becka." Maggie pulled a crystal ashtray from one of the drawers of the hutch and returned to the table.

"Your mother and father havin' their coffee in the livin' room," Becka said as she unloaded her tray.

"You are the chef, *Madame?*" Laurent stood up from his chair.

"I cooked it, if that's what you mean." Becka hid a smile.

Laurent kissed the tips of his fingers with a loud smacking noise. "*C'est magnifique!* It was better than anything in Paris or on the *Cote d'Azur, absoluement.*"

Grinning, Becka hugged the tray to her chest and backed out of the room. "Well, I'm glad you liked it. G'night, Miss Maggie."

"Goodnight, Becka. You outdid yourself. It was delish plus."

The cook exited the dining room with a loud swish of the swinging door.

Maggie thumped down the Waterford ashtray in front of Laurent. "What were you saying about being here on business?"

Laurent looked at her with surprise. "I have no business except for you, *ma petite.* I am here to be with you."

Maggie felt a flush of pleasure creep up her throat to her face. She scraped some breadcrumbs from the table and emptied them into Laurent's ashtray. "How long are you in town for?"

Might as well come right out with it.

Laurent frowned. "I'm here to be with you," he repeated. He looked around the cavernous dining room with its dual hanging chandeliers. "You do not live here."

"No. The cops made me move out until they're done with the...crime scene."

"How long?"

"I can move back day after tomorrow."

"We will move back then." He shrugged as if it was all just so simple.

Maggie felt a thrill run through her when she realized he wasn't leaving right away. She also couldn't help but imagine a few scenarios in her head where the two of them would be together in bed again. She must have telegraphed what she was thinking by a blush, because Laurent grinned knowingly at her.

"You know," she said, trying to change the subject and get a better handle on her emotions. "I never did get straight what it is you do for a living. I mean, can you afford to just take time off like this?"

Laurent poured her coffee and then his own before answering. He held up the china creamer and she shook her head.

He poured a hefty dollop of cream into his coffee. "I am *en vacances, oui?* On vacation?"

"And then you'll go back to France?"

Laurent touched Maggie's chin gently with his thumb and forefinger. "Don't worry, okay? I am here today."

Great. One of those live for the moment types. Maggie sipped her coffee.

"You have been through very much. To have a sister die..." He shook his head and clucked his tongue.

"I intend to find out who killed her." Maggie was surprised to hear the words coming from her mouth. Up until that moment, it hadn't occurred to her that she would do anything but wait to hear from the police.

"*Comment?*" Laurent set his coffee cup down in its saucer and held her gaze. "The police will find out—"

"No. They won't. They don't care."

"It is their job."

"Laurent, you don't understand. The cops are busy chasing psycho nut cases right and left in this town. There's one guy who's been raping people near my own neighborhood—"

"Mon Dieu!"

"To the cops, one more weirdo is just one more weirdo."

"Merde! Maggie, if I had known..."

"Well, this has been a particularly bad summer for crime in Atlanta. The guy who strangled Elise—"

"I think you are upset, Maggie. You need to forget a little bit. All this about strangling and—"

"I can't forget." Maggie's eyes hardened. "God, Laurent, you just need to look at my mother's face. *I* put that look there! If I'd have told them Elise was back, if I'd just picked up the damn phone. I should have driven Elise straight here that very first night."

Laurent frowned but let her talk. He seemed to know she needed to. She clutched her starched damask napkin with her fists.

"And well, okay, so I didn't. I'll go to my grave regretting it, but there's no reversing it. That's done. But I'm trying to tell you that it's the *cops* who are going to forget. And then the bastard who killed Elise will have gotten away with it. And I'll *never* be able to look my mother and father square in the eyes, or myself, or—"

"D'accord, d'accord, all right, then. *Je compris."* He leaned over and lifted her effortlessly into his lap. "But you will work with the police, eh? You will see what they have?"

"Yes, of course," Maggie said, completely flustered and surprised to find herself nestled in his arms, her legs draped over his strong forearm. His shirt smelled like sun and citrus.

"And Laurent will help, okay?" He touched her chin so she would look at him. "I can be very resourceful.*"*

She shook her head in amazement. "I just can't believe you're really here."

The big Frenchman shifted her in his arms so he was leaning over her, his face just inches from hers. Maggie felt her stomach do flip-flops in anticipation of the kiss she knew was coming. He leaned in closer and whispered conspiratorially. "But first I think we find where we are to sleep tonight, *oui?"* His eyes twinkled and Maggie heard herself laugh for the first time in two days.

That night, and the following two nights until they moved out, they spent wrapped in each other's arms in Maggie's childhood bedroom. Even at the risk of disapproval from her parents in the midst of their grief, to stay apart had been unthinkable. Laurent held her, petted her, consoled and loved her until the early hours of the morning. They slept little and parted discreetly before breakfast.

At Laurent's insistence, until the morning they drove away from her parents' house and headed toward Maggie's apartment in Buckhead they did not discuss or think about the details surrounding Elise's murder. He had been emphatic.

Just before leaving the small double bed they shared that first morning in Maggie's room, Laurent held her and carefully, lovingly, laid down the ground rules. "You will attend to this matter after we leave, yes?"

"By *this matter*, you mean find the guy who killed my sister?"

Laurent gave her a baleful look that Maggie was already becoming an expert at interpreting. All language differences aside, it meant he knew that *she* knew perfectly well what he meant.

"For two more days," he held up two large fingers before her, "we will eat and make love and take walks, yes? And play with little Nicole and you will be with your parents and you will not think about killers or murder or why the police are so stupid, eh? This you will do?"

"Laurent, I can't just turn my brain off!"

"Two days, *chèrie*," he said, still holding up his fingers. "I will distract you very much but you must work with me, eh? Take these days to heal with your family. Nobody else comes in. Agreed? No police. No killers. Agreed?"

Maggie exhaled in frustration. She couldn't help but think that catching Elise's killer was the fastest way to feel better about losing her sister. And she was also pretty sure that every day she waited was a day lost toward finally feeling no pain again.

But Laurent was insistent. Later, when she was sinking into a tepid bubble bath after an exhausting day spent in the garden, picnicking and hanging hammocks with Laurent and Nicole, it occurred to her that he had been that way in France, too. He was so agreeable and malleable she always had the feeling that *she* was in charge, when all along it was Laurent guiding her.

She didn't know if that scared her about him, or made her hunger for him all the more.

Chapter Ten

Laurent placed the bag of groceries on Maggie's marble countertop. The bag was straining with gleaming bulbs of eggplant, peppers and tomatoes. He rubbed his hands together and pulled from the bag a bottle of olive oil, a baton of French bread and a bunch of green grapes.

Maggie watched him from the doorway of the kitchen. "Where did you get all that stuff?"

He turned to look at her, as if caught by surprise. "Oh, Maggie, there you are!"

"Here I have been all morning, Laurent. It's you who's been out doing God knows what. What is all that stuff there?" She smiled at him.

Laurent continued to unpack his groceries. "You are eating frozen dinners all the time, *non?*" He waved in the general direction of Maggie's freezer, as if to imply even owning a freezer was somehow a shameful thing.

"Not all the time." Maggie peered around him at the groceries. "I eat Cheerios in the morning sometimes."

"*Mon Dieu,*" Laurent muttered. He held up a white block of cheese wrapped in plastic wrap.

"What's that?"

"*Fromage de chevre.*"

"Goat cheese."

"Very good, *chérie.*"

"I hate goat cheese."

"Mix it with your Cheerios. It's good for you."

"Cheese isn't good for you." She wrapped her arms around his middle. "The whole world knows this, except the French. Fact is, we've been keeping it from you."

Laurent tossed the cheese onto the counter and turned to face Maggie. "You and the whole world?" he said, smiling down at her.

"We're very close." She rose up on her toes and kissed him, then laid her head against his broad chest and felt the strength and security of his arms around her.

They had been allowed to return to Maggie's apartment the evening before. Maggie felt uncomfortable living in the place where her sister lost her life. Laurent was clearly doing everything in his power to soften, if not erase, the connection.

"Your asparagus is wilting," she said teasingly.

"Not possible," he said, giving her bottom a squeeze before releasing her and turning back to his groceries.

"You know, I haven't told anybody else this, but the body I identified in Cannes? The one I said was Elise? The cops told me it was an accidental death but it wasn't. There was a bullet hole above her ear."

"*Vraiment?*"

Maggie noticed that Laurent, who stood with his back to her, had stopped chopping.

"Why do you think the cops ruled it an accident? I mean, when there was obviously a bullet hole in the head?"

He shrugged. "Addicts, prostitutes…they are not valuable to the police in a town of so much wealth and influence."

"Just couldn't be bothered, you mean."

"*Exactement.*"

"But it does make me wonder if maybe I wasn't the only one mistaking that body for Elise's."

"You think the Cannes murder was supposed to be your sister?"

"I don't know. Is murder common in Cannes?"

"I think not. But among the society the young woman whose body was found, perhaps more so."

"Every time I try to imagine who could have killed Elise, I come back to a single question: *Why Elise?* And if I answer that question, I always come up with the same answer."

"Gerard."

"That's right. Gerard. He's the only one with a motive. If his wife and child were going to be together and, presumably, happy, don't you think it fits with his character profile that thought might drive him wild? The notion that they didn't need him. Were, in fact, going to be better off without him?"

Laurent frowned and looked unconvinced. "Did you tell the police about Gerard?"

"Yes, but I didn't get the impression they were listening. They did take down his name and stuff."

"They will question him."

"I suppose so."

"*Absoluement.* But I think, perhaps, they will think his reason to kill her is a little *façile.*"

"You're wrong, Laurent. You, of all people, ought to know about crimes of passion."

"*Moi?*" He sounded startled.

"Yes, being French and all."

"Ahhh, *oui,* of course."

"I mean, Gerard had a child by Elise. He lived with her for nearly five years. She was beautiful and she rejected him by coming here to her family. Did I tell you how he just opened up the car door and dumped her out onto the pavement? Yeah, Gerard is definitely my number one suspect."

"You must not speak with him."

"Laurent, don't be silly."

"I am *sérieux*, Maggie. *Je l'interdis.*" *I forbid it.*

"Oh, settle down. Honestly." Maggie felt both annoyed and flattered by Laurent's attempts to command her. "If I talk with him, you'll be there. Okay?"

He looked unhappy with the compromise.

"I probably can't even find him. Meanwhile, I need to talk to people in the apartment building. And don't tell me the police have already done that, because I'm still doing it, okay?"

"*Bien sûr.*" Laurent turned to observe her as she picked up her house keys.

"Look, I'll be back for lunch, okay?" Maggie continued to stand in the doorway, and realized that, for some reason, she wanted his blessing.

He turned and looked at her. "You must do it."

An hour later, she was back.

"You are not being gone very long, *chérie,*" Laurent said cheerfully.

"Nobody saw anything."

Laurent slid a golden crescent of fluffed egg onto a stoneware dish, sprinkled on a few sautéed peppers as garnish and set it down in front of her at the kitchen table. He put his hand against her cheek. "Do you want me to come too? I will tell them: 'You better answer her questions! Or I can be very *méchant.*'"

"I don't think it would help, but thanks." Maggie picked up her fork. The eggs were light and fluffy and she realized she was hungry. "I shouldn't assume people want to help, I guess." She took a bite. "Laurent, am I going to get fat living with you? Because I can't afford a whole new wardrobe."

"Oh, I talked with your *papa*. When you are working tomorrow, I will go with him to his club."

"Really?" Maggie stopped chewing.

"Is it a surprise to you?"

"Well, yeah. Dad never brings my friends to his club. I mean, I don't think he's even brought Brownie."

As Maggie looked at Laurent and wondered what in him that had resonated so strongly with her father, there was a knock at the door.

"That's funny," Maggie said. "People have to buzz you from outside. They can't get inside to knock on your door." She threw down her napkin and started to get up.

Laurent was ahead of her. He went to the front door and swung it open. *"Oui?"*

The man in the hall seemed startled to see Laurent. It was the young man from the last apartment Maggie had visited. He and his wife were newlyweds, both recently unemployed. He'd mentioned they probably would have to move back in with her parents soon.

"I...I wanted...is Maggie here?" He peered nervously into the apartment, clearly intimidated by Laurent. Maggie jumped up and hurried to the door.

"Yes, I'm here. It's Bill, right?"

"Yeah, listen..." He glanced up at Laurent. "We're heading out now, but I remembered something that, if it matters—"

"What? You heard something?"

"Yeah, I forgot about it until just now. I mean, there was so much excitement and everything the night of the...you know...and the cops were asking all their questions, so it just went outta my head."

Maggie nodded eagerly. "You want to come in?"

He shook his head and looked down the hall, as if someone was standing at his doorway waiting for him. "I remembered I saw this guy in the hallway that afternoon. I'm pretty sure it was that afternoon. Might have been the afternoon before, you know?"

My God, Maggie thought. *Had he seen the murderer?*

"I mean, he just does deliveries, you know? So I thought, no big deal. And I don't want to get anybody into trouble, okay?"

"What do you mean, deliveries?"

"From the grocer next door. Sometimes he'll send his boy out to deliver stuff, only he's not really a boy, more like..." and he tapped his head as if to indicate the person might be mentally unstable.

"I see." Maggie was already thinking of her next step. "Thank you. Thanks for taking the time."

"No big deal. Bye." He turned on his heel and was gone.

Laurent ushered Maggie back to their cooling luncheon. "It is a good clue, yes?"

They reseated themselves and Maggie watched Laurent tuck into his omelet with enthusiasm.

"Yeah," she said, thoughtfully. "I really think it might be."

The shop around the corner from Maggie's apartment was a harmonious hodgepodge of sewing notions, eyecups and prophylactics, with creaking wooden display bins filled with fruits and vegetables. Although it was not more than five minutes walking distance from Maggie's apartment, Maggie had only been in the place a couple of times in the four years she'd lived at The Parthenon. It was so much easier just to swing into the parking lot of Winn-Dixie on her way home from work. Driving past the little neighborhood grocery, she'd always gotten the impression that only the elderly residents of the area shopped there. She'd seen them trudging along the sidewalk in front of the place, their wire and wicker baskets, and occasionally their walkers, banging against their knees.

Maggie pushed open the shop door, hearing as she did the off-kilter tinkle of the bell that announced another customer. The place smelled of Ivory soap and soft fruit. Maggie wondered how in the world it managed to survive in a neighborhood where all the real money hopped in BMWs and shopped for their Wheaties in strip shopping centers. Surely, the old-timers she saw doddering about the neighborhood weren't enough to keep this place afloat?

"Can I help you, Miss?"

The proprietor came from behind the soda counter, wiping his hands on a towel that he'd tied in front of his slacks. His sparse gray hair capped a wise old head, it seemed to Maggie. His eyes didn't smile so much as they drilled. They were drilling now.

"I'm Maggie Newberry. I live next door and wondered if I could ask you a few questions?"

"If I can."

"You have a delivery boy?"

"Why?" He cocked his head at her like a bird watching a caterpillar.

"I think he may have seen something that happened in my apartment building and I'd like to talk with him about it."

"Who says he saw something?"

Was she mistaken, or was he becoming a lot less friendly?

"Someone who saw him there."

"Well, why not just ask the someone who saw him there what they saw?"

"Look, will you help me find the guy, or not? I just want to ask him a few questions."

"Boy's slow. Wouldn't harm a fly."

"I just want to talk to him."

The man rubbed his hands across his eyes and then scratched the back of his neck. "The police have already talked to him and me both. This wouldn't be about that again, would it?"

"It was my sister who was killed."

He didn't respond.

"And I was wondering if I could ask him what it was he saw."

"Well, he saw nothing."

"Okay." She waited.

"Didn't see a thing. That's what he told the police."

"But he was there that day? I mean, he was seen there the afternoon of..."

"I have no idea."

"Look." Maggie had about had her limit of the exasperating old cuss not cooperating. "You're his boss. Don't you keep some sort of schedule of the stuff that gets delivered? You know, Mrs. Brown's order sent out 3:15. Stuff like that?"

"I don't know a Mrs. Brown."

"It was just an example."

"When someone calls in an order I just put it together, ring it up and have Alfie take it to the address. I don't have to write it down."

"His name's Alfie?"

"That's right." He looked less smug now. Obviously he hadn't intended to give that much away.

"Is Alfie a teenager?"

"Seems to me a bogus air conditioning van parked out front of The Parthenon for half a day is a hell of a lot more suspicious than a poor half-witted boy."

"There was a fake air conditioning repair van parked out front?"

"You'll have to ask the police about that. I've answered enough questions. Kindly leave Alfie alone. He had nothing to do with this business. Now, if there's nothing else I can help you with…" He turned abruptly and disappeared behind a towering stack of what looked like blue Milk of Magnesia bottles.

Maggie stood for a moment in the middle of the aisle, smelling all the conflicting fragrances and odors, and then left the shop. She hesitated in front of it, not sure of what to do next. The sun had burned off the briefly pleasant morning and was now relentlessly attacking anything and everything that cowered below. She pushed up the sleeves of her thin sweatshirt and was sorry she wasn't wearing her sunglasses.

A fake air conditioning repair van? What did that mean? What in the world would that have to do with Elise?

Clearly, she was going to have to ask Detective Burton to do a better job of keeping her in the loop as he'd promised.

She sat down on the stone bench under the large sycamores in front of her apartment building. The bench, coated with moss and graffiti, was used primarily by Maggie's elderly neighbors, who rested themselves as they made their laborious pilgrimages from pharmacy to lonely apartment room. Maggie had never noticed the pretty bench before.

She tried to imagine where the van would have parked. There was really no spot since the building sat so close to busy Peachtree Road.

Why would a sham repair van be parked in front of my apartment building?

Chapter Eleven

"We hope you know we're all thinking of you, and that we're so terribly, terribly sorry about your sister." Gary spoke from the head of the conference room table, supported by muted murmurs from the rest of the office workers.

"Thank you," Maggie said, letting her eyes fill without embarrassment.

"We sent flowers to your parents," Deirdre said, looking down at her doodling as she spoke. "Since we didn't know when the funeral was going to be."

Maggie cleared her throat and smiled shakily at her co-workers. "It's going to be a memorial service. Just for family."

Deirdre handed Maggie a condolence card showing a seagull soaring over an ocean wave. "We all signed it," she said, still not looking at Maggie.

"Thanks, Deirdre. Thanks, all. That was kind."

"Right," Gary said, clearing his throat. "And now on to business." He gestured to Deirdre to begin reading the traffic sheet.

Obviously relieved to be on safer ground, Deirdre's voice became perky and confident.

"The EMI brochure needs to have copy by the end of the week." She looked at Maggie who nodded.

"I've already started on it."

"And I've got the layout due at the same time because of the tight deadline on this."

"Pokey?" Gary directed his attention to the art director. "Will that be a problem?"

Pokey tossed the schedule down in front of him. "Not if I have any interest in enjoying my weekend or having a life outside the office, I guess it won't," he said, his face twisted into a surly knot.

"Good." Gary nodded at Deirdre to continue.

"I have a problem."

"Yes, Patti?" Gary's voice was tight. He seemed to be concentrating on correcting some typo on the schedule in front of him.

"My problem is the new budget on the Calloway Toys commercial—"

"I haven't gotten to that yet," Deirdre said.

"Well, I've gotten to it right now," Patti hissed at her. "Gary, the new budget cuts the frequency nearly in half. Without the back-to-backs I'd set up—"

"Who's the AE on this?" Gary looked around the table.

"Uh, that's Linda," Deirdre said. "She's with a client."

"All right, we'll discuss it when she's back in the office. Next, Deirdre?"

"That's bullshit!" Patti said. "My new budget is due in Linda's in-box at two o'clock today. I have stations I'm having to renege on. I gave people my word! I'm having to lose discounts that I'd already figured into the budget, discounts that the client was counting on."

"Patti, I'm afraid you'll just have to redo the schedule with the new monies." Gary turned and stared at her, his face reddening with his effort to keep control of his temper.

"And bullshit though it may be, it is also the nature of the business." He looked at Deirdre. Patti gathered up her schedule and pens and stormed out of the meeting.

"Shall we continue?" Gary said wearily.

Two hours later, Maggie sat in one of the wicker chairs that lined the little office courtyard and waited for Gary to join her. The heat was cranking up with each minute she sat there. She removed her scarf and smiled wanly at a couple of female graphic artists from her office as they approached with their own brown bags and settled into chairs a few feet away from her. She watched them extricate their tuna salad sandwiches and little Charles Chips bags from their lunch sacks.

Laurent had packed a lunch for her of stuffed *courgettes* and roasted peppers. She carefully peeled the peppers off the wax paper before popping them in her mouth. The peppers melted in her mouth, offering only the essence of their flavor without the peppers' usual bite. *How does he do that?*

She'd already called him twice today. Twice just to hear his voice and remind herself that he was there, in their apartment, waiting for her. She'd have to resist calling this afternoon. Laurent would be with her father, at his club. She shook her head.

Curiouser and curiouser.

Living with Laurent was a total surprise, she decided. It was not as if she'd ever lived with a man before and so possessed some kind of control sample of cohabitation, but she'd had expectations. Concerns. Probably bred from answering too many *Does He Love You* quizzes in magazines at the hairdressers.

And Laurent had defied them all. He was accommodating, sweet, loving and strong. Did he dislike anything about the way she lived? Not seriously, anyway. Not in a way that wasn't teasing or playful.

The fact was, as frenetic and compulsive as she was —even without a murder investigation topping her To-Do list—Maggie found Laurent's soothing, caretaking ways a balm.

She had never had it to know she wanted it, and now she couldn't imagine living without it.

"Hey, sport. Why not pick a table right out in the middle of the blazing sun?"

Gary tossed down a plastic-wrapped sandwich from the building deli and sat down in a chair opposite Maggie's.

"We can move if you want."

"Patti told me she's in love with me."

"Patti *Stump*?"

"No, Maggie, Patti Page. Yes, Patti Stump."

"She *told* you this?"

"Loudly and without any mistake. Does this look like chicken salad to you?" Gary held out his sandwich to her.

"What are you going to do about it?"

"What do you mean?"

"Well, you can't pretend she didn't say it. Or is that exactly what you intend to do?"

"Why can't I pretend she didn't say it?"

"Gary, you're her boss!"

"Well, what am I supposed to do? Fire her? Put her in therapy? Set her up with one of my friends? Sleep with her? I don't know how to respond to this crap." He stood, running his fingers through his hair. "Darla was amused."

"Well, with anyone else it might be funny, but Stump? Let's face it, Gary, it's like having a bad-tempered Minnie Pearl with the hots for you."

"What do you recommend?"

"I recommend you have a talk with her." She saw his look of distaste. "Gary, no one ever said owning your own agency was going to be all rainbows and free beer."

"Well, that may be a moot point."

"How so?"

"I may not be the owner of this agency much longer."

"Thinking about firing yourself, are you?"

"I think I want to leave."

"Leave for where? Another shop? Are you kidding? What are you talking about?"

"I don't want this getting out to anyone, but I'm talking with Darla about leaving everything. I mean the agency, the city, the state, the country—just leaving."

Maggie stared at him.

"What with murders and maniacs roaming the streets, I'm worried half to death about Haley and Darla, and I don't seem to have much of a handle on what's going on here either."

"Gary, listen." Maggie reached out and touched him on the wrist. "Don't you think you're just a little overwhelmed right now?"

"I don't know. But I have to do something."

"Where?"

Gary shrugged. "I've been thinking about New Zealand. It has clean air and no drugs and, like, one murder per decade. And no guns. I think it would be good for Haley."

"*New Zealand?*"

"It's still in the 'just talking' stage," he said, not looking at her.

"Have you ever *been* to New Zealand?"

"Look, don't patronize me, okay? You know very well I've never been there."

"And Stump Lady?"

Gary covered his eyes and moaned. "Can't I just let it ride? She'll lose interest after awhile, and I just flat do not want to deal with it."

"Well, she's so daft she'll probably be hooked on Pokey by next week. I wouldn't worry about it, Gar. In fact," she gathered up her lunch debris and stood, "I wouldn't worry about anything if you can help it. Sorry, I have to run. I've got that copy I need to get to Deirdre."

Gary nodded and waved her away, but she couldn't help think he looked absolutely miserable. Once back upstairs in her office, she saw her cellphone vibrating against the desk. She snatched it. "This is Maggie."

"Don't tell me, you were going to call as soon the wedding invitations were printed."

Brownie. Maggie felt a lead ball settle neatly in the pit of her stomach.

"Hey, Brownie," she said softly. "How's it going?"

"Going okay, how about you?"

"Oh, you know..." God, she had dreaded this phone call. "I'm working through the thing with Elise. You coming to the service tomorrow?"

"Yeah, I talked with your mom."

Oh dear.

"She told me about your boyfriend."

"Brownie, I...."

"Hey, it's okay." He sounded so sweet and normal. "I wished you'd have told me, though. I mean, hearing it from your mom sucked a little."

"I know, Brownie, I'm sorry. I guess I didn't want to hurt your feelings."

"Hey, don't worry about it. I just wanted to make sure you were all right and to tell you I'll see you at the service tomorrow."

"Thanks, Brownie."

"Take care of yourself, Newberry."

"Yeah, you too."

Maggie sat back in her chair and stared at the wall. Between her conversation with Gary and now Brownie, she could begin to feel like crap very quickly if she allowed it. She took in a breath and let it out. She wouldn't allow it.

She checked the time to make sure she could get her copy assignment finished and on Deirdre's desk before the end of day, then picked up the phone and punched in the number for the Fulton County Police Department.

While she waited to be put through, she picked up the office condolence card and glanced at the signatures inside. Pokey's was practically unreadable. Funny, you'd think an art director would be too visual to end up with turkey-scrawl for a signature. Patti's was very precise, almost begrudging.

"Burton."

"Detective Burton? This is Maggie Newberry."

"Yes, Miss Newberry?"

"I'm calling to see if you have anything else you can tell me about Elise's death."

"Not at this time."

"Is it possible I might have a copy of your report?"

There was heavy sigh on the line. "Look, it's really a lot easier for everyone involved if you just let the police handle this. You will be notified as soon as—"

"It's just that I was really hoping to be a little closer to the investigation, as I'm sure you can understand. I didn't know, for example, that there was a fake air

135

conditioning repair truck parked out front of the apartment building during the time of the murder."

"That is incorrect information," Burton said, exhaustion dripping from every syllable. "The truck is not, at this point, related to the homicide."

"It was just coincidentally left there? I assume you haven't found the driver?"

"We have not. And we have no reason to believe, as I said, that it is in any way connected to—"

"Is it really so common to have bogus repair vehicles littered about the city to no real purpose?"

"You'd be surprised. The point is, Miss Newberry, that we have no new information at this time. I can suggest a support group or therapist to help you work through this. Relatives of victims of violent crime have a tougher time than people touched by other kinds of deaths. If you like, I can connect you back with the switchboard to be transferred to a department that can give you those numbers."

"Okay, good. Thanks." Maggie pulled a brochure with product facts on her current copy assignment out of her desk drawer and set it next to her computer.

"I wish you luck, Miss Newberry."

"Thank you, Detective," she said, flipping on her computer.

"Hold while I switch you."

Maggie disconnected while the line was ringing and dialed the Fulton County Police Department operator again, this time asking to speak with David Kazmaroff in Homicide.

"Kazmaroff."

"Hello, Detective, this is Maggie Newberry, Elise Newberry's sister. Detective Burton indicated you would have time to fill me in on the basic details of my sister's case so far."

There was a pause.

"He did?"

"Yes. He said he was too busy, but that you had plenty of time. I really appreciate it." Maggie had picked up on the tension between the two detectives, and now listened with relief as Kazmaroff switched his focus from the fact of her phone call to the arrogance of his partner suggesting he was busier.

The rest of her conversation with Detective Kazmaroff was hurried and rude, but it revealed, nonetheless, a lottery-winning cache of information. The detective made it clear that the police believed a drug dealing homeless person came in off the street, into Maggie's building, down the hallway and into her apartment. They believed that Elise's drug history made it likely that the killing was a drug deal gone wrong.

"What about Gerard?" Maggie asked Kazmaroff.

"We talked to him, and he alibied out. He was having a party in his hotel room with half the call girls in the metro area. It's confirmed."

"At two in the afternoon?"

"Miss Newberry, he is not a suspect."

"When did he go back to France?" She wasn't even sure why she asked the question. She assumed he'd gone back days ago.

"He is scheduled to leave on a Delta flight to Paris tomorrow afternoon."

"He's still in Atlanta?"

Before Kazmaroff had the chance to confirm the information and warn her not to approach him under any circumstances, Maggie was out of her desk chair, car keys in hand, the unfinished ad copy still sitting on her blotter.

Twenty minutes later, she pulled into the parking lot of the Hotel Nikko off Peachtree Road. She knew if Dubois was ever going to be considered a suspect she needed to come up with evidence soon. She hurried into the lobby, noting how close the hotel was to the Lenox Square parking lot where he'd taken her money and given her Elise. He probably just waltzed back over here afterward and had a six-course snack at her father's expense, she thought angrily.

She marched up to the front desk, asked for Mr. Dubois's room number and was told Dubois had checked out earlier that morning.

Her shoulders deflated, as if all the air had been squeezed out of her.

Now what?

She turned away and stood in the middle of the Hotel Nikko lobby. Could she catch him at the airport? She tried to calculate how many flights went out daily to Paris from Atlanta. What were the chances she'd see him there? Do they still page people in airports? Hartsfeld had over a quarter of a million travelers a day coming and going through the concourses. And unless she wanted to buy an international ticket, she wasn't even going to get close to wherever he might be.

She trudged back to her car and strapped herself in, sitting for a moment in the parking lot trying to think. A proper sleuth would probably at least go to the airport and try, but she knew it was as hopeless as it sounded. She'd missed him and that was all there was to it.

Maggie drove down tree-lined Peachtree Road past the old Sears parking lot, noting that everyone she knew still referred to the intersection that way even though there was a towering, glittering office building in place of the Sears parking lot, and had been for some years now.

At the traffic light in front of the Good 'ol Days outdoor café that now looked to be some kind of hardware shop, she pulled out her phone. It wasn't much, but in addition to telling her that Gerard was still in town, Kazmaroff had also let slip the fact Alfie lived with his mother, Carole Wexford.

While she waited for the light to change, she found the website on her phone for the Fulton County tax commissioner, went straight to the property records for the name *Wexford*, and had the address within seconds. As she did a U-turn and headed back up Peachtree in the direction of Saint Phillips Cathedral, Maggie knew it would take the taste of defeat out of her day if she could talk for just a few minutes to Alfie or his mother about where he was that day.

Earlier, when she was driving to the Hotel Nikko, she had worked to ignore the creeping feeling of guilt that she was doing something wrong. She knew for a fact Laurent wasn't available to come with her—he was out again with her Dad—but she was sure he'd understand the urgency and the timing involved.

On second thought, probably best just not to mention it.

Less than half a mile from her own apartment building, Juniper Street, where the Wexfords lived, was an older neighborhood made up of small, dilapidated crackerbox houses with blistering paint and stingy-sized garages that had once been sheds.

According to Kazmaroff, the police had questioned Alfie at police headquarters. Mother Carole had waited patiently during the interview and then taken Alfie home. No one had interviewed her.

Although hardly as exciting as the prospect of a confrontation with Gerard Dubois, Maggie still felt a nervous anticipation as she steered her car onto St. Juniper Street. While she expected Carole Wexford to be protective of her handicapped son, she also expected that, being his mother, she would have a clearer picture of exactly what her son had seen that afternoon.

Or done.

505 St. Juniper Street was less than six blocks from Peachtree Road. The Wexford cottage, with blue-gray cedar siding and a bright red door, stood out among the neighboring houses like a jewel in a basket of seaweed. Maggie parked in the bumpy driveway and made her way up the narrow walkway to knock on the door. Her approach had apparently been monitored because the door opened immediately.

"Yes?" The woman wore her jet-black hair in short, dated spikes that belonged on a much younger woman. Her eyes were framed in varying shades of green and purple eye shadow. Maggie guessed her age at about fifty.

"Good afternoon. My name is Maggie Newberry. Are you Mrs. Wexford?"

The woman looked at Maggie. "It's about the girl who was killed, isn't it?"

"She was my sister."

The waning afternoon light carved reliefs in the woman's face as she stood at the door. The lines cupping Mrs. Wexford's mouth were harsh and indelible. "Alfie already talked to the cops."

"I know. I just wanted to talk with you for a minute. I was hoping, maybe, that the two of you discussed what happened."

"He already told the cops he didn't see nothing."

"I know, but I just thought he might have told you some things...I mean, he communicates with you better than with other people, right?"

"Your sister was a goddamn bitch."

Maggie gaped at the woman. "What?" she managed to say.

"Your sister. She was mean to Alfie."

"Are you sure?" *Had Alfie spoken to Elise?*

"You don't understand what *mean* is?" Carole took a full drag off the cigarette she was holding.

"It's just that my sister was sick and had only been in town for a few hours."

"I ain't sure of the particulars. I know he was there doing his business and she was in the hall and they talked. And that's when she *verbally* attacked him."

"And Alfie didn't tell the cops this?"

Maggie saw a shadow move behind the woman and then form into a sweet-faced young man, who stood behind his mother, his hand on her arm. Mrs. Wexford ignored him. "He was too afraid. And if you tell 'em, I'll deny it and call you a filthy liar." She pointed her finger at Maggie as if for punctuation.

Alfie smiled shyly at Maggie and waved at her with just his fingers seconds before his mother shut the door firmly in her face.

On the drive home, Maggie couldn't help but think, irrationally but undeniably, that even though she'd only seen him for a moment the young man she just saw was nonviolent. Every intuition she possessed told her that Alfie could not have hurt her sister.

Twenty minutes later, Maggie arrived to an empty apartment and a note stuck to the refrigerator door.

Your father changed the time for me to come, ainsi it is tonight and not this afternoon.   I love you, chérie—Laurent

Maggie sat on the couch, feet resting on the coffee table, with a chilled glass of Sauvignon Blanc in her hand. Laurent's note remained stuck to the refrigerator door where he'd placed it. She was disappointed and sorry she hadn't called him in the afternoon after all. He could have accompanied her on her not very fruitful investigations. As it was, she longed to tell him of her discoveries, to see his thoughtful face as he listened to her theories and revelations. He would help her make sense of what she learned today.

The apartment smelled of sautéed garlic and onions, although the galley kitchen was tidied to a shine with neither a pot nor a dribble of olive oil to be seen. She imagined her Frenchman whipping up his lunch hours earlier and she smiled.   Although it was true she'd never read in any of the questionnaires or articles in *Cosmopolitan* magazine that said smiling all the time was a sure sign of compatibility, she assumed it was on the right track.

Had Elise been hateful to Alfie? Maggie set down her wineglass and got up to adjust the venetian blinds. It was dark now, and she didn't enjoy the thought of Peachtree Road traffic peeking in her living room window. *Maybe Elise had begun withdrawal and had been really testy? Maybe she hadn't realized that Alfie was mentally handicapped?*

Maggie resettled herself back on the couch and took a sip of her wine. And where does all this lead? *Could Alfie have killed Elise?* She tried to imagine the sweet man-child she had seen today angry enough to kill somebody. She tried to imagine him chasing Elise down the hallway to the bedroom with a wire outstretched in his chubby fists. She closed her eyes and willed the image away. It was too soon. Too soon to think of Elise's terror in her last moments alive.

The evening's rain had stopped and left fat droplets hanging by glittering threads from the small magnolia bush outside her living room window. She could see the branches, black and slick with the raindrops, tremble in what looked like a reasonable effort to dislodge them.

Maggie finished off her wine and glanced at the clock. Ten-thirty. She was glad Laurent was getting to know her dad, but she wished he'd come home soon. When her landline rang, Maggie frowned, assuming it was Laurent calling to say he'd be even later. She picked up the receiver.

"Hello?"

The voice rasped into her ear like a jar full of wasps. "How about if you're next on the list, bitch?"

Chapter Twelve

"You are ready to eat, *chérie?*"

Maggie smiled as she rummaged in the bottom of her clothes closet. She loved the whole *chérie* bit. "In a minute!" she called. She raised herself onto her knees and arched her back. The cops had been through every inch of her apartment with a flea comb, and although not the tidiest of people, they hadn't ransacked the place either. She knew the chance of finding any kind of clue behind a team of experts was pretty slim. She tossed a woolen sweater onto a heap on the floor of her bedroom that she had mentally marked "winter stuff." She wasn't sure why she should bother packing it away now. After all, chilly weather was only four months away. On the other hand, she wanted to make room for Laurent and his wardrobe.

Would he still be here for winter?

"It is getting cold, Maggie!" There was an extra sharpness to his voice, and Maggie noted that few things could flap the man except where it involved his stomach and the making, presenting and consuming of food. T h e aroma of garlic and sizzling peppers wafted delicately through the apartment.

"Coming!" She hopped up and raked the multiple dust buffaloes from her knees, and while doing so she saw the laundry hamper in the corner of the room. She knew the cops had gone through it and she flinched at the thought. She reached into the recesses of the wicker hamper and pulled out underwear, bras, and a pair of gym shorts. And the cardigan. It was made of lightweight cashmere, ripped at the elbows and frayed at the sleeves. Elise had been wearing it the night she dropped back into Maggie's life.

She grabbed the sweater and met Laurent in the dining room. He was already seated. She tossed the sweater down next to her and sat down. "Mmm-mm! *Qu'est-ce que-c'est?*"

"A little this, a little that," he said, pouring a pale pink wine into their glasses.

Maggie settled into her chair, marveling over the steaming and colorful plateful of peppers and thin slices of rosy lamb cutlets. "God, Laurent, maybe you should be a chef somewhere. This looks wonderful!"

"*Pfut!* In France, *tout le monde* cook *comme ça.* Everyone cooks."

"Yeah, but it's rarer over here. I'm serious, would that be something you'd want to do?"

"*Peut-être,*" he said dismissively, tucking into his meal.

She watched him enjoying his own cooking, his eyes flitting from time to time to smile at her but concentrating, for the most part, on his meal. Maggie couldn't fill in all the blanks about Laurent. He was intense and passionate in bed, but remarkably phlegmatic otherwise.

Sometimes even his words of sympathy or commiseration about Elise sounded rehearsed to her, almost false. It was, of course, his inability to express himself in English with any real depth or focus, she told herself. Still, it needled her in some part of her mind that resisted glossing.

Even during those painful months of no word and no contact, she hadn't examined too closely why she had loved him so quickly, or why she felt she needed to be with him.

It was as if thinking about it might reveal something to her that would make her continue to love him when she knew, deep down, she shouldn't at all.

"Laurent, I've decided I'm not logical when it comes to you."

"*Vraiment? C'est bon.*" He smiled at her and sipped his wine.

"Well, I'm glad you think so, but it scares me."

"I will protect you."

"God, who says stuff like that any more? How can you protect me against *you*?"

"Why do you need protection from me?"

"From how I feel when I'm with you, I mean."

"You think too much."

"That's what guys always say."

Laurent's eyes flashed and she detected a tic of irritation in his full lips as he set the wineglass back on the table. "I don't want to hear about your other guys."

"Jealous?"

"Phshht. How can I be jealous? You are mine, *n'est-ce pas?*"

Maggie felt a delicious tingle in her stomach. He was so disarmingly direct. It got her every time. "I am."

He shrugged. "So, I win. The other guys lose."

Maggie laughed. *Was it possible it was really that simple?*

She took a savoring mouthful, even closed her eyes to enjoy it more fully.

"Did you tell the police about the phone call?"

Maggie pushed a red pepper with her fork. The butter made a trail across her plate. "I left a message. No one has broken down my door to ask me about it."

"*Incroyable.*"

"I know. I went downstairs earlier today to talk to the night watchman but he was asleep because, of course, he

147

works nights, and his wife wouldn't let me wake him to ask him questions. So, I thought—"

"We will go and talk with him together."

"Thanks, Laurent." Behind him, she could still see the wreath of blue cigarette smoke from his *Gitanes* enveloping the bouquet of daisies and carnations he'd brought home.

"I'm just telling you, though," she said, "I *know* it was Gerard. He had motive and opportunity, you know? This wasn't random. Did I tell you the cops think it was some drug dealer wandering in off the streets? Gerard *knew* she was here. He came here, they fought and he killed her. It's so obvious. I just don't see why the cops don't arrest him."

"Oh! You have a parcel!" Laurent looked around the living room without moving.

"I got the mail, there was nothing."

"*Ah! Voila!*" Laurent moved to where a small box was sitting underneath a stack of magazines on the coffee table. Maggie pulled the paper off to reveal a small packet of stationary. A note, folded over, was jammed in between the pages. She opened it, aware that Laurent was reading over her shoulder:

> *This should be the last of it. Only prints on it belong*
> *to your sister.*
> *Sorry there isn't more at this time.*
> *Detective John B. Burton*

Maggie opened the stationary pad to the first page.

"It's a letter," she murmured. "Elise was writing someone named Michelle." She flipped a few pages. "It's not finished."

"Do you know Michelle?"

She shook her head. "It's written in French." She handed the pad to him.

She watched him scan the tiny, controlled hand on the page.

"She says——"

"Don't paraphrase it, Laurent, I need to know word for word what she says." Maggie tugged at Laurent's shirt pulling him back to the table.

"Dear Michelle," Laurent read aloud. "I have been missing you very much and hope that this letter finds you well and happy. I am with my sister now and I believe she will take good care of me. I wish you could meet her, Michelle. She is very..." Laurent looked up at Maggie. "I am not knowing this word in English."

"What word? Show me." Maggie jumped up and stood over his shoulder. He pointed to the word.

"I think, *peut-être*, it means, oh, *exotique?* Or, different?"

"She thought I was exotic?" Maggie looked out onto Peachtree Street.

"But she has the good heart and I am glad to see her face——oh, she says, *her dear face*——and I am glad to see her dear face again." He stopped reading and put the letter down. He touched her. *"Il a fini, ma petite,"* he said.

Maggie picked up the letter and read the words in French, not understanding them, and felt a tiny prism of awe at Elise's obvious comfort with them.

"Who is this Michelle..." She flipped the envelope over and read, "...Zouk? That Elise would write her? Will the police contact her, I wonder?"

Laurent shrugged and replaced his napkin in his lap. "Perhaps she is an old friend? The address is for Cannes, I think."

Maggie nodded, still holding the letter in front of her, her mind trying to remember something important. Laurent resumed his meal alone. Maggie suddenly jumped up and then crouched under the dining room table.

"Laurent!" she shouted. "Take a look at this!"

She knelt by his side as he sat at the table, the wadded up remains of Elise's gray sweater clutched in her hands. She thrust the filthy cardigan into his lap and peeled back the label at the neck with her fingers. In large silver script, the words *Chez Zouk Cannes, Paris* were revealed.

"This Michelle must have a boutique or something," she said. "Elise bought her clothes from her, don't you see?"

Laurent touched the label and then looked at Maggie. *"C'est important?"*

Maggie slumped back onto her heels, pulling the sweater across her knees. "I don't know. I mean, it's a connection, right?"

Laurent nodded, chewing his lamb slowly and watching her.

"I've got an address," Maggie said quietly, thinking hard. "And I've got the name of a friend. Maybe even one who's not a drug addict or a total loser." Maggie stroked the soft sweater.

She looked up at Laurent. "I need to go back to Cannes."

Chapter Thirteen

Later that evening, Laurent led the way down the darkened corridor of the basement of The Parthenon. Cobwebs hung in large wattles in the corners, dripping into his face as he and Maggie made their way down the hall. It was hard to believe someone actually worked down here, actually packed a lunch and hummed himself off to work only to arrive at the creepy bowels of a hundred-year-old building.

Maggie slipped her hand into Laurent's and squeezed it. She knew he didn't like the idea of her going back to Cannes—he'd made that very clear. She had worked to avoid the topic with him until she could make definite plans to go. It was very possible, she thought, looking up at him as they waited for the night watchman, that he thought she'd already dropped the idea.

"*Allo?*" Laurent called as they neared a doorway at the end of the hall, light spilling out onto the cement floor. "*Allo? Monsieur?*" They stopped in front of the door and peered inside.

"Mr. Danford?" Maggie called softly.

"With you folks in just a minute," a voice said.

Laurent and Maggie looked at each other and then entered the small broom closet of an office. A metal desk was shoved up against one of the cement walls. A half-sized window hovered over it. From outside the building, the window would be eye level with one's shoes, Maggie noted. Little had been done to make the office comfortable or attractive. No plants or pictures on the walls, no rugs across the cold and uneven concrete floor, not even a lamp with a shade to make the night watchman's station less wretched.

"You the girl whose sister was killed?" The man finally extricated himself from behind his six-foot filing cabinet and maneuvered around two metal folding chairs to stand in front of Maggie and Laurent. He held out his hand.

Laurent shook it. The man withdrew his hand before Maggie could shake it, too.

"Yes, that's me," Maggie said.

"Told the police everything. Didn't see nothing. I'm on duty at night, you see. Didn't happen at night, did it?"

He settled himself into a large swivel chair situated in front of the desk. Maggie thought he resembled Barney Fife with a touch of mange. His balding head supported long wisps of hair, witnesses to a losing battle. His eyes were bloodshot and watery, and Maggie found herself scanning the office for liquor bottles.

"No," Maggie said, turning her eyes back on the skinny little man. "But maybe you've seen strange people around at night. You know, shady characters that might be involved?"

Danford scratched the back of his head with a long, crooked finger. "Thought the cops said this was a spur of the moment kinda killing."

"*Monsieur*, do you know if any peoples come here at night? Bad people?"

Maggie wondered what the old guy would think of this big bruiser with the French accent.

Danford finished scratching and looked up at Laurent. "Sometimes I seen some weird characters around here. In the winter, mostly. Trying to get in to sleep it off for the night, you know? Someplace warm."

"And in the summer?" Maggie asked impatiently.

"Well, summertime's different. People want in for different reasons in the summertime. This drug dealer the cops was asking me about? He comes by from time to time. I reckon he's got a customer in the building somewheres, don't you? Else why would he keep coming by?"

"What's he look like?"

"Looks like crap, you want to know. Got this long, nasty yellow hair, you know how they wear it these days?" Maggie hadn't a clue, but she nodded encouragingly. "And clothes all ripped to hell. Big holes in the knees of his trousers, and his seat too, sometimes. Can't be making much money as a drug dealer, that's what I told Cissy. Cissy's my wife."

"This drug dealer," Maggie said, encouragingly. "Have you ever talked with him?"

"Told him to get his sorry ass outta the building once. That's talking to him, ain't it?"

"And he was okay about that?"

"He left."

"But he came back."

"I told you, he's got hisself a customer here. Must have."

"But you don't know who."

"I got my suspicions. And, no, it's nobody I'm gonna tell you about."

"Do you remember if he was around the night *before* my sister was killed?" *That would have been the night I brought her home,* Maggie thought.

"He was. Shuffling up the goddamn hallway on the third floor. I knowed he was there 'cause of the way he drags his feet, like he's drunk or something."

"And you threw him out?"

"That's right. About three a.m. No problem."

"One more thing. The cops said there was an air conditioning repair truck parked out back during the time of the...incident."

"Thought they said it was fake? And besides, I don't do no maintenance. I'm *security*."

"Yes, of course. It's just, I wondered if you'd ever seen it hanging around before?"

"No reason I would. I work nights. There ain't no fake AC repair trucks parked anywhere near my building at *night*. That'd be just plain stupid."

"Okay." Maggie looked at the man and then, helplessly, at Laurent. She'd run out of questions, and didn't know how to process the answers she was getting to the questions she had asked.

Laurent indicated the doorway with his head and Maggie sighed. Might as well.

"Thank you for your help, Mr. Danford," Maggie said stiffly. She touched Laurent's arm and they trudged silently back upstairs to Maggie's apartment. Laurent unlocked the door and Maggie threw herself down onto the living room couch.

She raised herself up on one arm and watched Laurent, who had seated himself in the large tub chair opposite the couch, his long legs stretching out and filling up nearly the entire floor space of the little room.

"Well, I'd say we're nowhere on this. I can't buy the theory that this drug pusher is the killer. It's too pat. I mean, what did he do? Go around rapping on doors: 'I say, is the lady of the house at home and would she be interested in some crack?' I mean, isn't it too much of a coincidence that he is a drug dealer and she was a drug addict?"

"You think the police have made up this theory?"

"I think they thought: dead junkie, on-premises drug dealer, let's put them together and wrap this case up."

"*C'est possible.* And Alfie?"

"I'm not sure he's tied into this at all. Elise was strung out and testy, they had a little ruckus, and Alfie probably remembers it worse than it was." Maggie shrugged. "I can't see him killing anyone."

"You do not know him very well," Laurent reminded her. "Coffee?" He got up and headed toward the kitchen.

"No, it'll keep me awake." Maggie pulled herself up to a sitting position and rested her feet on the coffee table. "Besides, he doesn't strike me as clever enough to do it and get away with it, you know? I mean, if Alfie killed her, wouldn't there be all kinds of circumstantial evidence leading right to his door? The cops would've picked up on it, surely."

Laurent poked his head around the corner. "The police have not questioned the *maman*," he reminded her. "They know nothing about his argument with Elise."

"Boy, they really did a slack job, don't you think?" She picked up a magazine and idly flipped through its pages.

Laurent came into the room with a small tray holding a china creamer, matching sugar bowl and two steaming mugs. Maggie removed her feet from the coffee table and he set the tray down.

"Will your office allow you to leave again so soon?"

Maggie sighed. They had fallen asleep the night before arguing about her intention to go back to Cannes.

For reasons that weren't entirely clear to her, Laurent was against her going.

Dead against it.

"It's been nearly six months," she said, reaching for her coffee, noting wryly that he had made her coffee anyway.

"You have the money? It is high season now."

"I'll put part of it on a card and get the rest from my Dad."

"Going back will open up the wounds again for your *maman*, I think."

"Laurent, I'm going so let's just put an end to this, okay? I'm *going*."

She could see by the way he narrowed his eyes that the argument was not by any stretch of the imagination ended. At that moment, however, the phone rang and she quickly picked it up. "Yes?"

"This is Carole Wexford. Alfie's mom? We talked yesterday?" The woman's voice was loud and easily heard, even when Maggie held the receiver away from her ear a good six inches.

"Yes, Mrs. Wexford, I remember." Maggie nudged Laurent's leg with her foot. He nodded to indicate he could hear.

"I got one more thing to tell you that Alfie just told me, but I got to have a promise from you that if I tell you, you won't be asking Alfie all about it."

"What is it, Mrs. Wexford?" Maggie watched Laurent with large eyes.

"Not until you promise me you won't come after Alfie asking him a bunch of questions. He's real upset about all this and he don't want to talk about it again."

"I promise. What did he tell you?"

"He told me he made an earlier trip to your apartment building that afternoon. He was delivering groceries that morning and saw some guy hanging out near the door where he fought with your sister later that day."

Maggie licked her lips. "Can he describe him?"

"He said he was dressed real nice. All slick and a jacket and all. He had reddish-brown, sorta curly hair, maybe balding, and he was a big guy. Maybe six-one. Wearing them sandals with socks that some people wear."

"Do the police know this?"

"You don't listen, do you? I told you, Alfie *just* told me. And if you ask him about it or go the cops, he's gonna deny ever being there, understand?"

"All right, Mrs. Wexford, I understand. Is that all?"

"Yeah, but remember, stay away from my boy, d'ya hear? I don't want to hear you been snooping around him."

"I'll leave him alone."

The phone clicked dead in her hand as the woman hung up on her.

"What is it?" Laurent took a sip of his coffee. "More clues?"

"God, I'll say," Maggie said as she put the phone back in its cradle.

"Alfie's mom just placed Gerard here on the day of the murder."

Chapter Fourteen

"How do you expect to pay for this, may I ask?" Gary shuffled through the Côte d'Azur brochures stacked on Maggie's desk.

Maggie, uncomfortable in a now too-snug knit dress, gathered up her maps and travel brochures and placed them in the bottom of her briefcase. She closed the case firmly. She was tired from a long, late night of feasting and lovemaking with Laurent.

"I intend to charge part of it to my MasterCard."

"The same card, I believe, on which you put that very expensive frock you wore to the Addies banquet a few months back?" Gary leaned against the windowsill next to her desk. He wore jeans and a light cotton sweater. Maggie noticed he wore leather moccasins instead of his usual wingtips. "The same card upon which you blew two hundred smackeroos last spring for that ungodly kitchen appliance you said would make your life complete?"

"The very one."

"Don't those people require payment periodically?"

"I'll worry about it when I get back."

"I see. The old worry-about-it-later credit plan. Yes, I think Darla subscribes to that too. Can't say it works very well for her either."

"Aren't you dressed a little casually today, *Herr* Boss? I mean, I didn't miss an interoffice memo, did I? This isn't the afternoon we all have to go out and do the lawn in front of the building or something, is it?"

"Ah, Maggie." Gary smiled and folded his arms. "Maggie, Maggie, Maggie. I'm going to miss that keen, snappish wit. That biting—some might say, corrosive—repartee. You'll have to write me a lot."

"Yeah, yeah." Maggie covered her eyes and felt a leaden weariness descend upon her.

Gary shifted uncomfortably on the windowsill. "You should support me on this. If I was to stay, I'd just go on being miserable, making everyone around me miserable. Besides, you'll visit us down there—"

"Are you kidding?" Maggie uncovered her eyes and stared at him. "It's ten thousand miles from here. It costs fifteen hundred dollars just to *get* there."

"Look, Maggie, I'm not doing this to drive you crazy or to break Darla's heart. I'm doing this because I have to. *I have to!* I'm dying here. How can I make it clearer to you?"

"Well, go then." Maggie bent over to scrape up the contents of her spilled folder.

"And you'll visit?"

"Sure." She tried to smile but gave it up.

"You know, Darla has a hissy fit if I even mention New Zealand, and we're scheduled to board the airplane in less than six weeks."

"You are?" Maggie gaped at him in astonishment.

"Did you think I was joking? Maggie, I am moving, *emigrating* with my family to Auckland, New Zealand. I am getting residency, a work permit and leaving the good ol' U.S. of A. Okay?" Gary tossed a paper clip at her wastepaper basket. "And Darla is a mess about it. Very unsupportive, if you want to know. And it would be nice, I'm just saying, it would be *nice* if there was one person on the planet besides my travel agent with whom I could discuss my plans and dreams."

"Six weeks. What are you going to do down there for work?"

He grinned broadly, his eyes alive and happy for the first time in a year.

Maggie left work on time and headed to the Newberry estate, where Elspeth opened the front door while Maggie parked. Her mother wore a soft cotton sundress with blue and purple violets on a white background, a pair of gold sandals on her feet.

"Have you changed your mind about dinner? Your father's home for a change."

"I told Laurent I'd be home."

"Call him. Have him come, too."

"I can't tonight. I'm just here to talk to Dad about something."

While her mother gave iced tea orders to Becka, Maggie went to her father's study, where he was sitting with the evening paper and a gin and tonic.

"Hey, Dad," she said, giving him a kiss.

"Well, hello, sweetheart." John Newberry's face lit up as his paper crumpled into his lap. "Your mother said you couldn't come to dinner tonight."

"I can't. I'm just here for a quick visit. Laurent is waiting for me at home for dinner."

"I like the man. He's got some very interesting stories to tell."

"Oh, really?" Laurent's story-telling abilities hadn't really come up much in their relationship. Maggie found herself intrigued.

"Ah, well, probably not the sort of stories a young man tells his lady love. Quite the scamp in his day, was your Laurent. Reformed by love." Her father straightened out his newspaper, folding it to a smaller size.

Although not surprised that Laurent had a mysterious past, Maggie was astonished he had shared any of it with her father, and that her father hadn't been alarmed by whatever Laurent had divulged. Couldn't have been anything too dangerous, Maggie decided, as she watched her father's pleasant face relax into a concentration of reading. Her father seemed fascinated by Laurent, and for some reason she found she wasn't entirely comfortable with the idea.

"I need to ask a favor, Dad."

He tossed the newspaper aside and gave her his full attention. "Shoot."

"I may have to return to Cannes."

He frowned. "Does this have to do with Elise?"

"It does. There are some answers about this whole business I think I can only get over there. I'd like you to trust me on this, and to lend me your Amex card for it, too."

"I see. Will Laurent be going with you?"

"No, he says he can't. He's got some private chef gigs you set up for him?"

He nodded. "It might be the beginning of a fine business for him. I've connected him with some friends at the Club."

"That's good, Dad. Laurent loves cooking, that's for sure. So, no, it'll just be me."

"How long?'

"Four days."

"Am I allowed to ask what you'll be doing there?"

"Dad, I'm not trying to be mysterious. But I know we all want closure on Elise's death, and I'm convinced we're not going to get it if we just sit back and let the Fulton County Police Department handle it."

Her father eyed her and then let out a long sigh. "Darling, I wish you'd believe your mother and me when we tell you we do not blame you for anything that's happened with Elise. How could we? The poor girl was on a collision course with her fate from the moment she took her first steps."

Maggie watched her father's eyes fill with tears and she felt more resolute than ever.

"It's not that, Dad. I just need answers. I can't move forward until I know why she was killed, and by whom."

"And you think you'll find them back in the South of France?"

"I've got a lead. I feel like I need to follow it."

Her father hesitated for only a moment, then took her hand and squeezed it. "There's an extra card in the desk, third drawer down."

Maggie leaned over and hugged him. "Thanks, Dad."

Maggie sat in her car in the back parking lot of The Parthenon and dialed the number she had found on the Internet for the Zouk Boutique in Cannes.

"Allo? Chez Zouk." A woman's voice came over the line clear and distinct.

"Oui, est-ce que Madame Zouk?" Is this Madame Zouk? Maggie asked.

"Comment?" Excuse me?

God, I was afraid of this. Why didn't I just have Laurent make the call for me?

But she knew the answer to that. Laurent had become singularly unhelpful any time she even mentioned going back to Cannes.

"*Madame Zouk. Je cherche Madame Zouk. Elle est la?*" *I'm looking for Madame Zouk. Is she there?*

"This is Michelle Zouk. Who is this?"

She speaks English!

"My name is Maggie Newberry, Madame Zouk. I am Elise Newberry's sister. Did you know her?"

There was a brief pause on the line. "*Oui.* I know your sister. She is well, I hope?"

"I'm afraid Elise has passed away, Madame. But I am going to be in Cannes in a few days and I was wondering if you and I could...if we..."

"I am heartbroken and saddened for you, Mademoiselle. Yes, come to Cannes. I would be delighted to meet the sister of my dear friend. I believe I have much to tell you about your sister that may lighten your heart."

Maggie was dumbfounded in her gratitude. "Thank you, Madame," she said, feeling tears threaten to overcome her. "I will call you this week as soon as I arrive. Thank you so much."

She sat alone in the darkened car for a moment longer, knowing Laurent would be starting to worry, but wanting to enjoy the bliss of connecting with one person on this planet who didn't seem to believe Elise was a degenerate low-life who got the only end anyone could imagine for her.

She dialed Brownie's number and he picked up on the first ring. "Brownie? Hey, this is Maggie. Sorry I've been out of touch."

"Maggie? Maggie who?"

"Very funny. I'm really sorry. I've been busy, you know, trying to figure out this thing with Elise."

"How's that coming?"

"Well, I have to admit not great. The cops are being no help at all. For example, I found out yesterday that Gerard—Elise's boyfriend—was at my apartment building during the time she was killed."

"Really? How did you discover that? Do the police know?"

"No, not yet. There are a few details that don't fit just yet."

"Like?"

"Well, Alfie said he saw Gerard *before* he got yelled at by Elise. Which would mean she was still alive when Gerard left."

"Why is this news significant then?"

"Because, Brownie, Alfie is mentally handicapped so he could easily be confused about who he saw when."

"That's convenient. You don't like the timeline, so you just punt to the fact that the handicapped delivery boy is an unreliable witness?"

"The point is, it's not important *when* he saw Gerard," Maggie said, feeling her annoyance with Brownie growing. "The timing of it can't be substantiated using Alfie because, you're right, he's unreliable. But the fact that he described him at all is significant. It places Gerard here at the building."

"Sorry, Maggie. I think you're so focused on wanting Gerard to be the killer that you'll see any evidence you find as pointing to him."

"Look, I didn't call to get your opinion of what I'm doing," Maggie responded, feeling her annoyance tip over into the full-blown anger category. "I just wanted to ask if you remembered anything out of the ordinary from that

165

night. Either around the parking lot or once you were inside the building."

"Not really. I do remember the cops were really pretty lax with me."

"Seriously?"

"They never checked my pockets or anything. I could've had a knife on me. In fact, I did have one."

"A knife?"

"You know the one I always carry? My Swiss Army knife?"

"They didn't frisk me either, Brownie. I don't they do that sort of thing. Anything else?"

"Sorry.. Look, Maggie, I know you feel like you have to do this because of the whole guilt trip with Elise and all, but you probably really ought to talk to someone. You know?"

Maggie let her building ire with him seep away. He was a good friend. He cared about her. She took a breath and let it out.

"I'm talking to a bunch of people."

"I don't mean interviews to find evidence. I meant —"

"I know what you meant, Brownie. And thanks. I appreciate it, but I'm fine. Really."

"So. How's the home life these days?"

"Fine, thanks. And yourself?"

"Okay, none of my business. Did all the rubberneckers at your building bother to clean up their mess when they finally wandered away from the show in your apartment?"

"They did make a mess, I know."

"When I showed up, it looked like the aftermath of a rock concert; empty potato chips bags, cola cans. Your neighbors are pigs, Maggie. Just saying. I picked up a bunch of garbage on my way out."

"Thanks, Brownie. Yeah, the cops said they filled two garbage bags full of trash just from the hallway that night. After they went through it, they asked me if I wanted it. They're just so helpful."

"Which reminds me, I picked up what I thought was a piece of jewelry in the hallway that night and forgot all about it until the other day. I must have thought it was valuable when I first saw it. I was going to turn it in to your building's lost and found."

"We don't have a lost and found. What is it?"

"I still don't know. A kid's toy, maybe? When I saw it wasn't valuable, I thought I'd give it to Nicole."

"You've still got it?"

"You can't seriously think this is important?"

"It's one more thing than I had fifteen minutes ago."

"It's nothing. Just a kid's toy."

"We don't have any kids in the apartment. What does it look like?"

"It's gold plated or something. Looks kinda cheap. I don't know...like a ring of some kind, but not for your finger."

"Can you drop it by my folks' house?"

"Is your apartment off-limits now that your frog boyfriend's taken up residence?"

"I just thought it'd be more convenient for you. Drop it off at my place if you want."

"I'll drop the thing off at your folks' place. If you're not there, I'll give it to your mom."

"Thanks, Brownie."

Later that evening, Maggie sat with her legs tucked under her on the couch in front of the light supper that Laurent had thrown together to keep them from starving until breakfast. Tiny sardines fried in batter, miniature onions swimming in some kind of spicy tomato sauce, raw carrots, artichoke hearts, radishes and, of course, the ubiquitous saucers of oil-drenched peppers and bread.

And since no meal was worth eating without *du vin*, there was a steadily breathing bottle of *Chateauneuf-du-Pape* to wash it all down with. Maggie wondered how long it would be before she started craving a cigarette and spending her mornings hanging around cafés, doing nothing but drinking *espresso* and watching the world go by.

She dipped a crust of bread into the trail of olive oil on her plate. Thirteen grams of go-straight-to-your-hips fat she thought as she popped the savory, sodden morsel into her mouth. She tried to remember the last time she had gone to an aerobics class or jogged around the block.

As soon as she'd walked in the door to her apartment, she'd greeted Laurent then gone straight to her laptop to book her flight to Nice and her hotel in Cannes. She hated the feeling she had while she was doing it—*surreptitiously* —because she knew Laurent was still so strongly against her going. But there was nothing for it. She had to go.

She prayed he'd get over it.

"It's all delicious," she said, smiling at Laurent next to her on the couch. They had taken their feast and spread it out on the coffee table in the living room. Tall tapers sputtered and dripped amidst their banquet setting.

"This is not cooking," he protested, refusing, as usual, to accept a compliment for pulling things out of a refrigerator.

"Doesn't make it any less tasty." She popped a final viscous artichoke into her mouth and wondered if he'd notice if she stopped eating. "Can I go over my notes with you?"

He nodded, a slight shimmer of oil lining his full lips. He reached for his wineglass.

"Okay. I've got a witness—Alfie—who can place Gerard at the scene around the time of the murder. So now Gerard has motive *and* opportunity."

"The police say—"

"I know, I know, that he was in his hotel room. But listen, I'd just given the bastard five thousand dollars. I'm convinced he could purchase all the alibi he wanted with that kind of money, regardless of what the police think. I just need to prove it."

"C'est difficile."

"Anyway, okay, that's Gerard and he's my number one suspect so far."

"And the drug dealer?"

"Laurent, the drug dealer did *not* murder Elise. That's just the cops' way of killing two birds: throw a scum-bag dealer in jail and wrap up the confusing case of a dead woman who happened to be a junkie."

She took a deep breath, knowing this next part was probably going to go a long way toward ruining their evening.

"When I'm in Cannes next week," she said, noticing Laurent frown immediately, "I'll visit Madame Zouk and also the Cannes Police Department. Surely, the French have something akin to the Freedom of Information Act over there? If the police have any records at all about Elise—or for that matter, the woman they palmed off to me as Elise and then conveniently cremated before anyone could discover the bullet hole in the side of her head—I'll be that much closer to finding the answers I need."

Maggie couldn't help but notice how disturbed Laurent looked. He'd even stopped eating.

"You are going to investigate the body you thought was Elise's?" His voice sounded flat, almost cold.

"Don't you think I should? I mean, I brought her remains home thinking they were Elise's. So who *was* she?"

"It was a mistaken identity," Laurent said, watching her closely over his wineglass.

"Maybe."

"Your parents have performed the DNA on her bones?"

Maggie shook her head. "It was going to take literally months for a private lab to do that, and I can't tell you how expensive it was. And now my dad doesn't see the point since we know for a fact she's not Elise."

"True."

"Are you okay, Laurent? You're not eating."

"I am only confused as to why this woman's identity would be of any value to you. She isn't Elise. And you know that."

"It's probably *not* of any value," Maggie said, reaching for a toasted round of bread and spreading a large dollop of aioli on it. "But since I'll be in town anyway, it won't hurt to ask."

"I wish you to not talk with Dubois."

Maggie looked at Laurent. He had resumed eating, but she couldn't help but think there was something going on behind his eyes. *At least he seems to have accepted I'm going.*

"Laurent, you know I need to make the police see that Gerard is our best suspect. That means building a case against him. Look at all the information I've found out just talking to people in the building and so on. I need to talk to Gerard."

"You will not talk with Dubois," he said flatly.

"Laurent—"

"*J'ai interdit!* I forbid it! He is a character *dangereux.* If he is killing Elise, then he can hurt you *aussi.*"

Maggie touched Laurent on the wrist. The outburst was something new. Laurent was normally so placid. She found the passion a tad thrilling on the one hand, but disconcerting on the other.   "Okay, fine. Then I'll just talk to Zouk."

Laurent eyed her carefully. "You will go all the way to Cannes and not talk with Gerard Dubois?"

"If you insist."

"I do. *J'insiste*, Maggie. He is a bad man. *Très mauvais.*"

"Okay, I won't approach him. I'll gather my information and build my case without talking with him."

He seemed to relax a little.

"In any event, I figure my best source is Madame Zouk anyway. If she knew Elise so well, then she definitely knew Gerard, too. I'm hoping she can help me prove that Gerard had a motive. If I can do that, and then bring Alfie's testimony in to place Gerard here at the time of the murder, I might have a case."

"I thought Alfie's mother said he would not testify."

"Details," Maggie said as she popped an olive in her mouth. "By the way, when are you doing that personal chef gig for the Club?"

She could see he was making an effort to let their previous conversation go.

"There are two events now. Your father has been busy."

"So you just go to people's homes and make them dinner? Is that how it works?"

He shrugged. "Like catering. Only for a family or, in one case, a couple."

"Dad said he can help you find all the work you want. I'm sure that's true, especially after they taste your cooking."

"*Peut-être.*"

Maggie's cellphone began to vibrate on the coffee table. "I hate phone calls at night," she said, standing to pick it up. "I'm always afraid of bad news."

"Hello? Oh, hey, how are you?" She glanced over at Laurent and his eyebrows shot up. *Qui?*

"You're kidding." Maggie sat down abruptly on the arm of the couch. "When?" Her hand went to her mouth and she gnawed a cuticle. There was a long pause, then, "Okay, yeah, I will. Thanks a lot for calling. No, I know you will and I appreciate it. Thanks, Detective. Bye."

"Well?"

"That was Detective Burton. He says they've got somebody new for Elise's killer."

"What happened to the drug dealer?"

"Huh?" She looked up at him, her mind a confusing tangle of thoughts and feelings. "Oh, he didn't mention him."

"*Zut! Mon Dieu!*" Laurent squeezed Maggie's knee. "That is wonderful, is it not? Maggie?"

"Burton said this guy just walked in and gave himself up this afternoon."

"Who is it?" Laurent poured her another glass of the heady red wine.

She tried to shake the labyrinth of confusing new questions out of her mind. "It's nobody we know. Just some guy. Some faceless whacko who's done it before. Nobody we know."

Chapter Fifteen

"Promise me you won't talk about the price of mangos in Auckland." Darla squirmed in the passenger seat of Gary's BMW and rearranged her headband in the visor mirror. "Let's just be normal for a change, what do you say?"

Gary smiled at his wife. She looked good. She seemed happier, more relaxed since they made the decision. He knew *he* was.

"Maggie knows we're planning to move to New Zealand, Darla. I've been discussing it with her all week."

"I'm surprised she hasn't called me yet to suggest prices on a semi-private at a good mental hospital."

"She supports me in this, Darla." Gary pulled into the parking lot at The Parthenon. "Something you would do well to emulate."

"She doesn't have to live with it. She doesn't have to wake up to your 'G'day, mates' and listen to the price of kiwi fruit as it rises and falls in the world market. We are *not* moving to New Zealand, Gary, and you are making us both look like idiots!"

Maybe he'd rushed that assessment about her happiness. Come to think of it, he thought, she looked bloody tense. "I won't mention mangoes," he said, pulling into a parking spot.

"Thank you."

"And perhaps Maggie won't mention her latest obsession."

"What are you talking about? I thought Laurent was going to be at dinner with us."

"I'm talking about her *other* obsession. The one about tracking down her sister's killer. It's all she talks about anymore."

"Well, it gives her a sense that she's doing something. She must feel pretty helpless."

"I know how she feels."

"In that case, you could probably suggest to her that she do something more constructive than tracking down Elise's killer. Like, say, moving to the Antipodes instead."

"Very amusing, Darla. I hope you're going to be a little less riotous during dinner. And why is it, exactly, we need to meet this guy? He'll be gone and out of her life in three months. Why invest the time in him?"

"You don't know he'll be gone and besides, it's to show support for Maggie. So she knows we accept him."

"I haven't even met him yet and I can tell you I don't accept him."

"Well, doesn't that just say a lot about the kind of person you are? You're judging him without having met him?"

"Trust me," Gary said as he locked the car and peered up at the ominous looking building Maggie called home. "When this all shakes out and he's dumped her and gone on his way, just remember who called it."

Maggie removed the candles from the fireplace mantle and set them on the table. She flattened the heavy cotton napkins out with her hands and placed them to the left of the four forks at each place setting.

"You know, I can't believe they've latched on to this new suspect, someone who clearly fits their new favorite theory that it was all random and not connected to any kind of motive or anything—"

"Maggie." Laurent appeared in the doorway of the kitchen, filling it. He was wearing jeans and a short-sleeve tee shirt. His eyes looked tired. He held a wooden spoon in one hand.

"I know, I know. No one wants to hear about this."

"It is not that. But perhaps just for the evening…"

"Yes, yes. Keep it light. No talk of murder and motive. Got it."

"Maggie, you will stop it now, *s'il te plaît*." He shook his head and wagged a finger. She remembered the first time he had done that, how sweet and sexy and possessive it had seemed to her.

It still did. "I love you, Laurent," she said impulsively, not knowing the words were coming until they were out.

Caught in a half-turn on his way back into the maw of the steamy kitchen, Laurent stopped and faced her again. *"Je t'aime, aussi, chérie,"* he said, a smile edging across his face.

Maggie ran to him and wrapped her arms around him. His grin telegraphed loud and clear that he was already calculating the possibility of moving her into the bedroom before the guests arrived.

"I'll stop talking about murder and death at least for the duration of our dinner party with Gary and Darla. *Je promis*," she whispered.

"Merci." He tossed the spoon in the sink and reached down to cup her bottom with both hands.

"Your *roue* is roiling."

"*Merde*." He released her and returned to the stove to snatch up the little pot of bubbling paste from one of the gas burners.

"You know, Gary's probably going to be on this Kiwi kick of his. Have I told you about that?"

"Of course." He lifted a ladle of the *roue* and plunged it into the hot broth in another pot on the stove.

A sturdy knock at the door brought Maggie around the dining room table and into the foyer. "Oh, that's them now." She gave her plum-colored tunic a quick pull over her capri pants and opened the door.

"Hey, guys!" Maggie and Darla hugged, then Darla pulled back and her face became serious.

"Maggie, I just wanted to say again I'm so sorry about your sister."

"Thanks, Darla, thank you. Hey, Gar."

Gary peered around the corner toward the kitchen. "Where is he?"

"Oh, God, you're not going to be weird tonight, are you?" Maggie turned to Darla. "He's not going to be weird tonight, is he?"

"Don't be silly. Gary? Weird? But seriously, Maggie, where is he?"

"He's in the kitchen." She raised her voice. "Laurent! Do you have a breaking point?"

"You mean he hasn't found that with you yet?" Gary quipped.

"*Un moment, chérie.*"

"Ohhhh, Maggie! You lucky creature! He calls you *chérie.*"

"I know! It's so cool."

"Oh, you girls are pathetic," Gary said. "Can I come in or are you going to make us get our hands stamped first?"

"Yes, yes. Come in. He's in the kitchen doing tricky things with flour and beef juice and stuff." She led the way to the dining room as Laurent came out of the kitchen with a bottle of white wine and four glasses in his hands.

He and Gary shook hands almost solemnly, and when they did the air crackled with the tension between them.

It hadn't occurred to Maggie before that moment that both men, perversely, considered the other a rival in some way. As if she had just witnessed a preview of the entire evening, she realized: *Gary and Laurent are not going to be friends.*

"*Enchanté,*" Laurent said, more to Darla than Gary. He put the wine bottle down and reached for her hand. He smiled broadly and handed her a glass of wine.

Gary took his wine from Laurent, too, and curtly nodded his acceptance. "So, Maggie," he said, turning his back on Laurent, "how goes the police investigation?"

"Not good." She ignored Laurent's look of disapproval and ushered them into the living room. "Sit down and I'll tell you a little about it. Are you just about finished in the kitchen, Laurent?" she called over her shoulder, not waiting for a reply. They settled themselves in Maggie's tiny living room.

"Okay," Maggie said. "I'll be brief."

"Oh?" Darla frowned.

"Well, you know, it's sort of a depressing topic."

Laurent entered the room, a glass of wine in his hand, but he did not sit down. Instead, he leaned against the archway of the door leading into the living room.

"Maggie is unhappy when she is thinking of her sister's death," he said, watching Maggie with eyes full of care and protection.

"It depresses me," Maggie agreed. "But I can't not do it, you know?"

Darla nodded sympathetically.

"I mean, I have to find out what happened and the police aren't doing anything."

"That is not true," Laurent said.

"All right, they're not doing enough for me." She took a sip of her wine.

"Gary said you got a bad phone call last week, maybe from the killer?" Darla leaned toward Maggie on the couch.

"Yes, I did. And I was so blown away by it that I didn't ask him any questions. I just hung up."

"What did the cops say?" Gary asked as Laurent retreated to the kitchen.

"I'll let you know when they get back to me. I left a message and they haven't responded yet."

"What did the caller say?" Darla asked.

"He told me I was next on his list, or asked how would I like to be next on his list...something like that. I don't remember exactly now. It freaked me out so much."

"Why are you still investigating? Didn't you say the cops have someone in custody for her murder?" Darla asked gently.

"*Exactement*," Laurent said. Maggie knew Laurent's comment was an extension of the heated argument they'd had earlier about why she still felt she needed to go to Cannes. Darla smiled as if she'd been praised for being good by a sexy professor.

"They do," Maggie said. "But they had someone last week, too. A homeless guy sleeping in the basement who had a couple of bags of weed on him so he got upgraded to murdering crack dealer."

"But this new guy confessed, right?" Gary spoke, but Maggie noticed he was looking at Laurent when he did.

"All kinds of people confess to things they didn't do," Maggie said. A quick glance at Laurent assured her it was past time to change the topic. His eyes practically flashed with frustration. "But enough about that," she said. "I think the thing everyone here really wants to hear about is the ratio of sheep to the population in Remuera. Gary, you have the floor."

An hour later, after a largely tense and laborious meal where everyone worked very hard *not* to talk about something that would inevitably upset someone else, Gary pushed his plate away and addressed Maggie. "Not bad. You're improving."

She gave him a warning look. "I didn't make it. Laurent did."

"Oh? My compliments to the chef." He smiled stiffly at Laurent.

"Don't be an ass, Gary," Darla said, her mouth full *of Boeuf en Daube Provençale.* "You *know* Laurent cooked it. So, so delish, Laurent," she said to him.

"*Je t'en prie,*" Laurent said, smiling at Darla.

"And that soup!" Darla scooped up another spoonful of her *Boeuf en Daube.* "I need the recipe for that, although I'm sure it's impossibly hard. Can you microwave it? You know, make it up early and then freeze it?"

"'Freeze it?" Laurent asked uncertainly.

"Oh, never mind. Keep it a secret from me. It makes it taste better."

Laurent replenished all the wineglasses and then returned to the table from the kitchen with a tray of sausage, cheeses, salad and thin slices of *crespaou*, a cold vegetable omelet smothered in tomato sauce and herbs.

"Well, finally," Gary said when Laurent set the tray down. "I was wondering when you people were going to finish feeding us."

Darla giggled drunkenly.

"Yes, well..." Maggie said, laughing with her. "The French definitely have the whole endless food thing under control. I told Laurent I'm going to look like a German *hausfrau* really soon now. He thinks I'm joking."

"Speaking of joking." Darla, sounding like she was one glass of wine over her personal limit, slid a slice of *crespaou* onto her plate and helped herself to a thick wedge of Brie. "What do you think about the idea of us *emigrating* to New Zealand?"

"I thought you didn't want me talking about that." Gary touched a piece of cold sausage suspiciously with his fork. "This is good stuff," he said, reaching over and pulling the wine bottle to him.

"*Chateau Cos D'Estournel 1982*." Laurent looked at him with surprise. "You are familiar*?*"

Gary shrugged uncomfortably. "I've heard of it."

"It all just seems so sudden to me," Maggie said, taking a pear from the basket of fruit on the table.

"Did you know that Auckland is the furthest point on the globe from Atlanta?" Gary said. "Except Perth."

"And I guess that's the whole point?" Maggie looked at Gary.

"I'm sick of being afraid for my family and reading about mass slayings at the McDonald's restaurants and drug killings in Cabbagetown."

"You act like it's an every day occurrence," Darla said, slurring her words.

"So your answer to that is to try your luck in another hemisphere?" Maggie cut her pear into small bite-sized chunks. "I don't know, Gary, it seems drastic. Don't you think so, Laurent?"

"I'm thinking it sounds like a *bonne idée*," he said, shrugging.

"I thought you liked America," Maggie said.

"I like wherever you are, *chérie*."

"Yeah, well, *I'm* thinking it sounds like the end of the world," Darla said, pushing her plate away. "Literally."

Maggie looked at Laurent and he covered her hand on the table with his. She felt the sudden and unmistakable peace of the unspoken truce between them.

Chapter Sixteen

Gary opened his office door and peered down the hallway. Awfully quiet for the afternoon of a great client victory, he thought. On the other hand, did they expect him to bring out the champagne every time they won a significant account? At least Maggie had to take back everything she'd said recently about his mind not being on the clients. Today's success story certainly threw *that* theory in the crapper.

He wandered down to Maggie's closed door and stood there, frowning. Deirdre passed him on the way to the copier machine.

"What's the deal with Maggie?" he asked.

"Private phone call, I guess. Should I buzz her to be at the condom meeting?"

"Stop calling it that, would you? It's a prophylactics client, for God's sake. You make it sound like we're practicing safe sex in the conference room. No, don't bother her. Let's assume she looks at her day planner."

Deirdre walked away but Gary lingered outside Maggie's door. *Ever since that frog came into her life, she's been acting strange. Even Darla said as much at breakfast today.*

Gary frowned at the closed door. She spent hours in the office ladies room messing with her hair, where she never used to care all that much before. She was never available for lunch any more. He grimaced. Probably because she's running home for lunch sex or something equally as unbalanced.

That was it. The whole situation was unbalanced. Out of kilter. Gary was determined that before he left the country he would make sure Maggie wasn't racing full-tilt down the road to sure destruction and heartbreak, as she currently was.

Unfortunately, giving her the real story about her hulking Franco boyfriend was the only way to do that. Sure, she'd be mad at first when he told her what he'd seen the night of the dinner party. But eventually she'd realize how foolish she'd been. It might take awhile, but he knew eventually she'd thank him for it.

He paused for a moment to imagine what she'd say when he told her about the prison tat on Laurent's left bicep he'd recognized peeking out of Dernier's shirt.

"Gary?"

He turned, embarrassed at what he must have looked like, staring at Maggie's closed door as if he were going to use mind powers to open it. Patti stood in the hallway, her laptop tucked under one arm.

"You okay?"

He flushed. He had successfully avoided seeing her alone for four straight days. He wasn't proud of it, but there it was.

"Oh, hey, Patti. I must look like an idiot just standing here in the hallway."

"We've all been there. Half the time I go into the supply room I have to ask myself, *now why did I come in here?*"

"Exactly! Yes. Thank you."

"I just wanted to say…"

No, no, no! Can. Not. Deal. With. This.

"…that I'm sorry about some stuff I said the other day. I feel like an idiot, and if you can rewind the memory tapes on that afternoon, I'd appreciate it."

"Oh, sure, Patti. Hey, good metaphor. Memory tapes. You know, for a media buyer? Anyway, of course. Hey, how about that client win, huh? Pretty exciting."

"Really exciting," she said, smiling.

Unless he was badly mistaken, Gary could tell Patti was just as relieved as he was to be out from under what had been said that day.

*****

The man glared at Gerard from across the café table. All along the *Rue de la Clignancourt*, shopkeepers were opening their doors and beginning the morning ritual of hosing down the patch of sidewalk in front of their stores.

The *Sacré-Coeur* was just visible in the distance, its bone-white onion dome dotting the horizon like a bright exclamation point. Every time he saw the cathedral, Gerard thought of his grandmother, that ferocious old crow, who every Sunday would drag him and his brother— unprotesting but unwilling—up the hundreds of steps to Mass. He could still feel the pinching grip of her withered old hand clamped on his wrist.

His eyes shifted away from the church and back to his companion. He eyed the filthy bundle of flesh and clothes across from him.

"As I have said before, Vadim, I have not seen Nadia in more than six months. And even then, we were merely acquaintances."

"Of course," the man said. "That's understood. You wouldn't be alive at this moment if it were otherwise."

Gerard licked his lips. He had been a fool to think they wouldn't look for him in Paris.

"Her father believes you were one of the last people to see her before she disappeared."

"Surely *disappeared* is a bit dramatic? Perhaps she went back to Russia."

"Her family there says no."

"Then she ran off with a lover."

"*Did* she run off with a lover, Monsieur Dubois?"

"Well, *I* don't know. Why do you assume anything at all happened? Nadia was a free spirit. Unpredictable. Who is to say where she would go?"

"She left her little dog that she loved so dearly. She left her father and a two million euro *pied-a-terre* in St-Tropez. Her spirit was not *that* free."

"But, if you haven't found a body, and I assume there have been no reports of suspicious deaths along the Côte d'Azur, why do you assume the worst?"

"It is true there have been no reports of unidentified bodies, accidental or otherwise, on the coast. None except for your own poor wife, of course," the man said, grinning obscenely at Gerard. "But a body is not a difficult thing to make disappear, if one is determined."

"Look, like I said, I haven't seen her in months. I have no idea where she might have gone."

"My employers are prepared to be kind, Monsieur Dubois, to have the truth in order to go forward."

Gerard hesitated. "I can ask around, Vadim. See if anybody has seen her." He raked a hand through his thinning, reddish-brown hair.

"You do that, Monsieur Dubois." The man's watery eyes blinked malevolently at Gerard. "You do that as quickly as you can."

It's as if he already knows, Gerard thought as a sudden, terrible coldness began to seep into his bones.

But how could he?

Chapter Seventeen

The skirt of Maggie's stiff cotton sundress spread out in a fan against the lawn. She drew her bare legs up under her and sipped from one of the frosty glasses of lemonade Becka had just armed everyone with. Laurent stood a few yards away in khaki trousers and a black polo shirt, holding the reins of Nicole's pony. Nicole, her jodhpurred legs sticking out awkwardly, sat woodenly atop the Welsh pony. Laurent spoke to her in French and Maggie enjoyed hearing his fluency for a change.

She hated to admit that Gary might be at least a little right on that score. He had lately done more than hint that the very sexy French accent Maggie was so enthralled with was a pretty big roadblock to basic communication. She wouldn't go that far, but from time to time she did find herself yearning for a more complicated exchange between them.

Yesterday, when they were trying to agree on which movie to download for viewing, Maggie had been appalled to see Laurent zero in—not to the foreign films, as she had expected—to the horror/sci-fi section of the online store. They had actually argued about it.

"I can't watch this stuff, Laurent."

"Pour quoi pas?" Why not?

"It's garbage."

"Ahhh."

"I mean, come on, Laurent, blood and guts pouring out of a dead man's eyeballs? It's gross and meaningless."

In the end, they'd compromised. Maggie promised not to make retching noises during his shows, and Laurent resolved not to sigh too heavily or yawn during the British drawing room mystery that she wanted to see. After all, it could've been a lot worse, she mused. It could have been a Jerry Lewis movie.

As she listened to him now, talking fluently to Nicole, she made a silent vow to take a French class at the local community college. Soon.

She turned to her mother, who was seated on a white wrought iron bench next to her.

"Do you think she enjoys that?" Maggie asked.

Elspeth shaded her eyes against the sun and smiled at Laurent. "Watch her left foot, Laurent. She looks like she's a little lopsided."

Laurent waved a finger in Elspeth's direction to indicate he had it under control. He trotted up and down the lawn next to the pony. Nicole clung to the saddle like a tenacious but somnolent jellyfish. Her little face appeared to be screwed into a squinting mask of concentration, which was an improvement over her usual blank stare.

"Why do you need to go to Cannes?" Elspeth spoke to Maggie, but her eyes were on her granddaughter. "Laurent mentioned that you are planning another trip overseas." Elspeth took a sip of her lemonade and then patted her lips with a lace-trimmed cotton handkerchief.

"I was going to tell you."

"He said you were going because of Elise."

Maggie cleared her throat and winced into the sun. "Well, sort of."

Elspeth turned and looked at her daughter. She wasn't smiling. "Maggie."

Maggie sighed. "Look, I don't know how to explain to you why I feel I need to go. I just do, that's all. Elise was writing a letter before she died and I want to talk to the woman she was writing it to. I know it sounds feeble, but I think it's worth a trip."

Elspeth set her lemonade glass down on the bench and stood up, applauding the approaching twosome.

"*Très bien, Nicole!* Our own little National Velvet." She touched Maggie's head. "I love you, Maggie. Possibly more than anything on this Earth." She turned on her heel and walked back into the house.

Astonished by her mother's words, Maggie stared after Elspeth's retreating back. Her lemonade glass was dripping blotches of condensation all over her skirt.

"You are getting wet, Maggie," Laurent called to her. He picked Nicole up and deposited her on the ground next to her pony and led the beast to where Maggie was sitting. He tucked the reins under the pommel and let the pony graze while he flopped down next to her. Nicole moved to where Laurent was seated and lowered herself to a spot beside him.

"She seems to like you," Maggie remarked.

"*Ah, mais oui!*" Laurent patted the little girl's hand. "We are very fond of each other, *n'est-ce pas, mon petit chou?*"

"What else did the detective tell you?" Laurent asked, smiling at Nicole. Burton had called Maggie as she and Laurent drove over to her parents' house that afternoon. Burton had called it a "courtesy call," but as far as Maggie was concerned it had been pretty devoid of any actual courtesy. Or content for that matter.

Maggie flicked away the droplets of water that had pooled in fat beads on her dress. "I did more telling than he did. He said this guy they have looks good for it and they're going for an indictment and then to close the case."

Laurent pulled out some grass and sprinkled it on Nicole's lap. She looked at him somberly. "And so you told the detective everything you know?"

"Well, you heard what I told him. All about Alfie and how Gerard was at my apartment that day."

Laurent nodded without looking at her.

"And it meant nothing to him! I mean, I practically have a video tape of Gerard killing Elise, and they don't care." She looked guiltily at Nicole and then lowered her voice. She shook her skirt free of remnant grass blades. "They got their guy and they're not interested in any more 'facts.'"

"Tant pis, Maggie." Too bad.

"Yeah, *tant pis,* all right." She stood and gave her dress a shake. "Come on, let's take Nicole inside. I'm starving and it's mostly your fault."

"Comment?"

"Your cooking. It's stretched my stomach. I used to eat like a bird. Now, if I don't get multiple course meals on a regular basis, I feel like I'm on a starvation diet. Thanks a heap, Laurent. I hope you like your women hefty."

Laurent hopped up easily for someone of his height and bulk. He caught her by the waist and swung her effortlessly into the air and back down again. He kept her pinned in his arms.

"Not too bad," he said judiciously.

She smiled, loving the feeling of his strong arms around her.

Nicole sat quietly between them, staring at the torn grass bits scattered across the lawn and on her bright blue dress.

Later that evening, they returned to Maggie's apartment. The summer was giving way begrudgingly to the first signs of autumn, and the heat of the day had completely dissipated. Maggie was exhausted, which was what she would cite as her defense for what happened.

She slipped out of her skirt and pulled on cotton shorts and a tee shirt while Laurent prepared a late night repast for them. She was determined not to remind Laurent of her upcoming trip. A part deep in the back of her brain couldn't come up with a good reason why he was so set against her going. It didn't feel like worry or even his usual protectiveness that seemed to be the impasse. For the life of her, she couldn't put her finger on what it was, only that it had become the first and only real problem they were having trouble getting past.

Now, as she sat curled up on the couch, a glass of wine in one hand and a warm *Croque Monsieur* in the other, she felt inextricably drawn to this man who had entered her life—and the lives of her family—so effortlessly and left her breathless with longing and desire.

"Laurent?"

"Mmmm—mm?" He looked up and smiled. A question mark hovered in his eyes.

"Do you have any ideas about our future together?" Maggie was surprised as the words came out of her mouth. She had not expected to say them out loud. She wasn't so unaware, however, as to not suspect they hadn't been hiding out in her head.

Laurent finished chewing and removed his napkin from his shirt collar. He placed it down on the coffee table and scanned the remains of their finished supper. It occurred to Maggie that Laurent, who always seemed to know what to say, when to get excited, when to let something pass, was a little uncomfortable.

"Of course."

"You'll get work over here?"

"Perhaps I will get a job as the French chef at Burger King."

Maggie blinked at him when he said this. *Was he being facetious?* "I was just wondering about a timeline for us is all. How long were you thinking of staying?"

"You are wondering how long we will last? Of course. Living with a French lover is one item on your bucket list, *non*?" He did not soften the words with a smile.

Vaguely aware that his English seemed to have improved, Maggie was horrified at how quickly the conversation had gone wrong. Even so, she was too angry to do anything but sputter, "What are you talking about? That's not what this is."

Laurent made a grunt of disgust. "*This*. Always you are misunderstanding me. I am talking about Maggie not making room for me in her life." He waved away her attempts to speak with an impatient hand. "Do not tell me you emptied a drawer for me, I am not talking about drawers. I am talking about your *life.*"

Maggie wrapped her arms around herself and stared at him. "I see," she said, stiffly. "I had no idea you felt this way."

"*Bien sûr!*" he exploded. "This is the *problem*. You have no idea. You want to continue as you are and be the independent single girl, *n'est-ce pas? Ach!* You are so *Américain...*"

"Well, excuse me for being so *Américain*. I'll try in future to be a little more Libyan, or would my being a tad more *French* be good?" She began picking up dishes. "That's what this is really all about, isn't it? Me being some simple-minded French girl who'll spend hours plucking her eyebrows and starving herself bony while whipping up heavy creamed sauces for her big Frenchman."

"You could not possibly be French," Laurent said with a shrug.

"I hate you."

"*D'accord*. As you always say, I can live with that."

"Great." Maggie whirled around and stomped toward the bedroom. "Why don't you live with cleaning up this mess in the kitchen while you're at it?"

"That would be different than usual?" he called after her. The door slammed between them.

Later that night, as Laurent lay snoring softly against her, Maggie watched the moon through her window as it broke loose from behind a diaphanous shred of cloud. She touched his sleeping face. The fight had been stupid, but it had also felt somehow necessary. It helped to put to bed finally and forever her concern that their language gap was only allowing them a shallow relationship. After the fight, she would never have to worry about *that* again.

She looked at his sleeping profile. Even with a scant one hundred words of common vocabulary between them they were still able—as able as any other couple—to have a silly fight about nothing.

When he had finally tapped on the bedroom door and entered, she could see from the frown on his face that his making the first move was as far as he was going to go with the reconciliation. Relieved to have at least been offered an olive branch—if somewhat hesitant—Maggie had reached out to him.

She looked at the alarm clock on her nightstand; it was a little after two a.m. This wasn't the first night Laurent had fallen asleep easily after three or four cups of strong Brazilian coffee, while Maggie fidgeted and tossed after her one meager *café au lait*.

She eased away from his sleeping form and got out of bed. Making sure not to wake him, though she didn't think anything short of another charge up the Bastille could, she gathered up a pair of jeans and a sweatshirt and closed the bedroom door behind her.

She set up her laptop on the dining room table, poured herself a glass of milk and rummaged in the cabinets until she found a few Oreo cookies. Rationalizing that she needed the cookies to go with the milk, that she needed to make her sleepy, she pulled on the jeans and sweatshirt over her filmy silk chemise.

"What is it?" Laurent's sleepy voice came to her from the bedroom.

So much for her assumption he was a sound sleeper. She walked to the bedroom door. "Nothing, go back to sleep," she whispered, then turned and sat down at the dining room table to sort out her thoughts with the investigation so far.

Laurent appeared in the doorway, dressed, his hair mussed and full about his face, his eyes squinting against the light in the dining room.

"Oh, Laurent, go back to bed. I didn't want to wake you."

"I am not sleeping good when you are gone," he said, holding a huge hand up to contain a yawn.

She saw him looking around the dining room and she hoped he wasn't going to make them something to eat.

"I will go for cigarettes," he said, tapping his tee shirt pocket as if to show there were none where they should be.

"Really? Laurent, it's past two in the morning."

He shrugged, now more fully awake, and tucked his wallet into the back pocket of his jeans.

"There's an Amoco station open on the corner, down Peachtree," she said, turning back to her laptop.

"I will be back," he said, kissing her before disappearing out the door. Maggie tried to sense if there were any vestiges left over from their fight. She could feel none from him. No emotional hangover, no recriminations.

Was it true what he said? Was she not making room for him in her heart? She thought she was so gaga over him she was downright foolish in most matters that concerned him. She ate when she wasn't hungry. She drank when she knew she'd already had too much. She trusted him implicitly when there was no real reason to do so after the very short amount of time they'd known each other.

Whoa. Where did that come from? She rested her fingers on the keyboard and stared ahead. Was she afraid she trusted him *in spite* of herself? Was there something going on underneath the infatuation and the passion— something Laurent detected—something in her that was resisting him?

Every single person in her life, with the possible exception of her father, who had his own form of infatuation with Laurent, had dropped comments or asides to the effect that she was getting in too deep too fast. Her mother, Gary, Brownie...even Darla had exhibited surprise to see the two of them moving so fast.

As usual, Laurent was several strides ahead of her. He knew what she had only begun feeling in a distracted, unformed way—that she wasn't quite sure of him. Somewhere not so deep down she hadn't forgotten that there had been no word from him for six months. And no explanation as to why not.

What could she possibly do about it? She couldn't ask him to move out. She didn't *want* him to move out. Her mind flitted back to a moment a few hours earlier under the covers at the height of their make-up sex. She blushed at the thought and stood to shake off the feeling. It was a wonderful feeling, to be sure. It was also a feeling of loss of control.

Maggie opened the dining room window, which looked out over the back parking lot and adjacent woods. It was a cool night, unusual for late August. Aside from the reputational splendor of living at The Parthenon, Maggie had been drawn to this apartment building because it felt like a little bit of country in the heart of the city. It, and a few residential houses in the neighborhood, shared a fair-sized tract of woods. The stand of trees was thick and forbidding though, protected by some stubborn dowager who'd owned the property for generations and refused to sell to developers.

Peachtree Creek flowed through the forest and Maggie had seen raccoons and foxes in it. Once, after she moved in, she had indulged in a little exploration in the woods. For a few moments she'd felt like she was somewhere on the Appalachian Trail; she'd also been stung by a bee and hadn't gone back in four years.

Tonight, the moon cast an eerie incandescence over the wooded patch. Blackened tree limbs were elongated by shadows and stretched out in all directions like skinny witches' arms beckoning her. She shivered and enjoyed the comfort of her little lighted nook in the darkness.

Suddenly, from where she stood at the window, she heard a noise from outside. She took a breath and held it, but all she could hear was the blood pounding in her ears. The wind seemed to have risen. She could hear it moaning in the trees. And then the sound again, like a dog in pain.

She pulled on her sneakers and stuck her keys and a small flashlight from the kitchen drawer in the pocket of her jeans. As she closed the apartment door behind her, the hall lights, triggered by her movement, blinked on. Maggie ran down the hall and pulled open the heavy outside door at the end of the corridor.

The moon, although not quite full, kept her path lighted making her flashlight unnecessary. She hurried to the opening of the woods in front of her dining room window. When she glanced up at her apartment window, she was surprised to see her dining room illuminated clearly and distinctly.

"Here, boy," she called. "Where are you, puppy?" She wished she'd picked up her can of mace instead of the flashlight. She heard the dog whimper directly ahead of her. Clicking on her flashlight, she moved through the trees and into the opening of the woods, toward the sound. As the darkness engulfed her, she strained to hear in spite of the thundering of her heart in her head.

Then she saw it.

A scruffy little terrier with floppy ears and big dark eyes was tied to a small sapling across a six-foot ravine. Her emotions seesawed between relief at having found him and trepidation that human hands had clearly put him there. She could see a representative trickle of Peachtree Creek at the bottom of the ravine. A few miles away it would turn into a proper creek, but here it was just a moving, damp creek bed.

She grabbed at branches and rocks as she slid her way down the steep side of the slope to the bottom of the muddy creek bed. The puppy squirmed against its bonds and watched her approach with large, frightened eyes.

"It's okay, boy," she said, trying to keep herself calm as much as the dog. "I'm coming." Her light flashed spasmodically along the leaf-choked side of the ravine. She took a couple of steps up the other side, her fingers reaching for the little dog and his rope. She pulled at the hemp twine but it held fast. The puppy whimpered again.

Maggie knelt down on one knee near the puppy and pulled out her house keys.

"It's all right, boy," she said, using the teeth of her keys to saw at the twine. She reached for the animal and it cried out. She shone the light on him and saw that the dog was covered in blood.

Maggie gave the weakened piece of twine a sharp jerk and pulled it free of the tree. She quickly picked up the animal, ignoring its cry, and tucked it against her.

It was then that she heard the other noise.

It was the sound of movement in the woods above her, the movement of something heavy treading on leaves and sticks. The sound of someone trying to be stealthy.

Fighting the urge to panic, Maggie clutched the dog and climbed up the steep side of the ravine. The dog trembled against her. Her mouth was dry and she could feel the beginnings of terror start to unravel her mind. *Who was out here?* She reached for a hanging root and hoisted herself a few feet higher up the ravine. As she neared the top, her hands were trembling and clumsy with fear, her heart fluttering in her throat.

She sensed her assailant behind her before she heard him. She tried desperately to climb the last few feet up the ravine before he could reach her, but everything felt as if it was moving in slow motion.

She was only vaguely aware of dropping the puppy. She heard it cry as if from a long distance. She smelled a light fragrance, like violets or lily of the valley. And then a blinding pain crept up from the back of her head, and the dark, damp ravine bottom of Peachtree Creek rushed up to slam into her face.

Murder in the South of France

Part III

Eliminating the Impossible

Murder in the South of France

Chapter Eighteen

The dog, just a puppy, was nestled in Maggie's arms where she lay on the couch, both of them enrobed in a thick afghan. Laurent had bandaged the worst of the dog's cuts—his feet were missing several toenails and there were a few shallow slashes across its rump—and fed him, of course. Now it slept deeply and peacefully, as if it hadn't been tortured and beaten the night before, tied to a tree and thrown down a ravine.

Maggie touched its floppy ears and smoothed a hand over its brow but the dog only twitched and slept on.

Maybe, on some subconscious level, she had believed the suspect Burton had in custody really had killed Elise. And maybe she really did think—deep down—that the maniac who'd been gallivanting all over Buckhead last summer was the same guy, and so now the streets were safe again. What other explanation could there be for the fact that she had gone into the woods last night?

That was pretty much what Laurent wanted to know, too. In fact, the tone of his questions ran a wide gamut, from reasonable soft-spoken ones to thundering what-were-you-thinking ones. If Maggie thought she had seen him upset before last night, the man had totally rewritten the chapter on frenetic worry since then. The way he carried on, she wondered if he'd ever allow her out of his sight again.

But whatever the reason was, the fact remained that she hadn't felt particularly afraid to go running around in the woods in the middle of the night. And the cold truth was that foolish decision had nearly cost her her life.

If not for Laurent.

He had returned to the apartment and found her gone and begun an immediate and noisy search of The Parthenon grounds, which awakened the night watchman as well as a good number of the residents. He had likely succeeded in scaring off Maggie's assailant, too.

Maggie picked up the icepack and held it to the back of her head. Laurent had found her lying crumpled at the bottom of the ravine, a large, swelling knot on the back of her head, the wounded terrier cowering by her side. He had insisted they spend the rest of the early morning in the emergency room at Piedmont Hospital to confirm that Maggie would not lose her memory or begin reciting chants in Urdu at some point in the future.

She was released with the assurance that, although painful, she had sustained only a mild concussion. As she sat in her living room, her head banging like a kettledrum being attacked by a shovel, it felt anything *but* mild.

Laurent entered the room, his eyes clouded with concern. He held a steaming mug of tea and a small flask of amber-colored liqueur. Wordlessly, he placed the tea in front of her and handed her the brandy.

"I feel like I'm in an old Bette Davis movie," she said, wincing as she drank the brandy. It hurt to tip her head back and the fluid burned in her throat.

"You have called Gary?" Laurent sat down on the couch.

She nodded and deposited the icepack in a bowl on the coffee table.

Laurent had called the police from the emergency department, but Maggie insisted he not report it but speak only to Burton or Kazmaroff. Laurent left a message.

That was six hours ago and they had yet to call back.

As she watched Laurent's face, so full of helpless anxiety and frustration, she felt a sudden urge to tell him not to worry. She would promise to stop asking questions and stop trying to find out what happened to Elise. She knew their lives would settle down if she did. And surely her love for Laurent was big enough that she could give him that much? She watched him with guilt and caring and said nothing.

The phone rang and Laurent picked it up. "*Allo?*" He handed it to her. "It is Brownie."

Maggie accepted the phone as Laurent took the empty brandy glass into the kitchen. After she hung up, she padded barefooted to the kitchen. She wore a faded pair of navy sweat pants and a light cotton sweatshirt. Laurent was peering into the refrigerator, his back to her, rigid and expectant.

"He wants to meet me for lunch tomorrow."

"Ah, yes?" Laurent looked over his shoulder.

"You don't mind, do you?"

"I don't mind, *chérie*. We French are secure!" He turned toward her.

She moved forward and slipped easily into his arms. "Good thing. Makes up for my wobbly American ways."

He tilted her chin up with his fingers and kissed her on the mouth. "Perhaps a little food would help?"

"No food," she said firmly. "Oh! What about the dog? He needs to be seen by a vet."

"*Monsieur* Danford will take him today."

"I don't know, Laurent. Do you trust that guy? He'll probably chop him up for a stew to cook on his hot plate or something down there."

"He is happy to earn a few dollars to be of assistance to us, *ma petite*. He will take the dog and return him safely."

The outdoor buzzer sounded. Maggie looked questioningly at Laurent, who shrugged. She pressed the intercom button. "Yes?"

"Miss Newberry? It's Detectives Burton and Kazmaroff. Will you let us in, please?"

Maggie sat on the couch next to Laurent, a mug of tea in her hands, the sleeping puppy in her lap. Opposite them, in mismatched tub chairs, sat Kazmaroff, in his cool chinos and Vuarnet sunglasses, and Burton, precision-pressed and held together like a rubber band around a bundle of nerves.

"As you know, we have a suspect in custody who has confessed fully to the crime."

"Can you tell me his name?"

"Robert Donnell." Kazmaroff opened his flip-top smart phone and began reading from it. "He works as a bank teller at a Fulton County National Bank branch in Buckhead, where he has been a teller for twelve years. Preliminary questioning of his co-workers revealed he was thoughtful, considerate, but a little standoffish. He has no girlfriend and has never been married. He has a cat, but no friends or acquaintances outside of work. Most of his co-workers were not surprised at that."

"So what you're saying is he just randomly killed Elise for no particular reason."

"It's what *he* is saying. Yes." Burton rubbed his hands together and made a squeaking popping sound with them. "Miss Newberry, even a psycho thinks he's got a reason to kill. I mean, it may be a nuts reason, but it makes sense to him."

Maggie felt tired all of a sudden. She wanted to go take a nap...for the rest of the week. She felt a chilling nimbus of loneliness envelope her as the detectives appeared to subtly retract any help or support. "And what about the attack on me last night?"

"The attack—which we are of course investigating—doesn't appear to be connected to our case."

"How can you say that?" Laurent's voice boomed out impatiently, causing Maggie to look at him in surprise.

"Be-because we have our suspect for her sister's murder *in custody*," Kazmaroff said uncertainly. Maggie noticed that both detectives reacted to Laurent's question as if the dozing bear in the circus had just slipped his chains.

"Maggie's sister is killed and two months later Maggie is attacked and it is a coincidence?" Laurent was standing now.

"Look," Kazmaroff said, standing too. He gave Laurent a conspiratorial smile that suggested he would now tell him some inside dope, man to man. Maggie began to see why his partner couldn't stand him. "I don't know what city in France you're from, but there is a lot of crime in this city. We average two fatalities a rush hour every single day. Did you know that?" He looked at Maggie and she couldn't help but think she detected a note of pride in his tone. "We rank in the top ten cities across the country for homicides."

She bit her tongue not to say *unsolved*.

"So if you're asking could your sister be murdered one month and you mugged the next and those crimes have absolutely nothing to do with each other?" He addressed this last comment to Laurent. "Absolutely."

Maybe Burton picked up on the fact Laurent looked like he was inches away from wiping Kazmaroff's unctuous smile off his face with his fist, because he put a hand out as if to calm everyone down.

"We are certainly going to investigate who did what to whom last night, you can be sure of that. Okay?" He looked at Laurent as if that might reassure him.

"What about the phone call I got last week saying I was the next victim?"

Burton looked at her in confusion. "You got a threatening phone call?"

Laurent threw up his hands. "*C'est ridicule!*"

"Yes. I left you a message that I got a phone call saying I was next," Maggie said. "Sounds pretty connected to me."

Burton glanced at his partner and the two of them began to move toward the door. "We'll pull the records on your landline to trace the phone call, okay? I guarantee you it was just a flake and it'll show up as the home number for a little old lady with nothing better to do than watch true crime re-enactment shows and try to spice up her life. I'm sorry, but in my experience most people are just no damn good."

"So you're saying you think the call was not specific to me. Nor the hit on the head, which I have to tell you, *feels* incredibly specific to me."

He stood. "I know. Again, I'm sorry. But my partner is right on at least one point." He looked at Maggie and the now awake dog in her lap. "Buckhead isn't as safe as it used to be. That drug dealer—the guy we originally held as a suspect for your sister's killing?—still hangs out around here, so I wouldn't take any more midnight walks in the woods. Even without psychotic killers on the loose, you can't afford to play Anne of Green Gables in a big city like this. Okay?"

Maggie nodded politely at him while she wondered if they could arrest her if she asked Laurent to throw them out on their shiny polyester keisters.

When she closed the door behind them, Laurent went out onto the small stone balcony that faced Peachtree Road to smoke. Maggie ran a comb through her hair. She looked awful, she decided, as she stood in front of the bathroom mirror. A tiny vein under her right eye, normally imperceptible, was vivid against her white skin—an unmistakable sign of weariness and stress. After splashing cool water on her face, she gave her cheeks a brisk rub with a rough towel to bring back some color. She still looked awful.

Laurent appeared in the hallway. She could smell the scent of tobacco on him as it clung to his clothes and hair. She eased past him and went to a chest of drawers in the dining room. Laurent followed her. He leaned against the dining room table, his arms crossed, and watched her.

Maggie pulled out a large leather photo album and began flipping the pages.

"They are trying to tell us that Elise died for no reason. That she was just some random body that happened to be in the wrong place at the wrong time." She stopped and then tugged a color snapshot out from the plastic pages.

"You are going out?" he asked.

"Not right away. But I have to ask Alfie a question," she said. "Where are *you* going?" She noticed his cigarette pack was in his shirt pocket, which usually meant he was going out.

"I did not think you would feel like going out so soon."

"Laurent, you don't have to ask my permission to go somewhere. And you certainly don't have to stay here and babysit me."

"I am taking the dog to Monsieur Danford downstairs. Then I have an engagement with your father *pour dejeuner.* I am happy to break it, *chèrie,* but I thought you were feeling better."

She hesitated. She knew the two of them were becoming close. *Was Laurent looking for a father figure?* She really didn't know much about his family. Was his father even still living? She touched his arm. "I'm glad you and my dad are getting along so well. I'm just surprised, I guess. He never spent much time with any of my friends before."

He leaned down to kiss her. "You will be careful, eh? And then come back and go to bed?" He held her chin in his hand.

"Yes, yes. *Je promis.* Listen. Don't tell my dad what happened last night, okay? He'll just freak and there's no point. Oh, and please tell him I don't want you knowing any stuff about my teenage years or anything."

"*Pfut!* We have covered all that many weeks ago." He scooped up the puppy and held him in the crook of his arm. Before he left, he gave her one last knowing smile.

Maggie went into the bedroom to pull on jeans and a tee shirt, and then into the kitchen. Laurent had made ham and cheese sandwiches using a slightly runny Camembert instead of Swiss slices. She took one of the wrapped sandwiches from the counter, poured a glass of juice and sat out on her balcony.

It struck her as bizarre that here she was eating a ham sandwich, with Laurent off to keep a lunch engagement, and just last night she'd been knocked unconscious into a ditch. She touched the knot on the back of her head.

Maggie tried to see the attack in elementary terms. Had she—as the cops seemed to think—merely interrupted a dog abuser during his moment of gleeful torture? Or had someone been watching her through her apartment window and used the dog to lure her out? Was the attack meant for her? More importantly, was it connected to Elise's death?

She drew the photograph out of her pocket and stared at it. The photographer had caught Elise looking annoyed and unsmiling. Maggie tried to remember when it was taken. After a tennis game, maybe? But Elise wasn't dressed for tennis.

She couldn't remember what was going on in the picture to make Elise frown, but what she *did* know, what she believed in every fiber of her being, was that when she showed this picture to Alfie this afternoon he was going to say he'd never seen the girl in it before. And if that was true, then it meant there was someone else who had frightened him that day.

She finished off her sandwich and looked around her apartment. She thought it looked lonely and too quiet. Had she already gotten used to the little puppy's presence in the small flat?

Or was it Laurent's presence she now needed as much as she did oxygen in the air?

She left the apartment and walked to the front of the building to the little stone bench, which sat a few yards away from a bus stop and the grocery store. And she waited.

It wasn't long before she saw him come out of the store, his arms cradling a box of groceries. She hated to accost him. She knew, as gentle as she would be with him, that he would still be upset. She glanced at the photo of Elise and her heart broke all over again. Upset or not, she had to know. She got to her feet and intercepted Alfie before he was even on the sidewalk to The Parthenon.

"Hey, Alfie." She smiled and tried to look surprised at seeing him.

He stopped walking and began pulling on an ear and blinking rapidly. His eyes darted everywhere at once.

She held up the photo before he could speak. In her experience, something visual always prompted an innate curiosity in practically everyone. She'd learned that from years of dealing with—and manipulating—advertising clients. She'd yet to have it fail her.

"Can you look at this, Alfie?"

Instantly, his eyes flickered to the photo. He stopped and stared at it, then up at her. "Pretty," he said.

He didn't recognize her.

"You don't know this lady, do you?"

He shook his head in confusion. "Is she waiting for her groceries?"

"Nope." Maggie tucked the photo into her pocket. "No, she is not. Thanks, Alfie. Have a great day." She turned and walked back to her apartment. The police hadn't shown Alfie a picture of Elise.

And he had never laid eyes on her until today.

Chapter Nineteen

Gary hung up the phone and tapped the base of it with a mechanical pencil.

Mugged! In her own parking lot. Wait until Darla heard about *this*. She'll be calling Qantas Airlines herself.

With Maggie out for the day and not in next week because of her trip to France, he realized he wouldn't have a chance to tell her face-to-face what he knew about Laurent. And now, what with being a victim of a crime, he could hardly deliver the news to her over the phone. There was nothing for it. It would have to wait.

He stood and raked up the venetian blinds on his window with a jerk of the cord. The full blaze of the morning sun shot through the window.

Mean temperature in Auckland in summer is 78 degrees with less than ten percent humidity. He turned away from the sight of cars and trucks moving at a slug's pace on the street below.

Situated on an isthmus, the views of harbor and beach are enjoyable from every vantage point of the city.

Gary leaned over his desk and engaged the public address system. "Attention, everyone," he said into the speaker. "There'll be a short meeting in the conference room in ten minutes." He felt a rush of adrenaline push through his veins. He'd been waiting for this.

The point of no return. The crossed over line.

He straightened his tie and patted the pockets on his blazer. He knew what he would say; no further preparation was necessary. It was annoying that Maggie wasn't here, but he'd describe it all to her later.

He jumped at the knock on his door, which pushed open to reveal Patti's blonde head popping through.

"Hey, Patti. What's up?"

"I can't make the meeting, Gary." She entered the room, her clothing, as usual, making its entrance first. A loud bow was knotted in her hair, something ruffly and pink. *Wasn't there an age limit on women wearing bows in their hair?* Gary wondered.

"Can't make it? Why not? It's important."

"Well, I've got a job interview," Patti said, her lips pressed tightly together.

He stared at her and then relaxed. She was obviously baiting him. She wasn't going anywhere. This was the usual manipulative Patti crap they'd all endured for the last four years. A perverse part of him—the part of him that was almost free—wanted to drop to his knees and scream, *"God, Patti, no! You can't leave!"* He got a grip on himself with effort.

"Okay. You don't need to be there."

"I've decided to leave the company, Gary," she said, taking a step toward his desk.

"So have I, as a matter of fact."

Her mouth fell open in surprise. "What?" she sputtered.

"That's what the meeting's about. To announce that I'm leaving."

"Because of me?"

The suggestion was so absurd Gary nearly laughed in her face. Instead, he paused as if considering it and then shook his head. "No, Patti. I am not leaving because of you. I am leaving..." He turned and waved a hand at the scene outside his window. "...because of everything." He liked the sound of that. Maybe he'd use it in his speech to the others. "But I wish you every kind of luck. I don't think you've been happy here either, and it's probably a good idea you're looking elsewhere."

It was true. The freedom he felt by cutting his ties— even by breaking the news to just one person—was profound. He felt energized, yet relaxed, capable of talking honestly about anything.

He felt great.

Patti continued to stand there in front of him in her ridiculous dress, her arms pressed in a Joan-of-Arc fold across her chest, her eyes burning with some indecipherable passion. "Well, that's it, then."

"I wish you luck, Patti," he said again. He felt more in control than he ever had before. He watched her shoulders sag beneath her dress, her head sink.

"Thanks, Gary," she said in a voice softer and more sincere than he'd ever heard from her. She held out her hand to him. "I hope you find what you're looking for, too."

"Just a little peace," he said. "And I will."

She moved toward the door. "Take care of yourself."

"You too," he said, buoyed with his factory-fresh, hither-to-untried ability to handle any situation. He smiled at her until she closed the door behind her. Then he turned for one last look out the window, patted down his suit pockets again, and went out to tell the rest of the world.

Chapter Twenty

Maggie rolled over in bed and saw Laurent was already awake and watching her.

"Morning," she said. He smiled. "You've got that thing today, don't you?"

He nodded and she noticed he was already drinking coffee. A second cup sat on the side table.

"You been up long?"

"No, *chérie*. Just long enough for coffee." He handed her the cup and she took a quick sip. As usual with everything about Laurent and everything he touched, it was just right.

"They're expecting us tonight at six," she said.

"I will get the *cadeau*."

"*Cadeau?* Oh, Nicole's birthday present. Will you have time? That'd be great if you would."

"No problem."

"You okay, Laurent?"

"*Je t'aime, chérie.*"

"*Je t'aime* you, too." She paused. "I'll be back from France before you know it."

"*Je sais.*" *I know.*

"I leave here tomorrow afternoon, I'm back Wednesday night."

Laurent narrowed his eyes. "Almost not worth the jet lag."

"Yeah." They sat quietly for another moment. "Did you take the dog out this morning?" Danford's wife had returned the animal to them late last night. He had been professionally stitched and bandaged. The woman shoved the dog into Laurent's arms along with a bag of veterinarian prescription drugs with a rushed, "The instructions are on the label," before she disappeared down the hall.

"Oui."

"I hated having Danford take him to the vet. Next time, I'll do it myself."

Laurent frowned. "You are not thinking of keeping the dog?"

Maggie sighed. "I'd love to, but I can't. The apartment doesn't allow animals over ten pounds." She turned to look at the animal curled up in a brand-new dog bed in the corner of the room. "He's probably over that now. No telling how big he'll get."

Laurent took their empty coffee cups and set them aside. He pulled her effortlessly into his arms and her mouth met his naturally and easily. After the kiss, she whispered, "Last night was fun."

"I was important to make sure there are no long-lasting damages from your head."

"I think we definitely determined that. Although I'm pretty sure I saw stars at one point."

"Très amusant," he said, a smile tugging at this full lips.

"You're not nervous about doing your chef's thing at lunch today? Everything's under control?"

Laurent laughed. *"Bien sûr.* Everything is under control." In one fluid movement, he turned so that she was on her back and he was positioned over her. He leaned down to kiss her again, and Maggie let out the same small sound of appreciation and relish that he himself often made when enjoying something particularly delectable.

*****

Elspeth Newberry picked up the newspaper, careful not to get newsprint on her fingers, and placed it at her husband's breakfast place. The headline shouted: *Local Banker Confesses to Buckhead Murder.*

"Good morning, my dear." John Newberry turned from the breakfast buffet in their dining room, his Belleek plate sparsely adorned with a scrambled egg and a melon slice. "I didn't know you were up." He kissed her absently on the cheek as he set his plate down.

John's thick shock of white hair was trimmed neatly in a cap around his head. His eyes were cerulean blue and a pink flush was on his high cheeks. Last night's schnapps and a generally happy disposition contributed to his good coloring. He was a man happy with his world. He never doubted the future, never regretted the past. As a result, he thoroughly appreciated his present. He was a man with the incredible propensity to always feel in step with life. It showed, too, in his overall affect, in his relations with others, and in his nights of sound, dreamless sleep.

Elspeth sat next to him at the long table set with china and silver for a simple Friday morning breakfast for two. She poured his coffee from a large silver pot and then added a small amount of skim milk to it.

He frowned. "Honestly, El, what could a speck of cream hurt?" He knew it was a waste of breath, and his wife didn't bother responding to him.

"Did you see the headlines?" she asked.

John looked at the solitary melon slice on her plate. "Is that all you're having?"

"The police say he confessed to it. There's a picture of the man. He looks a little like Uncle Jim."

"Hmmm." John took a bite of eggs and glanced at the newspaper. "Who is he?"

"They say he is a bank teller at a Buckhead bank." Elspeth sighed and poured her coffee. She took it black. "A Robert Donnell."

John wiped his mouth with his napkin and placed a large hand over her small one.

"And how, exactly, does it affect us, my dear? Elise is gone and all the suspects in custody in the world will not bring her back."

Elspeth withdrew her hand and picked up a spoon to carve open her melon slice. "It affects us, John, as long as we still have a daughter alive and living in Buckhead."

John looked at her with surprise. "You think Maggie is in danger?"

"I know she still lives in the apartment where her sister was brutally murdered." She looked at him. "If you took the time to read the story you'd see that the media seems to have reason to believe this confession is not authentic, which would mean the maniac who actually killed Elise is still on the loose."

"The media is trying to sell papers. They don't know squat. And as for Maggie, she's living with that great big brute of a Frenchman, for pity's sake!" he said, not hiding his exasperation. "Practically his only full-time job is to look after our daughter."

"I'm not sure what I think about Laurent Dernier," Elspeth said, returning to her melon. "There's something about him that doesn't feel right."

John took a sip of his coffee. "Well, I think I can set your mind at rest about that point at least. It is my belief that Laurent is the one stable, *normal* thing that our daughter has had in her life for a long time."

"And what do you call Brownie?" Elspeth pushed her fruit plate away and stared at him.

"I'm not saying anything against Brownie. I always liked the boy. But he wasn't right for our Maggie and I wouldn't have liked to have seen them get together."

"I can't believe you're saying this. Brownie comes from the finest family."

"I'm not saying he doesn't."

"He adores Maggie." Elspeth looked around the room in agitation. "He has practically grown up with her."

"All I'm saying is the girl doesn't love him and I don't blame her. Nice chap, but I'll pass on the son-in-law part, if you don't mind."

"I cannot believe you are saying this," she repeated. "And you'd rather have this...Laurent Dernier, instead, I suppose?"

"I would."

"He doesn't have a job! He barely speaks English."

"Maggie understands him. Come to that, *you* have no trouble understanding him either."

"I'm not against Laurent." Elspeth stood up from the table, her gold bracelets jangling softly as she did so. "But I think to compare him to Brownie is preposterous."

"I quite agree."

"I cannot believe this is what you would want for your daughter——an unemployed foreigner. Charming and handsome, yes, but marriage material for Margaret? You must be mad." With that, she turned to make an elegant exit, in complete possession of the last word.

Newberry replaced his napkin and finished his coffee. He grimaced and added more milk to the cup. Idly, he flipped the paper to the sports section and got up to find a small sausage on the quickly cooling buffet table.

*****

Laurent kept his eyes fixed on Nicole. She sat stiffly, a starched white petticoat peeking from under her velvet tunic. Her hair, shiny and soft with a simple wave someone had put in it, was caught up by a blue velvet ribbon, which draped down her back. Her eyes were flat and stared unseeingly at her mirror-bright black patent leather shoes.

"Nicole is *six ans* today," Laurent said softly. He lifted her chin and smiled encouragingly at her. "A big girl now." She stared dully into his deep brown eyes.

"She's a little tired tonight, Laurent dear," Elspeth said as she straightened the candles on the dining room table. Laurent and Nicole were seated in chairs lined against the far wall. The butler's table with Nicole's birthday cake—a sugar castle of icing and roses—was placed next to them.

"We've been shopping today and wrapping prezzies and helping Becka in the kitchen, haven't we, darling?" Elspeth didn't look at Nicole when she spoke, but continued to straighten and re-position the immaculately set dining table of crystal and china. It was set for five, although Elspeth had been tempted to add another plate for the one person who would never show.

"Oh, that is *formidable,*" Laurent murmured to the girl. "You have been getting many beautiful things today, yes?"

Maggie appeared through the swinging doors that led to the kitchen carrying a frosty highball glass. "Dad's got the drinks and stuff in the library, Mother. Is that okay?"

"That will be fine, dear."

"How are you two doing?" Maggie walked over and sat down next to Nicole. "Happy Birthday, darling." The girl continued to stare at Laurent.

The doorbell rang and Maggie put her drink down. "I'll get it."

Brownie stood on the other side of the Newberry threshold, dressed in a sports jacket and razor-pleated trousers.

"Brownie—"

"I can't come in. I just stopped by to give you this to give to Nicole." He pushed a stuffed giraffe into Maggie's hands. "So tell her 'Happy birthday from Uncle Brownie.' That is, unless you've already told her I've died or something, and in that case, forget it."

"Don't be an ass. Why don't you come in and give it to her yourself?"

"Can't. Got someone waiting in the car. And this is for you."

Maggie tried not to look toward the darkened interior of Brownie's BMW, its engine still running, parked in the circular drive.

He pressed something cold and hard into her hand. "It's what I told you I found in your apartment."

"What is it?" She looked at the strange, circular piece of jewelry.

"You're asking me? Look, I gotta run."

"It's a scarf ring," Maggie said. "It looks like one of my mother's."

"Mystery solved. Great. Later, Maggie."

He turned and hurried down the wide flagstone steps of the mansion's verandah.

"Thanks, Brownie. Thanks from Nicole, too."

Maggie watched as he opened his car door, illuminating the car's interior. The woman waiting for him was young and pretty. Maggie dropped the scarf ring into her purse on the foyer marble-top table and returned to the birthday gathering.

"Who was it, darling?" Elspeth was still retouching the flawless place settings.

"Just Brownie. He brought this for Nicole." She waved the giraffe at Nicole, who looked at it.

"She is very beautiful tonight, is she not, Maggie?" Laurent said.

Maggie touched Nicole's dress. "Very pretty, Nicole. *Très jolie!*" She turned to her mother. "What else did you get her?"

"That would be telling, darling. We don't want to spoil Nicole's surprises."

A loud crash sounded from the other side of the swinging doors and Elspeth sprang into action.

"*What* is the woman doing?" she said as she hurried into the kitchen. Maggie noted the sense of satisfaction apparent in her mother's voice. She took a long sip of her drink and listened as the ice cubes fell musically back into the half-empty glass.

"I can't believe you're going to do this." She said to Laurent, shaking her head.

"Your father said it would be all right." Laurent was watching Nicole closely. Maggie knew the girl had become special to him. It was as if there was already an existing kinship between them—their both being French? Maggie wondered.

"Yeah, but Dad said that without checking with my mother. She will flip out."

Laurent leaned back in his chair and Nicole dropped her eyes to her knees. He stood up with his hands on his hips. "Well, why don't we see*?*"

"Oh, Laurent, are you sure?" Maggie couldn't help grinning. This gift of Laurent's really was a disastrous idea. "I think we should warn my mother first." She realized that she found herself eager, in an impish way, to see her mother's reaction to Laurent's surprise.

"Your father is the man of the house, is he not? He is the papa?"

"Yes. But the *maman* will flip, all the same."

"*Pfut!*" Laurent waved away her comment with his hand and gave Nicole a quick kiss on the top of her head.

"*Un moment, chérie. Oncle Laurent* will be right back with a wonderful birthday present!" With that, he turned and exited the room. Nicole let out a long sigh that surprised Maggie.

"Hard day, huh?" she said with a smile, reaching for Nicole's small, cool hand.

Elspeth returned with Maggie's father in tow, a large drink in each of his hands.

"Hello again, Daughter," John said jovially. "Refresh that drink for you?"

"John," Elspeth said firmly, her eyebrows arched. She was all business tonight, Maggie noticed. This was clearly to be another family occasion whipped into shape, marched out in front of the video cameras and made to form into a proper memory of the moment.

Elspeth looked at Maggie. "Where's Laurent?"

"He had to go get our birthday present for Nicole," Maggie said cheerfully.

"Ahhh, yes!" Her father set down one of the glasses and took a healthy sip from the other. "The famous birthday present. Meanwhile, tell us about your upcoming trip."

"Well..." Maggie hesitated briefly. She crossed her ankles and straightened out the neckline of her knit dress. It was a deep blue, and she knew offset her dark hair nicely. "Laurent takes me to the airport tomorrow afternoon. I'll be gone about two days. If I need to, I might stay longer."

"And Gary doesn't mind, dear?" Her mother moved an errant silver fork on the dinner table to its proper place next to a plate.

"No. He's so wrapped up in his own plans to bolt the country that he really doesn't care. I mean, he's sympathetic and all." She shook her head. "But my leaving town is way down his list of priorities."

"What's wrong with him?" her father asked.

"He's going through a bad stage, Dad. He's worried to death about his family's safety with all the crime in town. This thing with Elise was actually the trigger."

"I can certainly understand that," Elspeth said.

"And taking over the company was more...I don't know...stressful than he thought it would be."

"So he's moving out of the country as a result?" Her father sounded incredulous.

Maggie nodded. "New Zealand. In six weeks."

"How does his wife feel about all this? What's her name?" Elspeth settled into the chair next to Nicole and took the girl's hand.

"Darla. Not great. I mean, she's not the one coming unglued. She doesn't want to leave."

"Poor man. I don't suppose he'd consider some kind of therapy?" Her father looked genuinely concerned and Maggie felt a rush of love for him.

"He thinks this *is* therapy, Dad. He thinks it's the epitome of mental health to be doing this."

"Poor lad." He shook his head.

Maggie's mother gave a sudden, small shriek and jumped up, dropping Nicole's hand. Maggie, sitting on the other side of Nicole, jumped up too, although she didn't know why. Her first thought was, bizarrely, that her mother had seen a snake curled up under the child's chair.

"What is it?" Maggie, totally bewildered, moved away from Nicole. "What happened?"

"Nicole!" Elspeth took Nicole by her thin shoulders and forced the girl to look at her. Only then did Maggie see the puddle of yellow pooling under Nicole's antique wicker chair.

"Oh, dear," Maggie said, looking at her father with dismay.

"Nicole, honey, are you all right?" her mother asked.

Nicole jumped up and wrestled free of Elspeth's grip. *"Laisses-moi tranquille! Laisses-moi tranquille!"* she shrieked, running from the room. Her voice, bleating and frantic, echoed through the house, room by room, until they heard the distant slamming of her bedroom door.

Elspeth sat, twisted around in her chair facing Nicole's exit route, her hands still in the air and her mouth open in a caricature of astonishment. Maggie gaped at her mother and then at the little puddle of urine on the imported Moroccan tile beneath the chair. She looked up in time to see Laurent walk through the doorway, the squirming terrier puppy in his arms, its front paws bandaged and a worried glint in its large dark eyes.

"Qu'est-ce qui se passe?" Laurent's brow puckered in confusion. *What's happening?*

"Well," John said, picking up the other drink from the table and bringing it to his lips. "I believe we just had a breakthrough."

An hour later, Maggie turned in the passenger seat to face Laurent as they drove through Buckhead back to her apartment.

"Peeing on the floor and running away screaming, 'Leave me alone!' *That's* progress?"

After the initial shock of Nicole's behavior, her mother had been downright joyous. So much so, in fact, the arrival of Laurent with the scruffy little dog seemed to have gotten lost in all the commotion. She sliced off a large piece of birthday cake, tucked a gaily-packaged gift under her arm, and disappeared upstairs to spend the rest of the evening with Nicole. And although she later admitted that Nicole hadn't uttered another word, it was clear that Elspeth felt encouraged by the incident. She even instructed that the puppy be put in a box with a warm blanket and a bowl of food in the kitchen until Nicole was ready to receive him. Maggie was thunderstruck.

She, Laurent and her father had retired to the library to eat cake and drink Wild Turkey for the rest of the evening.

Hey!" She said suddenly, tapping his shoulder as he drove. "Pull into Selby's for a sec, would you?"

"*Pourquoi*?" Laurent turned down the street where the advertising agency was located.

"I left a flash drive in my desk that I need for the trip. It'll just take a second, okay?"

"Of course." Laurent sighed and rubbed his eyes. After this was all over she'd make it up to him, she promised herself. She'd swamp him with attention the way she was sure most real French girlfriends do.

Laurent pulled the Accord into the office building's parking lot and stopped in front of the large double doors. He unbuckled his seatbelt, but she was already out of the car door. "No, darling, *pas de necessaire*. Don't even turn off the engine. I won't be a minute."

Maggie dashed for the heavy outside door and used her key to get inside. She stood in front of the lobby elevators, now looming like wicked maws in the vacant lobby, and glanced through the side panels of the building's entrance to see Laurent waiting patiently in the car. She punched the up button and the lift came immediately.

As soon as the elevator reached the advertising agency floor, she went to the front door and used her key to open the door. She was surprised when the key turned freely. It hadn't been locked. She slipped inside, closing the door behind her. *Had Jenny forgotten to lock up tonight? Who had been the last one out?*

The darkened receptionist counter looked sinister with its disorderly assortment of telephones, snaking wires, and magazines. Maggie scurried by, cursing herself for the forgetfulness that had prompted this mission in the first place. She ran past the art directors' cubicles and down the hall to her own office.

She groped for the light switch on the wall and was immediately assaulted with a bedlam of sensations, as if a terrible odor had been released with the flick of the switch. She stared into her office, her hand still wavering near the wall. Her desk was on its side, its drawers hanging open, reams of paper and open file folders erupting from them like great winged birds frozen in flight. Her chair was across the room, upside down. The filing cabinet had its contents scattered everywhere in a white, snowstorm of paper and manila envelopes.

Maggie felt her stomach lurch violently and she thought for a minute that she might be sick on top of the paper mess. She felt a strange creeping sensation on the back of her neck. One part of her actually thought she should find the jump drive, while another, more controlling, part of her wanted to flee—by the window, if necessary.

She turned and ran.

Sprinting down the darkened hall, clutching the office key in front of her like a protective talisman, Maggie cut through the conference room to the receptionist's alcove that led to the outside foyer and stumbled over what felt like an oversized bag of laundry. She fell face-first into the receptionist's desk, flinging her arms out in an attempt to catch her fall.

As she scrambled to her feet, cursing Jenny for leaving her gym bag in the middle of the hall, she felt the hard resistance of the "bag." Not wanting to know, but turning to look anyway, she saw a body slumped against the base of the desk.

It was Deirdre.

Maggie began to scream.

Chapter Twenty-One

Maggie got out of bed, leaving Laurent asleep, and padded into the kitchen. As she pulled the refrigerator door open and peered inside, the interior light sliced a wedge out of the darkness.

It was three o'clock in the morning. The police had allowed them to leave the office building just before one.

She pulled out a carton of two-percent milk, grateful she'd been able to convince Laurent to stop buying whole milk. She poured a stream of Hershey's chocolate syrup into a glass, added the milk, stirred vigorously, and took her drink into the living room.

Punching the buttons on the television remote control, she ran through her viewing choices: a sixties movie about a bunch of hippies intent on overthrowing the United States government, an old taping of a cooking show with Julia Child, a Spanish vocabulary lesson presented by a woman with a very strong Southern accent, and a fifty-year-old *Bonanza* episode she'd seen at least thirty times. Muting the volume for Laurent's sake, she settled on *Bonanza* and sank back into the couch with her drink.

Gary had come in to the office just before midnight. Maggie could still see his face, serious and nodding, shocked but not surprised. She thought he looked like one of those converts from some fanatical religious sect who is unable to conceal his pleasure when evidence of man's sins

235

is displayed so prominently. *He feels vindicated now*, Maggie thought.

Poor Deirdre. So happy to be a part of the advertising world, to be a part of its wit and glitter and hard work and excesses. The cops said she had probably surprised the vandal when she stopped by the office on a Saturday night, much like Maggie had done. Maggie closed her eyes to blot out the sight of the perky traffic manager propped up against the back of the receptionist's desk like some large, broken mannequin.

Kazmaroff and Burton had not been able to disguise their surprise—and unhappiness—at finding Maggie involved with yet another violent death in their jurisdiction. She could still hear Detective Burton's niggling question in her head: "What do you think he was looking for, Miss Newberry? In your office?"

What was the murderer doing in her office? Why was it trashed? What was he looking for? As far as she was concerned, it could still be Gerard. Did anyone know for sure he was back in France? Did anyone know for sure he actually left four months ago when he said he would?

Maggie thought of Gary's strained, unhappy face when he came to the office. He looked old, she thought. He looked almost…panicked.

She turned off the television and gazed at the blank screen, then closed her eyes and tried to imagine how Elise felt back on that afternoon, strung out and needy. Elise had come home. She'd screwed her life up and everyone knew it. Her parents knew it, as did her once adoring younger sister. Maybe even her little daughter knew it. And she was just sitting here wanting a fix so bad that nothing else mattered. Not her family, not Nicole, not tomorrow.

And then someone had snuffed out all her second chances. Just like that.

Maggie's eyes flew open and she suddenly felt cold. Reminding herself that she needed to try to get a few hours sleep before her trip tomorrow, she stood and stretched, hoping the action might incline her toward drowsiness.

Whatever Elise was feeling or thinking that afternoon, now nearly six months ago, it wasn't going to help Maggie now to find her killer. In fact, thinking of it only filled her with an immobilizing sadness. She picked up her empty milk glass, deposited it in the sink in the kitchen and returned to bed.

As she crawled into bed, Laurent automatically reached out with one arm to pull her into his chest, his warmth. When she let the strength of his arms cradle her, she felt herself letting go of her questions and her sadness, and a languid drowsiness claimed her.

In a few hours, she thought as she allowed her mind to be claimed by her exhaustion, the real heart of her quest would begin. Tomorrow would be the start of the revelations. If she found out nothing in Cannes about who killed her sister, she would at least find out who her sister had become. She would at least find out who it was who had died in her Buckhead apartment and left so many people so injured.

Laurent spoke very little as he drove her to the airport. He stood silently with her as she checked in and walked with her to Security, where they would part. Maggie had her own thoughts and the silence between them was not unwelcome. She knew he didn't want her to go. And she still didn't know why.

"Call me when you land," he said.

"I will. Good luck on your other two personal chef gigs. With everything that's happened—Nicole and Deidre —I haven't even asked you how Saturday went."

He put his hands on either side of her face and kissed her deeply. She moaned. "God, Laurent, don't kiss me like that when I have to get on a plane for seven hours and be apart from you."

"That is *why* I kiss you like that," he said, releasing her, the smallest of fleeting smiles on his face.

She turned and got in the security line. She wasn't surprised when she turned around a minute later to see that he was gone.

The stand-up café counter at the Nice International Airport held a dazzling array of pastries and breads. The confections were displayed in staggered tiers to tempt weary travelers as they trudged to and from their international connections. Maggie leaned against a stone pillar, munching a croissant and drinking strong coffee.

The flight had been tiring, with too much time to think. An hour into it she realized she had made a terrible mistake. She was taking an expensive trip back to France that her boyfriend was very unhappy about, and for what? Elise was dead! Was she going to make a citizen's arrest of Gerard? In France?

At two hours in, 50,000 feet and climbing, the whole idea of going felt like a really bad idea.

Dumping the remnants of her breakfast in a rubbish bin, Maggie hoisted the strap of her carry-on bag to her shoulder and dove into the bustle of pedestrians moving within the large airport. Within twenty minutes, she was settled on the shuttle bus heading to Cannes.

Deirdre's death seemed to have caused a bigger stir among Fulton County's finest than Elise's. At first, Maggie thought it was because Elise was a drug addict and the police have natural biases. But then she started to think that she didn't really know much about Deirdre. She'd graduated two years ago from the University of Georgia with a major in Advertising. She was easy to get along with, young, cute and funny—all immensely helpful for a career in advertising—but beyond that, Maggie just didn't know her very well.

The events of the last twenty-four hours and the burgeoning symptoms of jet lag combined to give Maggie a slightly hysterical feeling. She found herself wishing that Laurent could have come with her. Beyond the fact that she spoke very bad French, she missed him already.

Once in Cannes, she trudged up the few short steps to the concierge's desk at the hotel she had booked. She checked in and took the single, rattling elevator to the third floor.

In her room, Maggie unpacked her few things and put a call in to Laurent. She only had the energy to find a place to eat this evening and fall into bed. It seemed to ring a long time before he picked up.

"*Allo?*"

"Hey, Laurent."

"How was the trip?"

"It was good. Oh, I miss you! I wish you were here with me." Maggie settled back onto her bed and gazed out the tall, open French windows. "Is everything okay there?"

"Ah, *mais oui*. But I am sleeping the night without you and that is not good, *chérie.*"

"Not good for me either, trust me. I'll be back soon, though."

"Will you do anything today?"

"You mean about Elise? No. Today I crash. I just wish it was in your arms."

"Ça ne fait rien, ma petite." It doesn't matter.

"I love you, Laurent."

"Et je t'aime, aussi, Maggie."

After she hung up, Maggie kicked off her shoes and massaged her swollen feet before putting on a pair of running shoes. From her hotel window, she could see the sky was leaden with a threat of rain, so she pulled a thin rain jacket out of her bag.

It was late September, and while the sun was still bright in the South of France, Laurent had warned her that the nights would be cool. She slipped a credit card and a hundred euros in the front pocket of her jeans and left the room.

She deposited her key with the sullen young woman at the hotel desk, gave her a cheery *"Au revoir!"* and trotted down the hotel stairs with more energy than she felt.

The buildings that lined the narrow cobblestoned streets in this section of Cannes were ancient and jammed together. The crumbling eighteenth century architecture was testimony to the fact little had changed in this neighborhood in many years.

Café fronts and restaurants, one after another, heralded mostly seafood dining, with each restaurant advertising itself as better and more delectable than the last. *Couscous, coq au vin, pot au feu, soupe de poisons, paella.* The scent of baking *rillettes* and the ever-plentiful *croque-monsieurs* filled the air.

She fully intended to take it easy today. She would wait until she was recovered from jet lag before she tackled the famous red tape and confounding bureaucracy of the

French police and its departments. Besides, she'd already emailed her requests to them. She had meetings set up with two different people. They would either help her or they wouldn't.

For today, her task was simple. Find an awesome place to eat tonight that wasn't too far from her hotel, and find Zouk's shop. She had sent Michelle Zouk an email asking to meet with her tomorrow too, and while she hadn't heard back from her, she had been so friendly on the phone last week Maggie was sure they would get together somehow.

She hadn't stayed in or visited this section of Cannes when she had come before. Then, her father had insisted she stay in the five-star district along the water and so she had. While Laurent had taken her all over Cannes during their week together, she was sure they hadn't come here. It wasn't a bad area, really. But neither did it feel exactly safe. She made a note to make sure she was back at the hotel before dark each day.

Is Gerard in town? What if I run into him? Surely Laurent would have to understand if that happened.

She walked down the narrow pedestrian street and glanced up at the shuttered windows as she passed. Did the maids and bellmen for the ritzy hotels on *boulevard de la Croisette* live here? She glanced at her phone, where she had typed in the address for Zouk's boutique. She wasn't sure where it was, but she knew it wasn't in this neighborhood.

An hour later, she stood in front of the clothing store that matched the address she had. It was in a fashionable section of town, and from what Maggie could see in the darkened display window, the clothes looked to be colorful and of original designs.

The name of the shop, *Michelle Zouk,* was painted in cursive letters across the broad window that faced the *Avenues des Anglais.* In a discreetly placed placard in the lower left corner of the window of the shop were the words *Fermé pour la saison.*

Closed for the season.

*****

The man's fingers drummed nervously on the paint-chipped wooden desk, his fingernails bitten and scarred as if he'd actually chewed them completely off his fingers a time or two. Burton watched Donnell's mutilated fingers continue their drumming and vowed to stop biting his own nails just as soon as he had the nicotine thing kicked.

Dave Kazmaroff sat across the room—with its single table and three chairs—and balanced a legal pad on his knee. His stomach growled and he glanced at his watch.

"Come on, Bob, it's a simple question." Kazmaroff could hear the fatigue in Burton's voice. Usually it was a feigned weariness, designed to allow the suspect a certain false security to encourage him to lower his guard. Tonight, Kazmaroff doubted the weary tone was affected.

"I told you."

"Told us what? What did you tell us?" Kazmaroff chimed in.

"I told you that I was just walking along and—"

"Oh, give me a break." Burton tossed a pencil down onto the table and Donnell flinched. His baldhead glistened with sweat. Every so often, he would reach up and smooth the top of his bare crown with his fingers. It was a gesture that repulsed Burton.

"You were walking along and saw this apartment building and decided to go knocking on doors.

Man, if you don't start helping us out here..." The threat hung in the air.

"I don't know what you want from me!" Donnell's hands flew to his mouth, where he began to gnaw a forefinger with vigor. "I confessed to everything, didn't I?" His voice was muffled.

"Take your hands outta your mouth," Burton said.

Donnell jerked his hands back to the table.

"I said I did her, right? I told you *who* and *how*."

"And now we just wanna know *why*, Bob." Kazmaroff spoke softly to countermand Burton's roughness.

"Yeah, Bob," Burton said quietly. "*Why* did you do her?"

The man looked at the detectives with wide eyes, as if he didn't understand the question.

"Like, instead of riding your bike ten miles that day or, say, painting your living room, *why* did you go out and strangle someone you didn't know? Why?"

"Why?" he chirped back at them, a panicked look beginning to appear on his face. "Well," Donnell said, staring at his bad hands, "because she never really cared about me. That's why." He looked down at his shirtfront, resting his chin against his chest. "She only pretended to when he was around, but when he was gone she used to laugh at me or just pretend like I wasn't there."

Kazmaroff eased the front legs of his chair back onto the ground. "Who?" he asked.

Donnell looked up, his face a mask of misery and frustration. "Betty," he croaked. "You know? Betty?"

Burton restrained himself from screaming: *Betty Rubble? Betty Crocker? How would I know what Betty you're talking about, you stupid prick?!*

Kazmaroff said, "Your *mother*, Betty?"

Donnell nodded and buried his sweating face on his folded arms upon the table.

"I picked up the gun because she looked so much like Mother. I had to."

The gun? Burton covered his face with his hands.

"Oh. My. God. He didn't do it." Kazmaroff looked at Burton, who was standing with his hands over his face by the now sobbing Donnell. "He didn't friggin' do it."

Chapter Twenty-Two

Gary placed the newspaper on the kitchen table, knowing she was watching him from where she stood at the sink. He reached for his coffee, refusing to look at her.

"Any good headlines?" Darla asked quietly.

"Still complaining about the traffic on the Connector," he said, taking a sip of coffee.

"You'd think they'd be bored with that." She carried her coffee to the table and sat down with him. "They've only had the Connector about fifty years now."

Gary noted the distancing pronoun "they" instead of the more familiar "we" and felt a small bloom of satisfaction. *She was coming around. She was already starting to say good-bye to this place.*

Darla cleared her throat. "Anything about Deirdre in the paper?"

Gary shook his head. "Nothing much. You can't expect one little ol' murder to occupy more than a few inches of media space. Not when it's a full two days old now."

"Gary." She touched his hand and he was forced to look at her. Her eyes were sad. He hated to see it but he couldn't weaken now. He couldn't ease up on her when they were so close.

"What?" he said flatly.

"You talked to the police. What do they think happened to poor Deirdre?"

"Darla, I don't know, okay? Is there any more coffee in the pot?"

"But do they think it's the same guy? I mean, the guy who killed Maggie's sister?"

"Look, Darla, you obviously know more about it than I do so why are you—"

"Why are you acting like this?" Her face dissolved into an expression of frustration and despair. "I feel like I'm all alone in this, Gary," she whispered, reaching for his hand again.

Gary put the paper down and tried to show her a face of firmness and pity. He wished he didn't have to act, but he knew that if he was honest with her she'd start rationalizing why it all happened. She'd find a toehold in it all and then the battle to stay would continue. No, he couldn't let her backslide now.

"I guess when it comes to dying, we're all alone," he said.

"Gary!" She spilled her coffee in the saucer and he noticed that her hand was shaking. "Is that all you can say for poor Deirdre? That we're all alone when it's our turn to die?"

"I'm sorry," Gary said, pushing his own coffee away. "I didn't realize it was my reaction to Deirdre's death we were talking about. I thought we were talking about how alone you felt in dealing with it."

Tears rolled down her cheeks and he steeled himself to avoid comforting her. *Doesn't she know I'm doing this for her and Haley? That emigrating is the only way to save us all?*

"It could've been us, Darla. It could've been Haley, just as easily."

"What are you talking about?" She was crying, but the question wasn't real. She knew what he was talking about. Because she was afraid now, too.

*****

How can it be closed? Does that mean Zouk's not in Cannes? Maggie cursed herself for not following up before she climbed on an airplane and flew to France. Although, she reminded herself, there had been plenty of distractions.

She sat in a café on the same street of Zouk's shop and, after ordering a coffee she most certainly would not drink this late in the day, punched in Zouk's phone number on her cellphone. *Was this whole trip just one big* expensive *mistake?* If she didn't connect with Zouk, was it all for nothing?

"Allo?"

"Yes, Madame Zouk? This is Maggie Newberry, Elise's sister?"

"Ah, yes, Maggie. I have been waiting to hear from you."

"I'm actually in Cannes now. I just got in a few hours ago."

"Oh, *tut!*"

Zouk made a noise Maggie had heard Laurent make many times. It gave her an instant feeling of connection with the woman.

"Maggie, I am in Paris. I am so sorry. The season is over on the Côte d'Azur, yes?"

"Right, well, I'm just starting to see that," Maggie said as she watched the traffic on her street. Last spring this same street had looked like Mardi Gras there were so many tourists and cars, and shoppers. Today, it could be any sleepy backwater French village…with multi-million dollar hotels in spitting distance.

"Can you come to Paris? I am free tomorrow."

"Paris?" Could she do that? Maggie tried to think how complicated that might be.

"There is a train every hour from Nice," Zouk continued, as if interpreting Maggie's hesitation. "It is two hours on the TGV. I will meet you at my shop, yes? What time would be good?"

Am I really going to Paris?

"Er, yes, tomorrow would be…no, actually, I have some interviews tomorrow. Can we make it Wednesday?" She was supposed to be flying home on Wednesday. Maggie did a fast calculation. She would change her return flight to leave out of *Charles de Gaulle* and push it back a day.

"Wednesday is also very good for me. Shall we say two?"

"Yes, that's fine. Thank you, Michelle. *Merci*."

"Until Wednesday, Maggie. *Au revoir*."

Maggie sat in the café and drank the coffee—and two more—while her head buzzed with thoughts triggered by the change of plans. Later, after she'd trudged back to the hotel full of coffee and pastry as her dinner, she sat down on the bed and shook out a few postcards she'd bought on the walk back from a tissue-thin paper sack.

She thought about calling her mother, but decided against it. She was too exhausted, physically and emotionally, to be shoring up anybody else at the moment. Besides, she'd be home in a few days. And hopefully with some answers.

Her phone began vibrating on the writing desk in the corner of the room, and when she glanced at the screen she felt her spirits lift. "Hey, Laurent. I was just thinking of you."

"You have not crashed yet?" His voice sounded strong yet sweet. Maggie smiled just to hear his low rumble of a voice, all guttural r's and sliding z's. *So excitingly French*, she thought, and wondered, not for the first time, how much of her attraction to him had to do with his foreignness.

"No, I'm just about to. Have the cops come out with a line on Deirdre's killing yet?" Maggie ran a hand through her hair.

"Nothing they are sharing."

"Figures."

"So I will be at the airport at five, yes?

She hadn't been looking forward to this conversation.

"I had to push my flight departure back a couple of days, Laurent."

He didn't answer.

"Turns out Zouk's shop in Cannes is closed for the season, so she's in Paris. I'm taking the train up there to see her on Wednesday."

"You are going to Paris."

She now clearly heard the coldness that had been underlying his tone for the full conversation. She glanced at her reflection in the mirror that hung opposite the bed.

"I have to."

"You don't."

"Well, okay. I'm *going* to. I didn't fly all the way over here to say, 'Oh, not home,' and just leave."

"This is a mistake."

"I know you think that, but I don't know *why* you do." Maggie realized she was too tired to make sense. The last thing she wanted was to start a transatlantic fight when she was so jet lagged she couldn't see straight. "Look, Laurent, let me go, okay? I'm beat and tomorrow's a big day for me."

"Fine."

"I miss you. It's killing me to be apart like this."

"Then come home."

"I *am* coming home. Just as soon as I talk to these people."

"Who know nothing." His voice came across the line without emotion or energy.

"Well, I'll at least find out once and for all what they do know." She was surprised she still sounded coherent given how weary she was. They were both silent for a moment. "I'll call you tomorrow," she said finally. "And I'll be home two days after that. I love you, Laurent."

"*Et moi aussi,*" he said, almost sullenly.

After she disconnected, it occurred to her that she'd forgotten again to ask him about his cheffing gigs. *I must be the worst, most self-absorbed girlfriend on the planet.*

She picked up a postcard showing the *Isles de Lerins* and thought of her office back in Atlanta. She thought of Pokey and Patti, Bob and Jenny, Gary and the rest of them and how they must have reacted to the news of Deirdre.

She imagined the look on each of their faces when they realized little Deirdre wouldn't be showing up for traffic meetings any more. She felt so far away tonight from the people she cared about.

I should be with them. I should be sharing their grief in the office. My God, Gary is probably having a full-blown, living color nervous breakdown about now.

She looked again at the postcard with its picture of the *Promenade de la Croisette* and remembered the afternoon with Laurent at the abandoned house on the coast. Suddenly, from out of nowhere and for the first time since she'd met him, she had an unmistakable feeling of doubt trace down her spine. A question began to form unbidden in her head that she'd never fully considered before.

Who was he, really?

Chapter Twenty-Three

The City Morgue in Cannes was not in a nice section of town.

Far away from the celebrities and the fifty-*euro* sandwiches, the tanned bodies and the jewelry boutiques, it was a squat, new building set between two older factories. From what Maggie could tell, the factories were no longer in use. Coming here six months after her first visit was only a little less disconcerting. She wouldn't have to be identifying the bodies of any loved ones on this visit, but she went in this time knowing the people in charge were probably not really there to help her.

She stopped at the front desk and asked for Albert Donet. She had exchanged emails with Donet, who had been singularly unhelpful until she finally hinted that she might be arriving with more money than she could comfortably spend in Cannes.

The wait was brief. Before she had a chance to sit down, Monsieur Donet was walking down the stark hall toward the waiting room to greet her. He was younger than she expected. The assistant to the head Medical Examiner, Albert Donet was not friendly, nor was she absolutely sure he was in a position to give her any helpful information.

He did, however, speak English.

He ushered her into his office, a small rudely furnished room with barely enough space for the desk and a visitor's chair. Maggie pulled out an envelope with two hundred euros in it and slid it across the desk to him. If he balked at only two hundred, she had another two hundred loose in her purse. He glanced at the contents and made a face, but accepted it. His hands rested on a slim file folder on his desk. Maggie could see the tab label had a series of numbers on it instead of a name.

"How can I help you, Mademoiselle?" he said, looking like that was the last thing he was interested in doing.

"Thank you for seeing me, Monsieur Donet. As you know, I'm here to get information about the body I identified on April 10th of this year."

"*Oui.*"

"That body had a bullet hole immediately above the right ear."

He frowned and flipped open the file. Without looking up, he said, "*Non*. There was no hole recorded in the autopsy notes."

"Well, I saw it."

He shrugged. "The notes do not mention a hole."

"And, of course, we don't have a body to confirm it one way or the other because it was cremated without my instructions."

When he didn't respond, Maggie tried a different tact. "Can you tell me *why* the body was cremated, Monsieur Donet?"

"There must have been an order for it."

"Is it in the file?"

"*Non.*"

"Okay, well then let me ask you, what would you have done with the body if no next of kin showed up to identify it?"

"We would do a DNA test or dental records match. But labs are backed up nearly nine months. It would not be a priority."

"What if I sent you the box of bone and ash you gave me? You could run a test on those to determine identity."

"How do we know those remains are the same ones we gave you?"

"Really? You think I've got a garage full of random bones and ashes?"

"I do not know, Mademoiselle. But it would not be at all proper. You would need to go through official channels. You would have to first authenticate the remains."

"But that's why I'd be sending them to you, so you can authenticate them."

"I'm sorry, Mademoiselle."

"Okay, let's forget about that. Can you tell me how you knew to contact my family in Atlanta?"

"Someone else attempted to ID the body but was unable to do so, not being related. He gave us your contact information."

"Who?"

He flipped open the file and ran his finger down a text document. "A Gerard Gautier."

Gautier has got to be an alias for Dubois! Maggie felt herself get excited. "Who notified him there was a body in the first place?"

"No one. He reported his common law wife missing and was told to check the morgue. It is a standard procedure when a wife goes missing and there is no obvious lover in the picture."

"When did he report her missing?"

"I have no idea. You'll have to ask the police."

It appeared her two hundred euros worth of questions had run out. It was just as well. It felt as if she had paid more for dead-ends then any real answers. Dejected and unsatisfied, she thanked Donet and gathered up her purse. As she walked out of the dreary building, she felt a weariness descend upon her. She hadn't learned much from her interview with Donet, but she did walk away with a very big question in her mind.

Exactly who the hell was the poor girl whose bones and ashes were sitting on the mantle of the Newberry family home on Tuxedo Drive in Atlanta, Georgia?

Two hours later, after a wonderful lunch of *soupe de poisson* and a carafe of wine that made her think longingly for her bed, Maggie was otherwise ready for her second appointment of the day, this time at the Cannes *Commissariat de Police* on Avenue Isola Bella.

The detective with whom she had her appointment with was redolent of garlic and body odor, and had clearly had much more to drink at lunch than Maggie had. Plus, he was having a difficult time keeping his eyes off her chest.

"As I said in my email last week, Detective Jenet, I'm here in hopes of getting some information about my sister, who was believed killed in Cannes last spring."

"*Believed?*"

"Yes, you see, it turned out not to be her. As I said in my email, I'm trying to find out the whereabouts of my sister, Elise Newberry, last March."

The detective frowned and looked through his notes. He belched loudly. "She drowned in the Cannes Harbor and was claimed by next of kin in April of this year."

Maggie sighed in frustration. "Okay, well can we go back before that? An attempt was made to claim her body at the Cannes morgue by a man named Gerard Gautier the last week of March. I was told he filed a missing persons report through you. Do you have a record of that?"

Jenet turned to his computer and made a few entries onto the keyboard before scrutinizing the screen. Maggie was frustrated she wasn't able to see his screen from where she was sitting.

"Yes. Gerard Gautier notified the police on March 15th that his common law wife, Elise Newberry, was missing."

March 15th? The same day the body in the morgue was called in by an anonymous tip? Is it possible to believe this is a coincidence?

"Were there any other missing persons around this time? March 16th, say? Or 17th?"

He looked at the screen and seemed to be scrolling down. "No."

"Any time in April or May?

After a moment, he said, "There is a missing persons for a Nadia Golchek. Reported missing since March 12th."

"And she's still missing?"

"There doesn't appear to be any leads or unidentified bodies."

"What about the body that was brought in on March 15th?"

"That body was identified by next of kin as Elise Newberry."

"Yes, but as I've already said, it *wasn't* Elise Newberry. She showed up alive in the U.S. four months later."

"If you could have her contact us we—"

"Okay, I can't do that because now she's good and truly dead, but what I can do is give you proof that she died in June not March. If you can get the morgue to cooperate,

I can even get you the remains of Nadia Golchek so you can test them to confirm that's who she is so you can notify her family."

My question is how did this mix-up happen, and what does it mean?

"I'm sorry, Mademoiselle," Jenet said, licking his lips as if he wanted to eat her for dessert. "Speaking with the Cannes Medical Examiner's office would not be possible."

"Why is that?"

"We are not, how you say, on the same lines of communication. The channels are very complex and this would not be possible."

"Bureaucratic red tape."

"*Exactement.* If you were to get your attorney—and a French attorney would really be best—he might begin the process. I must warn you, Mademoiselle, something like this may take many months, or even years."

"Yeah, never mind." She stood and shook his hand, and felt a fierce urge to wipe it on her pant leg as soon as she left his office.

She was starting to see why people around here paid off officials to get anything done.

Later that night, after a quick but memorable meal of veal *piccata* and pasta, she put a call in to Laurent but there was no answer. She couldn't remember if tonight was one of his personal chef gigs. Because she needed to get up early to catch the train to Paris, she turned off her phone so she wouldn't be awakened by it, crawled into bed and fell deeply asleep with vivid dreams of her sister, Laurent, and an exotic Russian beauty named Nadia.

The next morning, she saw she'd missed a call from Laurent at one a.m. her time. There was no voice message. For some reason, an uneasy feeling had begun in the pit of her stomach when she saw the missed call at that hour (surely he knew she would be asleep), but she banished it. She dressed quickly and checked out.

Six thirty in the morning South of France time was ten thirty at night Atlanta time. She knew he would still be up. As she settled into the taxi for the drive to the Nice train station, she called him.

"*Allo*, Maggie," he said, answering promptly.

"Hey, sorry I missed your call last night. Was that after one of your cheffing gigs?"

"*Non.*"

"Okay, well, I'm on the way to the train station so that I can meet Michelle by lunch time in Paris. Do you want to hear what I found out?"

"*Bien sûr.*"

"I'm not at all sure how this relates to Elise, but I think Gerard—"

"Is he there? Have you seen him?"

Maggie paused and then said slowly, "No, because you asked me not to. I have no idea where he is. I'm just telling you what I learned from the detective at the Cannes police station and the assistant guy at the morgue yesterday. You know, Laurent, I have to say you are acting very strangely. I know you didn't want me to come on this trip, and it really hurts me that you don't understand how important it is for me to get closure on the whole Elise thing."

"That is not what this is."

"Oh, really? Then tell me what you think I'm doing over here."

"*C'est ne fait rien.*" *It doesn't matter*.

"Well, it does matter. You act like it's a personal thing against you or something."

"I think it is *idiotique*. It is a waste of money and is upsetting everyone."

"Well, it's certainly upsetting *you*."

"Pshtt."

Maggie had heard that snort before. It said a lot in one word.

"I'm *here*, Laurent. That part's done. Get over it."

Maggie looked at the brown scrub of the countryside as the taxi carried her to Nice. It irritated her that he wouldn't support her in this. She wanted to process what she'd learned and he wanted to hold grudges.

"Fine," he said finally. "Tell me what you learned."

"Thanks. Well, it turns out that Gerard reported Elise missing the same day that someone called in an anonymous report on a body floating in the harbor. That's a pretty big coincidence, don't you think?"

Laurent didn't answer.

"Well, I think it is. In fact, I think Gerard was the guy who reported the body and then tried to identify it as Elise to cover up the fact that he was also the guy who put a bullet hole in the head."

Maggie heard an intake of breath on the line.

"*Vraiment*?" he said.

"Don't you think?" she asked eagerly.

"*Peut-être*," he said, cautiously. "It is possible."

"I'll say it is. It makes total sense."

"But then where was your sister? He made a missing person's report on a person he knew was not missing?"

"She must have been someplace where he wasn't worried she'd be found, is all I can think. Obviously, I don't know all the details. But right now everything that I learned points to Gerard."

"*Oui*. Gerard as the killer of an unidentified body, but not of your sister."

Maggie sighed and slumped back in the taxi seat. "That's true. But in any event, I think I found out who the body was. A woman about Elise's age was reported missing around the same time. A Russian woman with a rich daddy, it seems. I googled her."

"There is a Russian mafia in Cannes," Laurent said slowly. "If this girl's *papa* is a part of that cabal, and Gerard really did kill her, it would be worth his life."

"Oh my gosh, Laurent, see how all the pieces start to come together?"

"*Oui, chèrie*, just not pieces that form a picture of your sister."

"Yeah, I know."

"I am sorry, *chèrie*, to have fought with you. I am missing you very much."

"And me, you, Laurent. So much. I'll never take a trip without you again. I'm too addicted to you. I'm going through withdrawal."

He laughed and she felt her whole chest bloom with pleasure to hear the sound.

"Take care, Maggie," he said, the warmth and love in his voice back just like it had never left. "And come back to me soon."

Murder in the South of France

Chapter Twenty-Four

Once at the train station in Paris, tired and unwilling to decipher the bus schedule that would take her the rest of the way to her hotel, Maggie grabbed a taxi and handed the driver the address of her hotel on the Left Bank. The driver, a large, malodorous woman lolling on a seat cover made of rolling wooden beads, seemed irritated either with Maggie's lack of bags or, perhaps, her destination. At any rate, she snorted continually throughout the long drive to *the Hotel de L'Etoile Verte* on *Rue Tournon*. Maggie tipped generously and left the taxi with relief.

The French windows in her room opened outward onto the roof, with Paris pigeons and a melancholy view of more Paris roofs. Spotting the unmistakable dome of *Le Panthéon* from her window, Maggie felt the energy return to her after her trip.

Leaving her hotel, she turned north onto *Rue Racine* and crossed to the area's other large boulevard, *Saint-Michel*. Along the way, Parisians appeared to be preparing for their midweek dinners with last minute afternoon shopping expeditions. Maggie wasn't surprised to see that most of those preparations seemed to involve food: the preparing of it, the selling of it, carrying it, and eating it— all on the busy, bustling streets in the heart of the Latin Quarter.

She continued down the *Boulevard Saint-Michel* until she reached the Seine, where she stopped and stared across the river. She had passed very near to Elise's first apartment, but had deliberately avoided going there. Not yet, she told herself. From the Seine, she turned east and walked parallel to the city's great river until she came to her destination, the *Cathedrale de Notre-Dame de Paris*.

The cathedral loomed magnificent and imposing before her, its twin towers as familiar and reassuring to her as if she'd seen them every day in Atlanta. Her mother had taken her and Elise to Mass here as children.

Now, standing in the square before the cathedral, surrounded by the ubiquitous lavender sellers, pickpockets and tourists, Maggie felt the same majesty and magnificence reaching down to her. She settled on a cold stone bench on the perimeter of the square and watched the famous church and its patrons for nearly an hour before she realized that, aside from her early morning airport croissant, she'd had nothing to eat all day.

Circling *Notre-Dame*, Maggie walked westward again, this time on the *Quai de la Tournelle Montebello* until she reached *Rue Dauphine*. She took a seat at a small café called *La Place Americaine*. She ordered the fixed-price menu of *paté* and roast beef with *pommes frites* and the house wine, which turned out to be a flinty dry white that tasted like bouquets of flowers, without the sweetness. To her relief, the waiter was pleasant and friendly.

She looked out onto the street as she ate her lunch and wondered which of the shops was *Chez Zouk*. The address she had was *ll Rue Dauphine* in the Latin Quarter. She guessed that Zouk's boutique must be only a few blocks from Elise's old flat here in Paris. Maggie had an image of Elise walking home from art classes and stopping in at Zouk's shop. *Probably caters to the bohemian-artsy crowd*, Maggie figured. Elise's style was definitely *not* Ellen Tracy.

After lunch, Maggie headed north on *Dauphine* until she reached the Seine where the *Pont Neuf* crossed over to the *Quai de Louvre* and the Right Bank. The wind had begun to pick up and she felt the rain in the air, although it wouldn't fall just yet. The river looked wild and angry. A block further south on *Dauphine*, she found the shop. It was small and looked quite old. The small display window showed antique jewelry amid dark cashmere drapes and sweeping skirts. Nice stuff, Maggie thought. A little on the black and spooky side, maybe, but then, that's Paris. A sign over the door read *Chez Zouk*.

The door opened before she had a chance to reach for the doorknob and Madame Zouk stood in the doorway. She was tall and slim, dressed in black with gray stockings and black velvet slippers. A thin web of black velvet caught her blonde hair up and carried it gracefully at the nape of her long neck. Michelle Zouk's eyes were dark and almond-shaped, her mouth full yet not too large for her delicate and finely boned face. She made Maggie think of a beautiful gypsy fortuneteller.

"*Enchanté, Maggie.*" Zouk spoke in a light, musical voice. She smiled and gestured for Maggie to enter. "You had a good trip from Nice?"

"Yes, thanks." Maggie stepped into the shop and noticed that Zouk locked the door when she slipped in behind her .

"So we are not being disturbed," she said. "If you will follow me?"

She led Maggie to a back room, where a table had been set for tea. The room was obviously used as a sort of sitting room, with a dark red velvet loveseat trimmed in tassels and ropy fringe parked in front of an antique coffee table.

Zouk gestured for Maggie to sit and she put her hand on the teapot. "You do not look like your sister."

"I know. Nor any of the rest of my family. I'm the changeling."

"Adopted?"

"No, no. Just a throw-back to an ancestor nobody looks like anymore."

Maggie took a sip of tea from the fragile teacup, its roses long faded from the translucent china rim. She waited and watched the Frenchwoman. It didn't seem odd to her at all to discover this exquisite creature was a dear friend of her sister. Elise, who had grown up in old-South Atlanta with white-glove parties and friends whose fathers were either colonels or reverends. And although Elise may have rebelled against the gentility and sterility of a Southern childhood, she'd nonetheless lived it.

"Your sister was my dearest of friends," Zouk said, sharing a sad smile with Maggie. *"Une amie de coeur,* you are familiar?"

Maggie nodded. *Friend of the heart.*

"She lived near here. Do you know that?"

"I did."

"Ah, but you want to hear what it is you do *not* know."

"Madame Zouk," Maggie said, taking a long breath. "I am trying to find out who killed her."

Their eyes met and locked. Zouk's long lashes fluttered briefly.

"Please, call me Michelle."

"I know this must feel very strange to you for me to turn up like this, but there are a lot of holes in my sister's life that, if I could fill them, might help me find out why she died."

"And you are looking for help from me to fill the holes."

"Well, if anybody can tell me what she was doing the last year, I figured it would be you."

"Yes, I can tell you." Michelle folded her hands in her lap, as if that was all she was prepared to say.

"Did you know I came to Cannes in April and identified a body as hers?"

"How is that possible?"

"Well, the body had been in the water too long to really identify it by its face, so I confirmed it based on the fact that Elise's bracelet was found on the body."

"Her charm bracelet?"

"Yes! You know about her bracelet? When I asked Elise how it was found on an unidentified body fished out of the Cannes Harbor, she said she thought she had sold it to someone named Delia. You know, for drug money."

Michelle looked like she had been slapped. Her hand flew to her face and her eyes filled with tears.

Maggie put her teacup down with a clatter. "I am so sorry, Michelle! I thought you...you must have known that Elise..."

"Yes, yes. She was an addict. I knew." Michelle took a handkerchief from her sleeve and dabbed at her eyes. "It's just that the last time I saw Elise, she was wearing the bracelet."

"Oh?"

"So if she sold it for drugs it would have been after that."

"When did you see her last?"

"In January."

"In Cannes?"

"No, my season does not begin down there until April. We met in Lyons."

"In Lyons? What was she doing there?"

Michelle gave a heavy sigh and looked out the doorway to the large picture window at the front of the shop. From there, she could just see the movement of shoppers as they walked down the street.

"I was older than Elise, but we were both *artistes* in our own ways. We met when she came into my shop one day after her art classes. When she was still living in Paris. We became friends. She wanted so much to be French, but it was her straightforwardness that I found so beguiling."

"She shot from the hip," Maggie suggested.

"*Exactement.* To be so beautiful and so honest is an intoxicating combination."

"Except she didn't always tell the truth."

Zouk laughed. "No, of course not. I wasn't talking of honesty in that way. Elise had many secrets and some of them were very bad. But we resonated, she and I." She glanced at Maggie to see her reaction. "I loved her very much."

"And Gerard?" Maggie prompted.

"When Elise met Gerard," Zouk said, her cheeks darkening in anger, "everything started to die for her. We saw less and less of each other until, *poof!* Nothing. He moved her to his apartment—filthy pigsty!—in Montmartre. She would write me. We lived in the same city, but she would only write me!" Michelle's eyes were wide and indignant. "Then, he dragged her and the child to the south."

"You met Nicole?"

Michelle got up to rummage through the drawer of a bureau standing against a wall in the cramped little room. She returned holding a small photograph. She examined it carefully and then handed it to Maggie. Maggie felt her heart squeeze to see Elise, a few years younger and smiling sweetly at the camera. In her lap was eight-month-old Nicole, a thin and pallid baby with large eyes and dark hair. Maggie scrutinized the baby's tiny face in an attempt to see a resemblance to the Nicole now living in Atlanta.

"May I keep this?"

Michelle sat back down. "Of course."

"I'm particularly interested in Elise's whereabouts earlier this year," Maggie said, tucking the photo carefully into her billfold. "Dubois filed a missing persons report on her when I have every reason to believe he knew she wasn't missing at all."

"Why would he do that?" Michelle frowned.

"Let's just say he needed an inconveniently dead body to be identified as Elise for his own purposes."

"*Incroyable.*" Michelle tossed a small wadded-up paper napkin at the tea tray. "*Monsieur* Dubois is a swine and a jackal."

"We're on the same page there, but can you tell me why he felt comfortable reporting her missing?"

Michelle nodded. "It is because he knew that for several months this year she ceased to exist."

"Ceased to exist? What are you talking about?"

"Elise was in a rehabilitation sanatorium in Lyons under a false name."

"What for?"

"To kick the drugs."

"You paid for that?"

Michelle nodded miserably. "Dubois knew she was there. So, of course, he knew it was safe to report her missing. But he must have come for her. All I was told was that she checked herself out."

"And I guess hearing that she sold her bracelet pretty much tells you she never got clean."

"Or if she did, it didn't last long when Gerard Dubois showed up again."

"I really would like to get this scumbag. Even if he wasn't the one who strangled her, he was definitely the one who killed her."

By the time Maggie had walked back to her hotel, she was too tired to eat. She had bought a *jambon* crepe at one of the outdoor kiosks, but it sat uneaten on her bedside table. Laurent hadn't called all day, but that was just as well. She was exhausted and her mind was spinning from all the things she had learned from Michelle.

She showered and fell asleep the moment her head hit the pillow.

The next morning after breakfast, Maggie dropped off her room key at the front desk and left the hotel, heading north again toward *Notre-Dame*. There seemed to be even more people out this sunny but cool Thursday morning, and Maggie picked up her pace to join them in their hustle. Their hurry and urgency was in sharp contrast to the numerous cafés filled with happily idle coffee drinkers arguing politics and philosophy. As she hurried along, Maggie had another twinge of missing Laurent and wished they were just another couple mooning over each other and a cup of *café au lait* at one of the crowded tables.

She hesitated when she reached *Notre-Dame* and had to fight the impulse to again take a seat on one of the stone benches in the cathedral gardens facing the Seine. The roses, in tender colors of pink and violet, were still in full bloom in early October, and the air felt cool and invigorating. Even at eight in the morning there were lovers strolling the sidewalk bordering the Seine, and solitaires reading *L'Express* and munching on crusty baguettes. Maggie forced herself to move on. Hurrying across the Seine on *Pont St-Louis*, she spotted a Metro sign and jogged down its steep stairs to board the train to Montmartre.

Maggie emerged from the underground station and entered a seedy world of cheap strip shows, porn cinemas and sex shops. Although still wearing its late-nineteen twenties Bohemian artist's garb of dark and sooty grays, Montmartre had long since become mired in the oily underworld of drug lords and panderers. The street she came out on was filthy. The few reputable shops sold leather-studded costumes or pizza by the slice, and *Ne Rodez Pas* signs hung from most doorways. *No loitering.*

As Maggie wandered through the squalid avenues, she could see the milky-white dome of the *Basilica Sacré-Coeur* peeking between the high apartment buildings. Her mother had taken her and Elise to Mass there as well. She wondered if Elise had ever taken her own daughter there.

Turning away from *Sacré-Coeur*, Maggie headed west up *Rue de Steinkerque*, passing two-penny instant portrait artists and paper etchers snipping out a living doing die-cut portraits for the few brave tourists gripping their cameras and fanny bags. Noisome, shabby hucksters flapped the air with "original" Montmartre landscape watercolors and etchings. Maggie kept her eyes on the next street block and trudged ahead.

She turned north onto *Rue des Martyres* and continued until it dead-ended into the *Rue des 3 Frères*, stopping only once to check the address on the slip of paper that Michelle had given her. There, at the intersection, was a small, dilapidated structure held together by what paint had not yet peeled off and the oil and grit of the neighborhood. *L'Hôpital de Martyrs*. This is where Elise had given birth to Nicole.

Once inside, Maggie had the feeling she was stepping back in time. The velvet, buttery smell of wood oil permeated throughout the reception room. So strong and pleasant was the scent, in fact, that it succeeded in blotting out any aural hint of medicine or antiseptics in the small hospital. The loose wooden-slatted floor was polished to a satiny gleam. The admitting desk was as tall and forbidding as was the severe-faced nun who manned it. Her eyes were small and unfriendly, and her broad face, though smooth and unlined, was still obviously the face of an old woman.

"Bonjour, ma Soeur," Maggie said as she approached the woman behind the desk. *"Est-ce que je vous demande une question, s'il vous plaît?"* May I ask you a question?

The nun, dressed in blue-black capes and a starched white headdress, looked at Maggie as though she did not understand.

Maggie berated herself for not taking Michelle up on her offer to come along and interpret. She had been so keen to do this alone, almost as if the errand was a crusade for a final understanding of her sister. Maggie took in a determined breath.

"Le archives de patients?" Maggie asked, smiling at the face of the stone wall in a habit. *"Est-ce que je peux voir le archives de patients enciente Americaine, s'il vous plaît? Pour l'annee de une mille dix-neuf quartre-vingt six,*

272

merci."   Might I see the files for any American patients giving birth six years ago?

The nun looked away from Maggie and flipped through a large book on the desk. Abruptly, the sister left her post altogether, leaving Maggie standing on tiptoe on the other side of the counter not knowing whether she was heard and understood or dismissed. She noted there was very little activity in the waiting room area. A young mother sat with her baby, both gazing as if hypnotized out the front window. The waiting room chairs were rickety and wooden, but brutally polished and oiled and topped with handmade green velveteen cushions. Maggie got a mental image of a whole convent full of women sitting around stitching green velour pillows for the hospital waiting room, when it was certainly cheaper to buy pre-fab foam seat pads. Her eyes met those of the young mother.

After a few moments, the stern-faced sister returned. She looked directly at Maggie. *"A quelle annee?"*

"Uh...deux mille uh.. zero cinq*?"* Maggie said.

The nun slapped a piece of paper and a pencil down on the counter and Maggie scrawled out the date and under that, the name "Newberry." The woman looked at it and then twisted on her heel and disappeared again.

Maggie turned to look around her and noted the bored young woman in the waiting room was now watching her openly.

Within moments the nun was back with a folder. She indicated that Maggie was to take the folder to a straight-back wooden chair to the immediate left of the counter, where the nun would be able to keep her in sight at all times. Maggie settled into the uncomfortable chair, smiling gratefully at the sister.

She opened the folder and found only one slip of paper inside. It was Nicole's birth certificate. It read: *Nèe 18 May. Mere: Elise Stevenson Newberry. Pere: inconnu.* Unknown. Maggie felt a surge of anger at Gerard's refusal to be accounted as the father and then corrected her emotion. The last thing any child would want was a document that linked her to that creep. Her face lightened into a smile. *This meant that Gerard had no legal claim to Nicole!*

In the middle of the certificate was the full name of Elise's baby, handwritten no doubt by one of the nuns, in full-flowery scroll: *Margaret Nicole Newberry*. Maggie stared at the words. Elise had named the baby after her.

Chapter Twenty-Five

Once outside, the sunshine hit her full in the face as the cool breeze of the late morning sent her hair billowing around her shoulders like a loose silk scarf. Elise had never told anyone Nicole's full name Maggie thought as she hurried away from the shambling old hospital. No one knew and no one would ever have known unless they came to this desolate street in degenerate Montmartre. Even Michelle hadn't known that Elise had named her only child after Maggie, her only sister.

Maggie touched the pocket that held the birth certificate she had stolen from the file before slipping out the door unobserved. Her mother would be glad to have this, she thought. She would be glad to safely file this document away in the Newberry archives along with all the other family documents.

She stopped at a stand-up pizzeria and bought a slice of pizza and a can of Coke and consumed her lunch as she walked down *Boulevard de Clichy*, a street as cheerless and ugly as any she'd found in Montmartre so far. Pigeons flocked and crowded her until she finally gave up the remainder of her lunch to them, scattering it in handfuls in the air and stepping away from the frenzy of feathers that resulted.

The address that Michelle had given her for Elise's old apartment was 1/2 *Bijoux* in Montmartre. She had been warned that it wasn't a proper street and didn't appear on any maps of the neighborhood, so she was prepared to have to hunt for it. Across from the Moulin Rouge, with its gaily-lighted blades, and before *Clichy* jammed into *Rue Caulaincourt,* Maggie could see the ghostly spires and columns of Montmartre Cemetery and she knew she was close. Michelle said that Elise would often write of the view of the cemetery from her flat.

Maggie approached it slowly, looking around, trying to find in the rows and rows of ancient, towering apartment buildings the window that might have been Elise's perch as she wrote to her friend, Michelle.

She looked for numbers by the doors but there were none that she could see. The very brick of the buildings seemed to envelop her. She began to feel suffocated, even nervous. Elise lived here? It was just one more wretched street in a whole wretched neighborhood. But the fact that Gerard could bring Elise here—where she would live with her baby, little Nicole—was, in Maggie's eyes, further evidence of the man's guilt and general uselessness as a human being.

The grim, stately stone markers of Montmartre Cemetery spread before her, its few large trees shading the dead, the celebrated and the wretched. Elise would have sat at her window in order to see the cemetery and to write Michelle, and she would have used this light by which to paint. Maggie felt a tremendous sadness and wished there were a place where she could sit down for a moment. To think that Elise had been living for three years in this slum, and her Atlanta family had never had a clue.

*****

"I went by Elise's Paris flat today." Maggie sat on her hotel bed, cradling her cellphone, a can of diet soda on the nightstand.

"Ah, oui?" Laurent seemed in a better mood tonight. She assumed it had to do with the fact she was leaving Paris in two days.

"It was just depressing."

"Your meeting with Michelle Zouk was helpful though, yes?"

"I don't know. I mean, I learned what Elise was doing this year and how her being in rehab made it possible for Gerard to pass her off as dead, but I haven't learned anything that relates to why she died in Atlanta, or by whose hand."

"I'm sorry, Maggie."

"Yeah, you were right. Coming was a mistake. It didn't help and I'm not sure I don't feel worse."

"You are leaving tomorrow, *oui*?"

"No, the day after, unfortunately. But my flight is a morning one so I shouldn't be in too late."

"Ach, I have an appointment in the evening. But I can cancel."

"No, Laurent. Is it one of your personal cheffing gigs? Just go. I can take a taxi to the apartment."

"If you are sure, *chèrie*. I hate not to see you immediately."

"You'll just have to give me a super warm welcome when you get home. *Comprenez*?"

"You will have jet lag."

"Well, as long as we're not talking trapezes or French maid costumes…"

"Très amusant, Maggie. We will leave those for the weekend, of course."

"Oh, I miss you so much, Laurent. I'm so used to processing everything through you, it's hard to have an independent thought."

"As if should be, *chèrie*."

"Je t'aime, Laurent."

"Et toi, aussi. Come home, *chèrie*."

After they'd hung up, Maggie sat holding the phone for a few more minutes. Slowly, she stood up, replaced the phone on the nightstand next to her bed and went into the bathroom to splash cool water on her face. It was only seven in the evening and she didn't feel like staying in her room, but she had no place she could think of to go. She tidied up her makeup and pulled a comb through her hair. She tied it back in a ponytail and stared at herself in the mirror.

She wore a thin black turtleneck and a pair of cotton slacks. Very French, she thought when she had packed them. Now, she just shook her head. She had circles under her eyes and the lipstick she'd brought made her look too corporate in spite of her outfit. Elise could've pulled it off, she thought with a sad smile. Elise could've pulled off looking sultry in clown shoes.

When her phone rang, she picked up and was delighted to discover it was Michelle.

"Bon soir, Maggie, do you have dinner plans for tonight?"

The restaurant they decided to meet at was a short walk from Maggie's hotel. Maggie noticed it was a classic Parisian brasserie, with polished wooden floors, deeply recessed paneling and moldings, lace café curtains and all of it lit by candlelight. Michelle had made reservations and was waiting for Maggie when she arrived.

Maggie still couldn't believe her luck at finding Michelle Zouk. It many ways, it was like getting a piece of Elise back. The sober, non-crazy piece.

Maggie ordered the veal, with a salad and a spicy eggplant gratin. Michelle ordered a bottle of Châteauneuf-du-Pape.

"I'm so glad you called," Maggie said as they waited for their meal. "I pretty much finished up everything I had to do in town, and now I'm really just waiting around until my flight leaves on Friday."

"Did you get your answers?"

Maggie sighed. "I guess I was hoping to find evidence that would indicate that Gerard killed Elise. I don't know how, really. And if I did, I'm not sure what I could have done about it."

"The police are not doing their job in Atlanta?"

"I really don't know what they're doing, to tell you the truth. They say they have someone in custody."

"Really?"

"Yes, but to accept their suspect as Elise's killer you have to believe that Elise was killed for no reason, that she was just random bit of violence. And I just can't go that far yet."

"Ah. You want her to death to have meant something."

"I guess so." Maggie took a sip of the wine. It was bright and velvety on her tongue. "I saw Nicole's birth certificate today. Gerard wouldn't give his name as the father."

Michelle shook her head as if to indicate she was not surprised by anything Gerard did. The waiter came with their salads. Michelle immediately cut into her *crudité*.

Like all French, Maggie noted, food was a serious business with her.

"I went to the neighborhood where she lived in Montmartre, too. I have to say it was disgusting. My mother would've wept."

"Monsieur Dubois has much to be responsible for, I'm afraid. Starting with moving her to that slum."

Maggie toyed with her food. "You know, Michelle, there was another murder that happened the night before I flew to Nice."

Zouk stopped eating. *"Another?"*

"She was a coworker and a friend of mine." Maggie felt hot tears spring to her eyes. It was true she and Deirdre never went out for drinks after work. She hadn't had her over for dinner, nor had she ever met her boyfriend, Kevin. But it felt like they were friends.

Michelle gave Maggie a pained look. "I am so sorry, Maggie. This is very hard on you."

Not half as hard as it is on Deirdre, Maggie thought, concentrating on her plate again. *Or Elise.*

"Anyway," she said, taking a ragged breath and reaching for her wine. "Since Gerard was probably in France at the time Deirdre was killed, I'm open to believing that he might not be involved in Deirdre's death. Maybe her murder was random. I don't know. It's all so confusing."

"Of course, I see." Michelle said. She caught the eye of their waiter and asked him to bring two *crème brulees*.

"Everything you told me about Elise being in rehab fits with what I learned in Cannes, but it really only shines light on *that* murder. Not the one I'm really interested in."

"You have no more work to do in Paris?"

"Not really."

"What if I was to tell you that Gerard Dubois is here?"

Maggie's fork stopped halfway to her mouth. "Gerard is in Paris?"

"*Oui*. And I know where you may find him."

Maggie's mind began to reel. She looked out the brasserie windows, then back at Michelle. "I kind of promised I wouldn't talk to him."

"Of course, very sensible. He is a dangerous man. I just thought you would want to know. But if there was some way you could talk with him in public, that would be good, *non*? If you like, I would be happy to accompany you. The dog would not have the nerve to hurt us together."

Maggie licked her lips and pushed her dessert away. *Gerard in Paris! I can finally get some answers.* Her mind raced as she remembered how vile he had been in their last interaction. She wouldn't be so naïve as to think it would be easy. But Michelle was right; together they would be safe against him.

"Was it your papa you promised? Because I can talk to him if you like."

"No, it was my boyfriend."

"Oh, these men of ours! They are so protective, *non*? They think we are little flowers that need to be carried around in a buttonhole, *comme ça*." She mimed putting a rose boutonniere in her lapel and smiled.

"Yeah, he's seriously protective when it comes to Gerard," Maggie said.

Michelle nodded and spooned into her *crème brulée*. Maggie noted that Michelle ate delicately, almost theatrically, holding the spoon in front of her after each dip into the pudding as if she expected to be photographed for

Paris Vogue. "But otherwise he supports you, yes? That is very important. Love is all very well…"

"He does. Mostly. I have to say he's losing steam with it though. He's French, by the way."

"Yes?"

"As a matter of fact, I met him during all this. When I came to Cannes to find Nicole, he helped me get her."

"How did you meet?" Michelle turned to the waiter and ordered coffees.

"It was through another guy, an Englishman, who my father was in contact with. Laurent was brought in to help us find my niece."

"Gerard has a brother named Laurent," Michelle said.

Maggie felt her stomach tighten. *What an odd thing for her to say.* "Well, I guess it's a common name, huh? Laurent's last name is Dernier, not Dubois."

Maggie watched Michelle put her hand to her mouth, her eyes wide with shock, almost as if a video had been slowed down. Maybe, on some level, Maggie knew what Michelle would say. Maybe a part of her had always known. She found herself wanting to reach out, to physically stop the words from coming out of Michelle's mouth.

"Your boyfriend's name is Laurent Dernier?" Michelle shook her head.

Maggie didn't answer. She watched Michelle's mouth as the words tumbled relentlessly out.

"Oh, *chérie,* is this possible?" Michelle whispered. "That is the name of Gerard's brother."

Chapter Twenty-Six

Maggie rubbed the sleep from her eyes but remained in bed. She had slept badly. When she'd finally drifted off, she heard the slow, harsh rumble of a Parisian service truck making its early morning delivery.

Laurent was Gerard's brother.

She felt a dull cramp in her chest as the words formed and images of him unfolded: Laurent lying to her, Laurent being "helpful" during her investigation, Laurent feigning ignorance about Elise and Nicole, Laurent listening patiently with such understanding and support during her frustrating months of questions and tortured bafflement.

Bastard! Liar!

She swung her legs out of bed with no intention of going any farther, but she forced herself to stumble to the tile-cracked bathroom to splash water onto her face. For a minute she wasn't sure she wasn't going to throw up into the hand-painted ceramic basin. As she looked in the mirror, she saw the tiny vein under her left eye begin to pulse.

She ran into the bedroom and snatched up her purse, pulling out the picture of Elise and baby Nicole. She held the picture, mouth agape, until she finally sank down on the bed. It had been there all along and she had missed it...or just refused to see it. The birthmark on Nicole's forehead was faint, but clearly visible. It extended into her hairline.

Elise's daughter had been born with a visible birthmark. An identifying one.

Maggie stared at the picture and thought of the little girl living with Maggie's parents. She saw Nicole's face at Elspeth's dinner table. She saw her mother's bright and loving face as she bent over the little girl in a conspiring, happy moment. She saw an image of Laurent holding Nicole on his knee and murmuring to her in French. So it's true, she thought.

She isn't ours.

Her thoughts returned to Laurent. *And he's known all along.* She felt an icy wave of nausea ooze through her when the realization came to her that the real Nicole was almost certainly dead. And that's something else that Laurent knew, she thought numbly, in blind disbelief.

And has known all along.

She spent the day walking the chilly streets of the Latin Quarter until the sun died and she had succeeded in exhausting her body, if not her mind. Looking up at the famous pointed bronze tower soaring toward the sky from the roof of *Notre-Dame*, Maggie sat on the cold, stone bench and allowed the agony of the last twenty-four hours to permeate through every molecule of her body. She watched the familiar façade of the cathedral, with its Gallery of Kings, and ached with a memory of her first visit here with her mother and Elise.

She remembered the Cokes and *pommes frites* they'd lunched on after Mass that Sunday so many years ago. Her mother had indulged her girls, her two bright, happy girls. She remembered Elise, already beautiful at thirteen, smiling coquettishly at the young brutish waiter and sipping her Coke as if it were Drambuie. Even then, Elise had a style and a vision of who she was.

Maggie gazed up at the screaming faces of the gargoyles and hellhags rimming the cathedral. Human, lunatic heads attached to hunching dog's bodies, wailing souls, shrieking griffins and goblins.

Laurent smiling, presenting Nicole as the long-lost relative.

Laurent standing in her mother's rose garden.

Maggie wrenched herself off the stone bench and stood, wavering, for a moment in the square. She walked quickly away from *Notre-Dame*, pushing past the lavender sellers and the Nikon-necked tourists, away from the sparrows bathing in the mud puddles and the pigeons staking out the stone saints in the cathedral gardens.

She crossed to the back of the church and headed south on *Rue Dante au Double*. The street was busy for a Sunday afternoon. Shops were closed on both sides. Banks and bakeries, sandwich shops and boutiques were tightly shuttered up.

She had left dinner abruptly last night, unable even to arrange to meet back up with Michelle to plan their confrontation with Gerard. Last night she just wanted to be alone, and to cry for a very long time.

She felt stronger today. She turned as the *Rue Dante* jagged westward, and then stopped. This was Elise's neighborhood, where she lived before Gerard got his hooks into her and moved her to the slum in Montmartre. Students were everywhere. Clean, well scrubbed, if disheveled, young people who scurried and playfully shoved each other on the sidewalks and looked like they had a place to go.

She walked to the intersection where she remembered seeing a sign for the Metro. She was surprised that she seemed to know where to go next. It was almost as if Elise was guiding her. She took the subway—never more aware of the filth and despair in each station platform as she passed. While changing trains in the cavernous, urine-saturated halls of the *Chatelet* station, a tiny Indian girl, half the age of Nicole, held out her hand and touched Maggie's skirt.

The child was making an appeal for money, but to Maggie it felt like the curious, investigative nuzzle of a wild animal that doesn't know enough to be afraid. She saw the child's parents sitting in dirty, stained sari and pajamas, a cardboard cigar box in front of them, filled with euros. She gave the girl fifty American dollars and smiled at her, as if it were the gift of a benevolent, spoiling auntie, not pity money for food begged from a total stranger.

She surfaced on *Boulevard des Capucines* and the Opera House soared into view.

To her left was the *Café de la Paix*, her destination. Its bright, striped awning stretched the full length of the block. She hurried toward it. Perhaps now all her pain could finally come together in one seamless ache. Perhaps now, here, where it all started, where Elise met Gerard and began the whole series of events that would hurt so many people, Maggie would be able to get the perspective she craved.

She stood at the door of the café and peered in, amazed at the number of people crammed into the overflowing outdoor seating area that eddied and bulged into the street. Her chances of getting a table without a reservation at the famous *Café de la Paix* were about as good as making partner at one of the larger law firms back in Atlanta—without a college degree.

The waiters, in starched white shirts and black bowties, scurried past her, balancing huge silver trays over their heads. The constant movement and noise was spellbinding.

And then she saw him.

In the massive, confusing jumble of smoking, drinking, masticating humanity, she saw the one person she expected least to see and, had she thought of it, should have counted on seeing.

Roger Bentley sat alone at a corner table, protected from the hubbub and cacophony by two barely visible earphones. He was engrossed in a hardback book and was drinking wine. His food had not yet arrived.

Maggie was moving toward him before she had time to realize what she was doing. She stood in front of his table, her hands clenched at her side, her mouth open to try to speak. Her frustration and anger rendered her painfully mute.

Bentley looked up and a smile spread across his face. He stood, placing the book on the chair beside him.

"Well, I say! Maggie Newberry. In Paris! What a surprise!"

"That girl isn't Nicole," Maggie finally managed to get out. She stared him in the eyes, eyes that danced and feinted, cajoled and convinced.

"Fine, just fine, and you?" Bentley looked behind her. "You're dining with friends? Alone?" He gestured to the empty chair at his table. "Join me. Well, I'll be switched. Maggie Newberry, in Paris."

Maggie placed her hands on his table. "Roger, I..." She didn't know what to say. He looked at her with confidence, even pleasure. Her anger began to evolve into confusion.

"Please, dear girl, sit down. You look all in. Been shopping? Have some wine." He reseated himself and waited until she sat down across from him. "Such a nice surprise, I must say. *Garçon!*" He waved over one of the speeding waiters and asked for another wineglass and a menu. "So, old girl, what brings you to Paris?"

Maggie took a deep breath. "That girl isn't Nicole," she repeated.

Bentley sighed and removed his earplugs. Maggie heard the faint strains of some sort of classical music before he turned it off. He paused for just a moment, then said sadly, "Ah, no. I'm afraid not."

The waiter brought the glass and menu, but Bentley waved the menu away. "The *mademoiselle* will have an omelet also." He turned to Maggie. "They're jolly good here. Like nothing you've ever tasted." The waiter departed and Bentley poured her glass.

Just like old times, Maggie thought in bewilderment. "Where is Nicole?" she asked bravely.

"That is hard to say." Bentley flapped his napkin out onto his lap.

"Is she alive?"

"I don't believe so, no."

"I see." Maggie felt her hands begin to tremble and she pushed them into her lap under the table.

"You must see it from my position, Maggie."

"You flimflammed me!" she cried, and then looked around at the other diners, who had turned their heads in their direction. She really didn't feel like making a scene in one of the world's most famous restaurants. "It was all a set-up," she said more softly. "Did you kill Nicole?"

"Are you serious? Maggie, really! I cannot imagine you would even—"

"Roger, I haven't got the energy for this bullshit of yours. I really don't. Maybe the *gendarmes* will have more patience for it, but I'm not up to it."

"Jolly well put. Yes, well. All right, from the top." He ran a hand through his dark-blond hair and massaged his jutting chin. He looked at her as if he were about to drastically cut the selling price on a set of china they were haggling over. "We took advantage, shall we say, of an existing situation. I knew the child had died—"

"You knew the murderer?"

"I'm not sure there really *was* a murderer, my dear. I believe the child died...naturally."

"I thought *natural causes* involved old age, Roger." Maggie felt warm. Her cheeks were flushed.

"I'm just telling you what I know, pet. The girl was dead. Maybe an accident, I don't know. What I did know was that her mother's family had money and they had never laid eyes on the girl."

"How did you know Elise hadn't sent us a photograph of Nicole?"

"Honestly, Maggie, you must think I just took up the business or something. I'm not a total *git,* you know. It was known to me that Elise was disinherited."

"That's not true!" But Maggie knew it was.

"In any event, the child was not bandied about in snapshots to doting grandparents. Am I wrong?"

Maggie didn't answer him.

"It was quite the ready-made scam, if I may say so. Something an artist dreams of. Rich family, dead main players...nothing but for a chap like me to step in and make it all happy and right."

"Is that what you think you did?"

"You were happy. Your parents, I take it, were happy?"

"And the little girl? Is *she* happy?"

"My dear woman! The child, who is an orphan by the way, was rescued from a ghetto of incest and poverty. Am I to believe that my taking her away from that and dropping her into the lap of one of the wealthiest families in Atlanta, Georgia was doing a disservice to the little mite?"

"My God." The tight feeling returned to the pit of her stomach. "She's been molested?"

"That was my understanding. Do you think I didn't enjoy the idea that her life—in one stroke—was going to change for the better?"

"She needs psychiatric help, Roger. She's in bad shape."

"No, my darling, she's in very good shape now. She's in your hands, isn't she?"

"You think you played God. You think you actually did a good turn?"

"I must say, I do. Your parents needed someone to help assuage their guilt over their daughter's disappearance and subsequent death—"

"What do you know about what my parents need?"

"You'd be surprised the things I have to know in my business. And little '*Nicole*' needed people to love and care for her. And not just anybody. As you pointed out, she needs special care now."

Maggie shook her head. "And Laurent? Where does he fit in to all this?"

Roger shrugged and took a sip of his wine. "He was my partner, that's all. A good chap, Laurent. He knew Elise and Gerard—"

"Don't lie to me, Roger! I know Laurent is Gerard's brother."

"You're not going to let me finish a full sentence, are you?" He smiled at her. Maggie glared at him. "All right, so of course he knew them. Anyway, that's the connection. Laurent knew about the girl and Elise's family having money."

"Laurent knew so much," Maggie said bitterly.

"Hmmm? Well, he's quite a capable chap, if you know what I mean. And very likable."

"For a criminal." She watched the sea of faces at the surrounding tables, faces laughing, smoking, pouting, shoving huge amounts of rich food into moving, chewing mouths.

"Great fun to work with too," Roger continued. "Good sense of humor. Haven't you found that? Aren't you two—as the French so politely put it—*à folie à deux?* Involved? I thought you were. Laurent gave me the impression that you were."

"He did?"

"He most certainly did. It's not true?"

"I don't know what's true. Nicole's dead, Elise is dead. And Laurent is a very mysterious equation to me. He lied to me."

"Dear girl. That's the nature of his business. Doesn't mean he doesn't care for you, or love you, come to that."

"How very strange you people are."

"'By 'you people,' I take it you mean non-Americans?"

"He could lie to me, cheat me, intend to continue lying and cheating me—and still love me?"

"Sounds jolly rude when you put it like that. But I dare say he's not interested in cheating you again. As for the lying, well, once you start, it's bloody difficult to pack it up if you see what I mean. He can't very well come clean on Nicole, now can he? I'm sure he doesn't relish living a lie the rest of his life with regard to her."

"But he could do it."

"Maggie, life isn't perfect. Or haven't you come to that yet?"

"I could have you arrested."

"Well, that's very nice, I must say."

"You cheated my family out of thirty thousand *euros*."

"I'm not giving it back, if that's where this is leading."

"I don't know what to make of you, Roger. I sort of like you, but you're a definite felon."

"You Americans and your backward charm. Look, Maggie, I've been honest with you, haven't I? Why not go back to Atlanta, go back to Laurent, and pick up the reins again? Let Nicole go on being Nicole and enjoy the fact that you and your family are doing your best for one of the world's downtrodden." He shrugged again. "I really don't see what else is to be done."

"Why did you bring me to Cannes to identify that body?"

"I was told that it needed to be identified as Elise Newberry and I was paid to contact the family in order to make that happen. I don't know beyond that."

"Was it your idea to find and give us Nicole?"

Bentley shrugged. "My job is to see opportunities where others see utilitarian necessity or fate."

"You're good at your job."

"Thank you. So does your family know yet about Nicole?"

"We didn't have her tested."

"No? Well, I'm not surprised. I could see from the start you were not the sort to love a child and then toss her to social services when she turned out not to be blood related."

"Shut up, Roger." Maggie turned away and looked once more at the frenetic crowd. *This is where Elise sat, she thought. This is where Elise felt at home and happy. This is where Elise met Gerard.*

She took a sip of her wine, aware that he was watching her closely. Still holding her glass, she looked at him with resignation. "A good year, I suppose?" she asked wearily.

"Of course, my dear," he said, reaching for his own wineglass. "Wouldn't expect anything less from ol' Roger, would you?"

She noticed that his eyes seemed to twinkle with real pleasure.

Her meal, which Bentley paid for, was a simple egg omelet with a healthy serving of the ever-present *pommes frites*. The omelet—fluffy, light, with barely a hint of the cheese, green pepper or ham that had gone into it—was, without doubt, the most exquisite thing Maggie had ever tasted.

Later, when she happened to see the bill the waiter planted in front of Bentley, she began to understand where her father's money went during Elise's first year in Paris. Her omelet had cost nearly ninety-five dollars.

After she left the restaurant, Maggie walked down the *Boulevard de la Madeleine*. Remorse had not been Bentley's tendency. He made no apologies for his behavior or his profession. On top of that, he behaved as if he genuinely liked her. She wondered if that was compatible with the kind of person he was or the business he was in.

She wondered the same of Laurent.

And so this was Laurent's work too. She had been afraid to ask Roger—in case he told her the truth—exactly how far he and Laurent were willing to go in their chosen profession. *Where did murder fit in? Blackmail? Kidnapping?*

She still didn't have the stomach to call Michelle. If it meant she didn't speak to Gerard before she left town, well, she wasn't sure she cared anymore.

In any event, tonight was not a night for negotiating grimy Metro stations with their late night clientele graduating from panhandling to a more forceful rendition of acquiring a stranger's money. She watched the golden glow of the Eiffel Tower twinkling in the distance from the back seat of a taxi. She wished she could see it without the veil of gloom wrapped around her.

In spite of the wine at dinner, she was sober and dispirited as she paid the taxi driver and ascended the entry steps to *Hotel de L'Etoile Verte.* The middle-aged man who handed her key at the desk seemed weary and world-soured.

"You have messages," he said, pulling out two pieces of paper with her room key.

She felt a sharp pang. Laurent had called. She had deliberately turned off her phone so as not to spend the day looking at his texts and missed calls. She trudged to the hall elevator, shoving Laurent's message into her purse. The second communication was from Michelle, asking Maggie to call her.

Not much of an investigative trip, really, Maggie thought as she punched the up arrow button for the elevator. *I found out everything except what I was looking to find.* She knew her parents must be wondering why she hadn't called them. She could almost feel Laurent's message in her purse vibrating insistently. She would have to talk to him eventually.

But God, not yet.

She was about to push the elevator button again when the doors jerked open. She stepped aside to let the occupant out, and when they didn't exit she looked up to see the sole occupant staring menacingly at her from the elevator's interior.

Gerard Dubois.

Chapter Twenty-Seven

He stood in the elevator for a moment, then stepped clumsily out and stood in front of her. Maggie could smell the alcohol rising from his rumpled clothes like steam. He looked at her through rheumy eyes as though he didn't know who she was.

But he knew.

"So, you're back," he slurred, blasting her with a vaporized mixture of cheap wine and garlic.

She made a face and took a step away from him.

"Whatza matter?" He leaned toward her in a threatening sway, as if he might topple over onto her at any moment. "You are in Paris to see me, *non*?" He licked his lips and grinned obscenely. "I am here."

Maggie was immediately visited by a vision of awful similarity: Laurent standing in her mother's garden, his hands open in a disarming gesture, his eyes full of love and relief to see her.

So, I am here.

She pulled her eyes away from the tottering, malodorous wretch blocking the lift doorway. As she did, she realized what she had known all along—Gerard was the key. He was always the pivot around which all the pain and confusion spun.

"Over here," she said to him, jerking her head to indicate the lobby.

"You are afraid of me, little peony?" Gerard sneered, but he followed her.

Maggie walked to the worn settee in the lobby and sat. He heaved himself down next to her.

"Madame Zouk told me where to find you," he said, his foul breath blasting into her face.

"I don't believe you."

"How are you thinking I am finding you, eh? The bitch told me where you were!" He smiled, displaying yellow teeth.

She willed herself to appear more in control than she felt. She took a long breath and exhaled slowly. "Did you kill my sister?"

He shoved his face close to hers but she did not retreat. His pupils were the size of pinpricks. "I will answer your questions, but you must pay me twenty thousand *euros*. Tonight."

"Sure. Fine. I'll go to the ATM right after we talk. Let's start with an easy one. Who was the body I identified in Cannes?"

Gerard looked at her suspiciously and then shrugged. "A friend of mine who had an accident."

"Nadia Golchek."

He blinked at her with surprise. "How do you know that?"

"It doesn't matter. How did she die?"

"I told you. An accident."

"I saw the bullet hole, Gerard. I'm prepared to give you the money you want, but I need accurate answers to my questions."

"We were drunk. It was unintentional."

"Unintentional."

"What difference does it make? The case is closed. The police don't care anyway."

"I thought it was her father that was the real worry."

Gerard's eyes flashed at her in wary fear. "He believes she is still missing."

"No, I'm pretty sure after all this time he knows she's dead, Gerard. He just doesn't have proof. And I'm also pretty sure people like that don't care about needing facts before they reach out to the guilty party."

Gerard began to sweat.

"So you and Nadia got drunk and somehow she got shot in the head—"

"We were playing Russian roulette."

"Charming. And then you remembered who she was and how her dying on your hands was probably going to get you killed, so you put Elise's bracelet on her, dumped her in the harbor, waited three days so she'd be good and unidentifiable, then called in a missing persons on Elise."

He looked at her with amazement. *"C'est ça."* That's right.

"And when they wouldn't let you formally ID her, you called Roger."

"I called someone who knew him."

I wonder who that might be.

"That bastard, Bennett! He stole my money! I will rip his entrails from his body and make him eat them in front —"

"You're pissed off because he took your game a step further by selling my family a fake kid in place of Nicole and you didn't think to do it. Yeah, it sucks to be stupid."

"I will kill him."

"Which brings me to the twenty thousand *euro* question." Maggie swallowed hard. "What happened to Nicole?"

"She is here in Paris. For a thousand *euros* I will bring her to you."

"Cut the crap, Gerard." Her hands tingled with her loathing. "I know the real Nicole is dead. I want to know, did you kill her?"

His eyes locked with hers. Then, his shoulders slumped forward and Maggie had an awful moment when she thought he was going to weep.

"It was an accident," he said. Maggie willed herself not to breathe.

He pulled out a crushed pack of *Gitanes* and stuffed a bent cigarette into his mouth. She waited while he lit it.

"I was drunk. She fell off the boat sometime in the night."

Maggie listened to his words, her heart pounding in her chest.

"Nicole and I lived on a little boat after I took her away from Elise." He blew a smoke ring at Maggie. "One night, she is falling over the side." He made a graceful gesture with his hands to indicate the soft fall of Nicole over the side of the boat. "Pshhht!" He simulated the sound of a small weight spilling into the stagnate water. "In the morning we are finding her little body." He dragged harshly on the filter. "It was very sad."

"Did Elise know?" Maggie began to feel cold and distanced from the lobby at the *L'Etoile Verte,* as if what she was hearing was from a television show, something unreal and unrelated to her. Her mind fought to stop the image of the four-year-old girl sinking to her death in the night-dark Mediterranean Sea with no one to know or care.

He made an abrupt gesture, as if waving away a fly. "She did not ask."

Maggie shook her sadness away. *No time for that*, she told herself fiercely. "You were at my apartment the afternoon Elise was killed. Do you admit that?"

"Of course. I came to remind her she was to get money for me. Drug addicts are so forgetful."

"How did you know where I lived?"

"I followed you when you drove away with her."

Maggie felt her skin crawl. "Why should I believe *you* did not kill her?"

"*Mademoiselle*," he said sarcastically, his tongue flicking out over the end of his cigarette like a snake's. "How would it help me for there to be *two* bodies identified as Elise Newberry, eh? You think I'm stupid?" He held Maggie's gaze.

"Well, why did you bring her home in the first place? I mean, as soon as you did we knew the remains we had weren't hers."

"I did not care what you thought."

"I bet you figured you needed to get Elise out of France before somebody found out she wasn't really dead. Which would make *somebody* wonder who really *was* dead. The cremation of Nadia was a nice touch, by the way."

He shrugged. "Paperwork mistakes happen all the time." He dug in his jeans pocket and pulled out a wax paper packet half the size of a deck of cards. He placed it on the sofa between them.

"What's that?" Maggie looked at the packet, then reached out to pick it up.

He grabbed her wrist and held it firmly. "It's extra."

She wrenched her hand away, forcing her dinner to stay in her stomach. Gingerly, she picked up the little packet. Inside was Elise's gold charm bracelet. A pony, a tiny artist's easel, a piano, a miniature book. Both girls had been given charm bracelets when they turned ten. Maggie lost hers on a Girl Scout camping trip the following year.

Their mother had added to Elise's bracelet over the years until Elise moved away.

The gold-braided bracelet made a soft tinkling sound in Maggie's hands, every loop filled with a tiny, bobbing gold charm. She kept her eyes on the bracelet. "Where did you get this?" Her voice sounded hoarse, full of emotion even to her.

"A friend of mine returned it to me."

A friend at the Medical Examiner's office.

Maggie looked at the bracelet. How was it possible that Elise had kept the bracelet? Through crack houses, whorehouses, and slums. All these years. And something so *bourgeoisie* at that. A blatant reminder of her boring, civilized Southern past.

She looked at Gerard, her fingers closing loosely around the packet of charms. "Why did you take it from her?"

He smiled. "Because it was important to her. She is always loving her beautiful bracelet. It is from when she was a little girl, *non*?" He grinned at Maggie, as if expecting her to agree with him.

She tossed the bracelet back into his lap. "Keep it."

"Only five hundred more," he said, frowning at her.

"I don't want it."

Gerard looked at her with a stunned expression on his face. "I cannot take less than five hundred *euros*!"

"Sell it on the street. Wear it yourself. I think we're done here."

"*Mademoiselle.*" His face turned into a wheedling mask of pathos and urgent need. He placed the bracelet delicately on Maggie's knee. "Three hundred *euros*."

"Let me ask you, Dubois, did you ever hit my sister? I mean, not that it matters. You did every other imaginable thing to her."

"I...no, I did not hit—"

"Liar!"

"I am not lying!"

Maggie stood abruptly, causing the charms to tumble to the rug in a muffled jangle. "You beat my sister, pimped her, got her hooked on drugs and now you expect me to *pay* you?"

"You promised you would pay me!"

Whatever drugs he'd done prior to coming to the hotel were obviously on the verge of kicking in. Gerard sat transfixed, staring at Maggie as she stood over him.

"Let me guess. You need money to leave France to escape a certain Russian father who wants to nail your gonads to the top of the Eiffel Tower." She glanced at the hotel desk. The clerk appeared totally disinterested.

"Oui, mademoiselle." Gerard scooted himself closer to Maggie. "It could mean my life."

He closed his eyes softly and seemed to go into a trance. Maggie bent down, picked up the bracelet and slipped it into her purse. Gerard's eyes fluttered open.

"Time to go," she said to him.

"Eh?" He snorted and looked around the lobby and seemed to have trouble focusing.

"You need to go, Gerard. I've called some friends of Monsieur Golchek's to give you a ride home because I think you're a little over your limit."

He looked at her in confusion and mounting panic. *"Golchek?"* He struggled unsteadily to his feet and took a few hesitant steps toward the door. The night clerk looked up from his magazine.

"You are giving me my money," Gerard said loudly.

"What I'm giving you, you worthless cretin, is a five-minute head start on the man who's coming for you. *Comprenez?*"

He cursed her, but turned and ran in the direction of the front door. "I will hurt you!" he shrieked as he struggled to wrench open the door and disappeared into the night.

The clerk gave Maggie a sour look and turned back to his magazine. The clock over his shoulder showed it was nearly two in the morning. Maggie walked to the elevator and punched the up arrow.

Now I can leave. I have talked to the devil himself and learned every ugly, useless answer to all my stupid, useless questions.

And I still don't know who killed Elise.

As she stepped inside the elevator, the exhaustion of her day bearing down on her, her thoughts turned back to the *other* little Nicole. The one who died without her *maman* on a warm summer's night in the South of France.

Maggie closed her mind to the image. She would put her grief away in the same little box where she kept thoughts of Elise and push it to the back of her mind, to be brought out and dealt with later—later when she was stronger. When she wasn't so tired.

Much later.

Chapter Twenty-Eight

"Well, I didn't want to say anything, Maggie, but I thought you should know."

Maggie sat in the lobby of her hotel, her bag at her feet, a cup of coffee on the table in front of her. She hadn't slept much the night before.

How many times had she seen that tattoo on Laurent? She had always just assumed it was a European thing. The design meant nothing to her. It wasn't colorful or pretty, just a small mysterious graphic she had traced with her fingers in languid moments in bed, probably hundreds of times.

"It doesn't matter, Gary. I guess you and everyone else were right on that score. I didn't know him very well."

When had she started referring to Laurent in the past tense?

"How was the memorial service?" she said, switching the subject.

"It was nice. I read a poem by Houseman. Deirdre's brother gave the eulogy. It was sad. Everybody cried."

"I should have been there."

"The trip not what you expected?"

"Not at all. Turns out I solved the mystery of who murdered the woman I *thought* was Elise in Cannes. Only trouble is, I'm not one inch closer to figuring out who actually killed Elise."

"Sorry, Maggie. But, hey, on a brighter note, the movers come in two weeks, and I'm meeting a guy in Savannah tomorrow who's interested in buying me out of the business. Don't worry. You'll be brought in on all that when it comes together. We land in Auckland the week after that. Haley is thrilled."

"And Darla?"

"Darla is committed to our going. Trust me."

"Got a job yet down there?"

"Got a bunch of interviews, and they're as good as got. New Zealand's economy has been in bad shape for a while now, but their advertising community is pretty healthy. Plus, they respect outsiders, probably more than they should. They put Yanks and the Brits in all their top spots."

"So, you're expecting to do well on the job market scene."

"I am," he said briskly.

"Gary, look, I'm not indicting you for moving to New Zealand, so I would appreciate it if you would ditch the defensive tone."

"Look, I'm sorry, okay? But I have to have a certain mindset to pull this thing off. I can't relax or the whole thing will fall apart. And, honestly, no, Darla is not leading cheers from the sidelines. She's going to New Zealand with the same attitude the penal colonists went to Van Dieman's Island."

"And you still believe—"

"With my whole heart."

Maggie sighed. From where she sat, she could see a couple of workmen across the street working to restring a shop's awning. One of the men reminded her of Laurent. He stood on the bottom rung of the ladder and yanked on a long rope pulley. She watched the gray striped awning flap open over the metal scaffolding.

"Well, that's important," she said. "Do what you gotta do, Gary."

"I fully intend to."

After she hung up, Maggie dialed Michelle's number, noticing that two more calls had come in from Laurent. Just seeing the calls—both with voice messages that she deleted—glaring at her from her phone screen made her want to throw up, but also made her want to hear his voice.

To guard against the impulse of answering the next time he called, she knew it was best if she shut her phone off until she was back in the States. Surely, she would feel stronger and better able to speak to him then?

When her call to Michelle went to voice mail, she hung up and dialed Jack Burton's number. He answered on the first ring.

"Burton," he said abruptly.

"This is Maggie Newberry."

She heard the overly patient sigh across the line. "Yes, Miss Newberry."

"I was just wondering if you had any news for me about…anything."

"As you know, I was not assigned to the case involving your co-worker and I have heard nothing on that front. As for your sister, well, we are still making inquiries."

"What about the guy you have in custody?" It hadn't occurred to her that they might still be investigating Elise's death.

"He was released."

Maggie found herself getting excited. "Okay, so now what? Do you have somebody you like better? And what about my crank call? You said you'd follow up on that."

There was a hesitation on the line.

Something had happened.

"We did follow up on it, and it turns out the call came from a burner phone."

"What the hell is that?"

"It's a disposable cellphone."

Maggie sat up straighter. "No little old lady is going to buy and discard a cellphone to get her jollies."

"No. We are reinvestigating the presence of the air conditioner repair truck that was parked at your apartment that day."

"What does that have to do with the disposable cellphone?"

The sigh he emitted made Maggie realize he was speaking against his better judgment. But he was speaking.

"They are both possible evidence of a contract killing."

A hit man?

"That doesn't make sense. Elise couldn't have been killed by a hired killer. That's just ridiculous."

"In any event, that is the lead we are currently following."

Did any of this even matter? Every lead these idiots followed ended with nothing. Every suspect they dragged in was as unlikely as the one before. And now they think a contract was put out on Elise? Next they'll be calling it a suicide!

"Well, thanks for keeping me in the loop." Maggie couldn't help letting her frustration peek through with her sarcasm. She felt emotionally drained. She just wanted to get on that airplane, take a sleeping pill and not think of anything for about six hours.

"Well, I'm sorry if we're not informing you at the level you would like," Burton said in a clearly annoyed voice, "but I did give all this information to Mr. Dernier a couple days ago."

*****

Laurent switched the telephone to his other ear. He stood in Maggie's small galley kitchen leaning against the stove, regarding the red plastic wall clock opposite him. He should have known the reason why she wasn't returning his calls. He should have known the minute she found that damn sweater with Zouk's name on the label.

"Non, merci, Roger," he said into the phone. "I am glad you called me."

"Well, I thought you'd want to know, old chap. Bit of a surprise for me, I can tell you, running into her like that."

"Mmm-mm, yes, I can see that." His tee shirt strained across his chest as he took in a long breath.

"Not sure what you'll want to do about it," Roger said. "She was dead keen to get to the bottom of this Nicole business, I can tell you. I'm afraid you're in for it, Squire."

Laurent sighed. "Well, thank you for calling, Roger. I will handle it from here."

"I know you will, old darling. Listen, I'm to Cap D'Antibes next month. I don't suppose you'd be interested?"

"Ach, non, Roger. Not this time, *mon ami."*

"Ahhh, well. Never hurts to ask. Take care of yourself, Laurent."

"Adieu, Roger."

Laurent hung up and turned to stare through the small kitchen window. The leaves from the cherry trees that lined the busy street below had just begun to fall. He rubbed a hand across his face as if to erase his very features. *Ahhh, Maggie,* he thought sadly.

*****

Maggie told the taxi driver to drive to the airport by way of Montmartre. A check on her cellphone had showed that her flight was going to be delayed by at least three hours.

Whatever.

So Laurent had taken the information from Burton about the threatening phone call and deliberately kept it from her. What other information had he known and concealed? Had he been steering her away from the truth all along? An unwelcome and nauseating thought occurred to her.

Burton thinks a professional killed Elise.

Laurent is a professional.

She dialed Michelle's number one more time, noticing as she did that she had another call from Laurent. In spite of the mounting evidence against him, she perversely felt her resistance to him, to his efforts to connect with her, weakening. *I need to shut this thing off!*

"*Allo?*"

"Michelle. Hey, it's Maggie."

"Maggie! Did you see him?"

"I did. He came to my hotel. Did you send him?"

"I knew you would be safe, *chèrie*. It was a public place. And you needed to talk to him."

"Yeah, well, it was very informative," Maggie cradled the telephone against her cheek as she watched the streets of Paris streak by. "He denied killing Elise, of course. But admitted to being responsible for the other death. I mean, this whole trip was nuts. I solved a murder three thousand miles away that means nothing to me, and I still don't know who killed Elise."

"Do not give up, Maggie."

"I *am* giving up. After what I've learned about Elise and...and Laurent, I just don't have the energy to go any farther."

"Perhaps Gerard did not strangle the life out of Elise on that night, *chérie,* but he killed her as surely as if he held the wire that tightened around her throat. He put an end to her art. He put an end to her friends. Elise was alive with her friends. She could not live without her art. She was an *artiste!"*

"I just don't think I care any more. Elise lived her life the way she did. Gerard or not. Trust me, Michelle, her responsibility for this disaster is in there somewhere. Let me ask you, Michelle..."

"Yes, *chérie?"*

"What do you think of Gerard's brother, Laurent?"

"I do not know the man very well. Only that he makes his living as *le voleur*...the conman. But what is it mattering now? Oh, I see. You must get to the bottom of this Laurent fellow, *absoluement!* There are too many questions, eh? But if it is love..."

Truly, the French are not like the rest of us, Maggie thought as her heart twisted in pain. She said goodbye to her new friend amidst promises to write and wished she could somehow believe the same philosophy. Then she turned off her phone.

Maggie told the driver to wait and stepped out of the cab. From where she stood at the entrance to the cemetery she could see oversized granite urns and what looked like miniature Washington monuments punctuating row after row of plain stones—which looked like a field of gray surfboards jammed into the ground. The wind picked up. White crosses jutted out from the hard ground. Stone angels and fierce cherubs guarded long-dead babies under the ghostly great trees, their leaves shed onto the patient graves and markers.

Montmartre Cemetery.

Maggie entered the cemetery through the arched gateway. She moved between the headstones, careful not to trample the flowers mourners had placed next to the graves, and took a seat on one of the many wrought iron benches. She thought for a moment of the ancient artisan commissioned to create these graveyard thrones.

She thought of her father telling her and Elise ghost stories when they were girls. Elise seemed to want to believe in witches and spirits and supernatural things. She had paid close attention to her father's stories, jumping at the appropriate spots, eyes widening in fright. Maggie hadn't seen the point. If someone was dead, he was dead. Elise told her she had no imagination.

Maggie turned to find the window of Elise's apartment in the building across the street. Gone forever, Maggie thought. Elise gone, her little girl gone. And here was Maggie, sitting in the scene Elise had painted maybe a hundred times.

Why had she come here? To say good-bye to Elise? Why not the Elise who had lived in the Latin Quarter? At least that was an Elise she might have understood. Not the drug-addled wretch who had lived here.

Maggie's eyes filled and she opened her purse to search for a tissue. And, of course, the Latin Quarter Elise was an Elise who hadn't felt at all understood. She was an Elise who'd packaged herself in such a way as to be accepted by her family—but who had compromised herself to do it. *This* Elise was the real Elise, Maggie realized. This Elise, who had lived in Montmartre and taken drugs and had brutal lovers.

Maggie's fingers found the little scarf ring Brownie had given to her at Nicole's birthday party. She thought of that little girl and her heart squeezed. What's to be done about all that?

She shook herself out of her blackening mood. Plenty of time for all of those questions back in Atlanta, she told herself,. She tucked away her tissue and held the scarf ring for a moment and thought of Brownie. Poor Brownie, who loved her so much and who she knew would never lie to her.

Suddenly, as she looked at the little gold-painted scarf ring in her hand, Maggie felt a realization so swift and undeniable that she snapped the ring in two with her fingers. Sitting there on that bench in Montmartre Cemetery with no one but the dead to see or hear, she emitted an audible gasp.

She knew who Elise's murderer was.

Chapter Twenty-Nine

Darla stared at the map of Auckland City propped up against her coffee cup. Gary had drawn circles on it to indicate areas where they might live, where he would work, where Haley might attend school. Darla touched a spot on the map. *Kohimarama.* She traced the line across Hobson Bay. *One Tree Hill. Onehunga. Te Papapa.* Her finger came to a stop at *Manukau Harbor.*

"Finding everything all right?" Gary leaned over the back of his wife's chair. He smelled of soap and coffee beans. "See, this is *Waitemata Harbor.*" He jabbed at an expanse of blue that divided the city of Auckland. "If I take the Bates job, I'll be able to see the water from my office. They've got a regatta every Wednesday in full view. That's what the headhunter said. Pretty neat, eh?"

"When will you be back?" Darla asked, picking up her coffee mug.

He shrugged and peered around the corner of the kitchen into the living room as if searching for something. "Tomorrow afternoon. I'll get there around eight or so. Meet with Bryant for dinner. God, it's going to be a late night."

"You think he'll buy you out?" The map crinkled noisily in her fingers. He thought it was taking her a long time to get it all folded up.

"That's the plan. Seen my briefcase?"

315

"Going to wrap up everything before Maggie's had a say?"

Gary stopped hunting for his briefcase and looked at his wife. "Maggie has no say, Darla. But she knows I'm talking to a guy. If it weren't for all this happening to her and her sister, I'd be tempted to sell it to her. I'm sure her dad has the money to loan her and she'd do a great job running the shop."

"I think Maggie wants a husband and kids."

"No reason she can't have that and an ad shop, too.

Darla stood up from the table and put a hand up to his freshly shaved cheek. "I love you, Gary," she said, beginning to cry.

He put his arms around her. "Believe in me, Darla. Believe I'm doing what's best for all of us."

She buried her face into his suit jacket.

*****

The gods must be holding their sides was all Maggie could think as she stared at the flickering battery indicator on her phone. It looked like fate was going to ensure she didn't break down and accept one of Laurent's calls.

Or anybody else's.

The taxi driver gave Maggie an impatient toot on his horn. Maggie glared at him as she hurried in his direction. Can't he see I'm coming?

"Un moment!" she shouted. It had taken a few precious moments to power her phone back up and, in her excitement, she'd dropped it in the dirt, costing her more time before she could punch in the call-back function to Burton's line.

"Sorry, Ma'am," the voice crackled over the telephone line to her. "Detective Burton isn't answering his page either."

Maggie shifted her phone to her other ear as she reached the cab and slipped into the backseat.

"I've got to talk to him." She closed her eyes in agony.

"You'll have to leave a message." The impersonal drone of the sergeant's voice made her want to scream. She took a deep breath and looked out the window as the taxi began to move.

"Look, tell Detective Burton *or* Detective Kazmaroff that Maggie Newberry called again, okay?" She paused until she was sure the man was writing this all down. "Tell them, please, that I know who killed my sister. *And* Deirdre Potts, too. Tell them that. And...and to page me at the Paris airport, okay? I'll be there in about thirty minutes and then for about an hour once I'm there. Charles de Gaulle Airport in Paris. Okay?"

I must be mad to think that redneck cop is going to call the airport in Paris, France.

Maggie watched her phone die in her hands, the screen going slowly to black. She sank back into the stained and lumpy backseat.

Thirty minutes later, she took a place at the back of the line that wrapped around the Information Desk at Charles de Gaulle Airport and glanced at the large clock over the desk. She had a full hour before she needed to go through security and find her gate, and still no word from Atlanta.

Why wasn't he paging her? My God! I said I've discovered the identity of the killer. Is that not strong enough?

Maggie eyed the woman manning the information booth and hoped she spoke English. Should she have left a message *naming* the killer? *Was it safe to do that?* She looked at the clock again. It was late afternoon back home. *Where were they?*

An uncomfortable image came to her mind of Burton crumpling up her message and tossing it away. *"Not that Newberry woman again! Why doesn't she give it a rest? 'Found the killer,' she says! Brother!"*

A garbled message in French came over the public address system, and Maggie strained to catch some semblance of her name being mentioned. She finally approached the counter. "My name is Margaret Newberry," she said breathlessly. "I am expecting a page."

"There have been no pages for you."

Maggie turned away from the counter, frustrated and defeated. She walked toward a wall of telephones that lined the long corridor leading to Security. She jammed a *euro* coin into one of the machines and dialed Burton's number again.

She had been crazy to withhold the name of the killer in her earlier message. She was so sure that Burton would doubt her word that she had wanted to tell him herself so she could outline her evidence.

But apparently not saying the name only seemed to ensure that Burton disregarded her messages. She just had to tell him what she knew and pray he would take it from there.

When the same bored Fulton County desk sergeant came on the line, Maggie was brief. "Look, this is Margaret Newberry again—"

"Detectives Burton and Kazmaroff are not in, Miss Newberry. They have not seen your messages—"

"Look, forget it. I have a new message."

There was an audible sigh on the other line. "Shoot."

"Tell Detective Burton this." Maggie licked her lips and watched the airport's travelers parade by her. "Tell him the key is Gary Parker. You got that?" Maggie turned away from the stream of airport travelers and faced the phone box. "The murders are all connected to him."

*****

A haphazardly taped flap of the box that held every piece of her wedding china began to slowly curl up, as if repelled by its own adhesive powers. Darla watched it from the kitchen table, where she was in the process of packing another box. She carefully placed a ten-inch ceramic Madonna and child, which she and Gary had found on their honeymoon nine years ago, in a nest of tissue and newspaper. The Madonna's head was cocked as if questioning her. *Are you really going through with this?*

Darla tried to imagine this box, with its fragile, hidden prize, in the bowels of some rusting tramp steamer making its tedious, laborious way across the Pacific Ocean, past atolls, uninhabited islands, radiation-cooked archipelagos, and ancient shipwrecks to the lonely little apostrophe of a country in the middle of the sea at the bottom of the world.

The house was quiet this afternoon. Although she had been tempted to keep her daughter home for company, Darla had allowed Haley to spend the night with a friend. The weeks were racing away when Haley would still be able to see her friends and Darla couldn't deny her.

"Your father and I would move without batting an eyelash," her mother, the stereotypical Army wife, had said earlier in the day when she had called to see how the packing was coming. "Guam, Germany, California..."

"I know, Mom," Darla had said, "but you and Dad did your moving before we kids were born."

"So? We certainly didn't plan it that way. The service won't let you, you know. You go when and where they tell you to go. And Gary needs to do this for his career."

Darla had wanted to rip the phone out of the wall. Was everyone ready to see her in a covered wagon, forging ahead to some primitive new land...at the bottom of the world? "He doesn't even have a job down there. He's just doing it out of fear."

"Darla, a wife should support her husband. Not snipe behind his back."

Darla wanted to weep, and she had already done plenty of that. She shoved another empty box onto the kitchen table and began rummaging around for more newspaper. Some days she thought she could really make it work, could stop fighting with Gary about it and just get in step with him. Other days, she cried.

*****

Maggie sat with her airline seat tray half-open and propped up against her knees, gazing blankly at the flight attendant as he methodically inflated life vests and indicated where to access oxygen masks.

She shook her head, remembering how she had wanted Elise's death not to have been random, not to have been for nothing. And now she knew it was so much worse than that. It wasn't at all random.

Except the person who was supposed to have died that day was Maggie.

Tears filled her eyes as she thought of all the days and months of believing the murder somehow had to do with Elise and her lifestyle. She had blamed the police for jumping at the prospect of a random drug dealer as the murderer, but she herself had been little better. She wanted so badly to believe it was Gerard because he was one of Elise's many bad choices.

It had never occurred to her that Elise might have died as a result of a simple mistake——the mistake of being in the wrong place at the wrong time.

Elise was killed by someone who wanted Maggie dead. When she'd realized in the cemetery whom the scarf ring belonged to—and so, who had been there at her apartment that afternoon—it all fell into place.

Besotted with Gary, Patti Stump had killed, or tried to kill, every woman close to him.

Maggie tugged on her seatbelt, although it was already fastened and tightened, and glanced at her seatmate. He looked to be a businessman, but she was still surprised that someone would travel transatlantic in a suit and tie. He smiled at her pleasantly and she tried to return the smile.

How many times had Patti seen Gary smile jovially at Deirdre? Or seen him ask her with real animation and pleasure how her weekend was? How many times did Patti watch Gary laugh at one of Deirdre's silly—usually unintended—jokes, all the while plotting to kill her? Maggie shivered. She had meant to kill Maggie as well.

The AC truck, the burner phone. If what the cops now believed was true, Elise *was* murdered by a contract killer——a contract killer who got the wrong woman.

A flush of rage seared through Maggie as she tried to remember Stump's reaction the next day at work after Elise had died. All she could picture was the woman sitting at the conference room table and tapping an impatient fountain pen against her spiral notebook.

It was *Patti* who had run into Alfie in the apartment hall and ridiculed him. Patti who made the obscene phone call, and then disposed of the phone. Patti who had attacked Maggie that night in the woods.

"You okay?" Her seating companion cocked his head at her and smiled. "Are you a little nervous about the flight?"

Maggie took a deep breath and nodded affirmatively. "Yes, I guess so," she lied. How else to explain the fact that she couldn't sit still and wanted to run up to the cockpit and jam her foot on the accelerator lever? *Get this crate moving!*

"The statistics are in our favor, you know." He had an English accent and Maggie found herself wondering what his business in America might be. He reminded her of Roger.

"Although I know that's little comfort where hysteria's involved." He raised his hand as if to pat hers and then obviously thought better of it. "We're quite safe, though, I must say. I shouldn't worry."

"Yeah." She smiled at him. "Thanks."

"The drinks cart will put you right," her companion said affably. Maggie nodded, then turned away.

All this time, sharing office space with the woman who murdered Elise—who would've murdered me if she could have. When her next thought hit her, it occurred so abruptly and with such certainty that she jerked upright against her seatbelt and gave a sharp gasp that prompted her seatmate to wrap his hand around her wrist. And although she could hear him making soothing noises to her, Maggie heard nothing of what he said.

My God, she thought, gripping the armrests.
Darla...

Chapter Thirty

Jack Burton stared at the blackboard facing his desk. He was tired and edgy and craving a cigarette. This case felt like it was unraveling at his feet, but with nothing at the end of the string.

Kazmaroff hit the door solidly with the palms of both hands as he walked through it and Burton jumped.

"So, you gonna answer her messages?" Kazmaroff asked as he settled himself in his desk chair. He scooted his chair out from behind his desk, the wheels squeaking annoyingly as he did so, until he too was facing the blackboard. "Still nothing, huh?" He nodded at the board.

"Unless you've thought of something between here and the can." Burton sneered. "And no, I am not calling Paris, if that's what you're asking." He tossed the chalk onto the blackboard tray and returned to his desk.

"Well, then. What do you think about her accusing Parker of being the guy?"

"That's not what she said, Dave. She said he was the key. Big difference."

"So you think she's got something?"

"All I know is we don't."

"I think she's crazy," Kazmaroff said, flicking a blond hair from his burgundy blazer. "I think she's got some idea that she's Nancy Drew or something, and she's pulled together a story in her own mind that takes care of someone at her office she doesn't get on with."

"We questioned everyone, Jack, right after the secretary got killed."

"The secretary didn't get killed. It was the traffic manager." Jack watched Kazmaroff closely.

"Yeah, okay, whatever." Dave jumped up and sorted through the pile of file folders scattered across his desk.

"You don't even know who you talked to?"

"Listen, I talk to a dozen people a day. Give me a break, okay? Oh, yeah, hey, that's interesting."

"What?" Burton forced himself not to go and look over the bastard's shoulder. "What does it say, man?"

Kazmaroff scrutinized the file folder contents. "I guess we didn't talk to her." "Who?"

Kazmaroff cleared his throat and shifted uncomfortably from foot to foot. "The media director. She wasn't available the day we hit most of 'em at the office, and when we went to the memorial service she said she was too broken up to talk."

Burton stared at him. "So we never got back to her?"

Kazmaroff scratched his neck and continued to look at the file. "Doesn't look like it."

"Whatever." Burton ran a hand through his hair. *There was no way a dumpy forty-five-year-old spinster with six cats was behind these murders.* And it only showed how truly desperate he was that they were even thinking of it. The murder at the apartment building had pretty clearly been a hit. That much they now knew.

"Did we get anything on the driver of the truck?" he asked Kazmaroff.

"Looks like he's disappeared down whatever hole he came out of. He's not in town at any rate."

"That's no big surprise. It's been six months."

"Who you calling?"

.

Dave looked up from the phone.

"*Don't* call the media director, Dave. That's ludicrous. We need to follow the line on the *driver*. You're getting as bad as the Newberry woman."

Kazmaroff hung up the phone and laughed. "Yeah, guess it just makes me feel like I'm doing something."

Burton stood and wrote the name *Gary Parker* on the board. Under that he wrote: *Victims: Elise Newberry (Maggie's sister). Deirdre Potts (Agency employee).* He tapped his lip lightly with the tip of the chalk stub. "She's not wrong about one thing though," he said, looking at the board. "Both victims *are* connected to Parker."

*****

"I'm almost positive they asked us to power down all our—"

"Yes, yes, I know. But this is an emergency," Maggie said as she dialed Gary's number into her seatmate's cellphone. The call went straight to voicemail and a wave of almost unbearable frustration came over her. She hung up and dialed a different number.

"Miss, really. The airlines take these rules painfully seriously as I'm sure you can appreciate. After 9/11—"

Maggie held up a finger asking for silence while she waited for Brownie to answer. *Please be home, Brownie. I can't think of anyone else who can help me now.* When the voicemail finally kicked in, she hung up and dialed Gary's house. This time the phone rang and rang but there was no answer.

She disconnected and sat, holding the phone in front of her, her mind racing to try to think of whom else to call.

"Miss?"

She turned to see a stern-faced flight attendant standing before her. "All electronics must be powered off and trays in their upright position for takeoff, please."

*****

Darla turned off the television and tried to savor the stillness of the house. It was no use. She missed her family. Her home felt strange and unfamiliar now, with boxes filling every room, obstructing every hallway. Already-packed pictures and photos left blank walls where reassuring loved ones had once stared down at her.

She pulled her cotton cardigan around her and went into the kitchen and made a bowl of popcorn for dinner. She wondered why Gary hadn't called yet. She had to admit she hadn't been acting much like the loving, understanding wife a husband would want to call. She braced herself against the urge to feel sorry for her current loneliness.

Moving away from a job she liked, from a school she was satisfied with for Haley, from friends she'd known since childhood, and from family right around the corner. Moving away from a lifetime of comfort and familiarity to a land at the bottom of the world. A place that saluted a queen and drank tea—but never iced—that revered windsurfing over tennis. A place she had never expected to visit, much less live.

The sound of the bell on the microwave ripped into her mood and she jumped a little. *Must be spooked.* All the bowls were packed, so she opened the steaming popcorn bag and ate a handful straight from the bag while standing in the kitchen.

What in the world is my life going to be like in Auckland, New Zealand? The dark windows of the kitchen reflected her image back at her. Through them, she could see the bare branches of the trees behind her house as they swayed gently in the blackened windows.

Suddenly, she heard a different sound. Not a quiet creaking sound of the house settling down for the night, or a gentle whistling sound of the wind spinning leaves against the siding. Darla heard a crunching sound that shouldn't be. A sound of slow furtiveness.

A sound from inside the house.

Murder in the South of France

Chapter Thirty-One

Gary rotated his head slowly, trying to work the strain out of his shoulders. He sat fully clothed, except for his shoes, on his Best Western bed. He'd arrived in Savannah an hour ago and had immediately taken a brief nap— something he rarely did at home. *The stress must be getting to me*, he thought as he massaged his neck.

He debated calling Darla but had decided against it. The five-hour drive had allowed him a peaceful respite he wasn't quite willing to relinquish. No sullen stares or recalcitrant answers to perfectly normal, even friendly questions. Just a five-hour stretch of road and radio. He wasn't willing to stir the numbness of his mind right now with the silent and not-so-silent accusations Darla would certainly feel obliged to dish out if he called.

It would be soon enough to call her after he'd had dinner with the prospective buyer. If all went well, he'd be in a good mood and better armored to endure her unhappiness. He got up from the bed to put on a clean shirt.

*****

Had these events always been on a collision course? Since when? Since Elise came back? Since Nicole was born? Since *Elise* was born?

Maggie lifted the gin and tonic to her lips and smiled politely at her seatmate. He'd insisted on buying the drink for her. They were four hours into the trip. Four interminably long, agonizing hours.

She still couldn't quite process the truth. *Elise hadn't died because of Gerard or because of her drug addiction.* She died because of a sickness in her own country. She died because someone had been psychotically jealous of Elise's less pretty little sister. Oh what a joke *that* was! That Elise would die because of a rival's obsession with *Maggie.*

If it weren't so heartbreaking, it would be the biggest laugh of all.

And what about Nicole? The damaged little waif who belonged to no one? Maggie thought of her parents experiencing one more loss, one more bone-crushing disappointment, and she took a long gulp of her drink.

"Plenty more where that came from." Her seatmate smiled over at her.

"You've been very nice to me."

"Ah, well, I've had a nervous flight here and there, myself."

"I'm not really afraid of flying, you know."

"The thought did occur to me. Want to talk about it?"

"Not really. But thanks." She pulled out the inflight magazine and flipped through its well-thumbed pages, not seeing the pictures and advertisements. The alcohol was helping to calm her agitation at being entombed in the slowest Boeing 747 on the planet, but it was decidedly unhelpful in avoiding thoughts of Laurent.

In fact, she was pretty sure she was going to start bawling any minute.

"I say, I can't help but notice that you really seem very upset. I'm happy to listen if it will help."

Maggie took a long breath. "It might," she admitted. "But you've got to promise not to call airport security as soon as we land."

"Are you being funny?" The man frowned and Maggie couldn't help but notice he looked a little less eager to listen.

"I wish I was. The fact is, I have information that a murder is about to take place. In fact..." Maggie tapped the man's wristwatch, making him flinch, "...possibly at this very moment. So you can see why I'm stressed."

He said nothing. Maggie noticed he inched away from her. "You probably want to be left alone," he mumbled, reaching for his own magazine.

Exactly. "Thanks for understanding."

Three more hours. Three more endless hours when anything could happen and Maggie was powerless to stop it. With Gary out of town, this was the perfect time for that crazy Patti to try something. Maggie rubbed her hands against her pant legs, but when the flight attendant came by she waved away another drink and asked for coffee instead. The booze was no longer helping her to calm down *or* deflect thoughts of Laurent. Might as well be as sharp as she could be for what was ahead.

Laurent.

What in the hell was she going to do about that?

Why did he follow me back? Why is he carrying on pretending to be my boyfriend? What is he doing here?

Did she have the nerve to report him to the police? What was she going to tell them when they asked her for the crime he had committed?

She slumped back into her seat and closed her eyes. Instantly an image of Laurent came to her. Smiling, laughing, giving her *that* look that always turned her knees to jelly.

What, indeed?

*****

"I guess it never occurred to you that you were holding him back?" Patti Stump sat at the Parker kitchen table, her spine rigid in the straight-back chair. Balls of wadded up newspaper lay on the table next to the dark, blocky form of a seventeen-round Glock pistol.

"I mean, did you even ask yourself if you were meeting his needs?"

Darla sat at the table facing the woman. Her hands were drawn behind her and bound to the slats of the kitchen chair. Her hair stuck out of her head as if she'd been dragged around by it. She stared at the woman. And at the gun.

"I didn't let the others talk. You should feel honored." Stump's eyes were mad and piercing. She wore a lavender pantsuit, the kind Darla hadn't seen since the sixties. The pant legs were flared and the trousers rode snugly on the woman's bony hips.

"You know about the others, right?" A hint of annoyance seemed to creep into Stump's voice. "Gary knows, too. Trust me, he does."

Darla cleared her throat but was afraid to speak.

"Sweet little Deirdre? Remember her?" Stump smiled. "What you probably didn't know is that Gary screwed her. I know. Annoying, right? But I took care of her. I was following her and saw her go into the office last Saturday."

Oh, my God. She killed Deirdre.

Stump's glance darted toward the kitchen appliances as if she were looking for something and then returned to watch Darla's reaction. "I'll bet you didn't know that Gary screwed her, did you?"

Darla licked her parched lips.

"We've screwed too, of course." Stump leaned across the table toward Darla. "He told me he couldn't stand you...that just to touch you makes him sick to his stomach." She stroked Darla's bare arm. "I'm sorry the little girl isn't here tonight." Stump stood, as if to search the house again to make sure. She looked at Darla and smiled. "I'll have to kill her too, of course."

Darla fought back the bile rising in her throat, wondering if sheer terror all by itself was enough to kill you.

*****

Gary dialed home as he stood in the hallway leading to the restaurant men's room. His buyer waited at their dinner table, with the Dover sole and Brussels sprouts. Gary tried to remember how many client dinners he had sprung for, enthused over, gushed during, and then rolled his eyes about afterward. That probably wouldn't change in New Zealand.

The buyer was not a bad sort. He was smart and he'd probably get along great with Maggie. Or was Gary just trying to allay any guilt feelings over selling before Maggie had a chance to disagree? He listened to his home phone ring a half a dozen times before she finally picked up. By then he had worked up a mild annoyance. *Give me a break. How long does it take to wander into the kitchen from the TV room?*

"Hello?"

Instantly, he knew something was wrong. Her voice was withered yet controlled. In a rush, all his terrors of the last six months came roaring back in living color to slam into his face.

"What's wrong?" He clutched his chest and felt his breathing coming in short, labored pants.

"Oh, Gary—" The fear in her voice slithered across the line and wrapped its cold tendrils around his neck.

He could hear her begin to cry—as if the sound of his voice was the only catalyst she'd been vulnerable to.

"Darla," he said hoarsely.

And then another voice came on the line. A voice that would awaken him time and time again for years to come in a screaming sweat from the deepest of sleeps, the sweetest of dreams. A voice he would remember until the day he died.

"It's me, darling," the voice hissed. "I'm here with wifey."

Gary was speechless. He tried to imagine the scene. Patti at his house, Darla hysterical... "What's going on, Patti?" he asked evenly, hoping he didn't sound as out of control as he felt.

"I'm taking care of business, lover."

"Patti, what are you doing *at my house*?"

"Don't worry, darling, I told you—"

"Patti, let me speak to my wife."

"Your *wife?* Your *wife?*" Her voice came across the wire like serpents writhing across dried leaves. "You can forget your *wife*, Gary. She's deadsville, okay? She's terminated, okay?"

*My God, my God, my God...*Gary felt his mind unraveling.

"I did little Deirdre too, or hadn't you figured that out? Maybe I overestimated you, Gary. I'm doing it for you, you bastard! Do you hear me? I did 'em all for you!"

Gary saw his buyer rise from his chair and look in Gary's direction. Gary turned his back. "My God, Patti. What are you saying? You couldn't have—"

"Couldn't have what? Killed someone for you? How about two someones? How about going on *three* someones?"

"Patti, don't...don't hurt Darla. If you care..." His mind raced. How fast could he get the cops there? Could he some how keep her on the phone while he called them?

"The bitch is as good as dead, okay? So forget that. What I want to talk about now is the kid."

Haley.

"You call the police or screw things up in any way and I'll kill her, too. Do you understand?"

"Let me speak to Darla, Patti...please." He felt tears spill out over his lashes and he felt so weak. So powerless.

"Behave yourself and it'll be the three of us. I'll be Haley's new mama. Screw me over, Gary, and I'll strangle her right now with her own Winnie-the-Pooh bathrobe belt."

He heard her small, guttural laugh, and he thought he would lose his mind. "Patti, please don't hurt my wife and daughter. I am begging you."

"Here. Say goodbye to your first wife."

He heard Patti laugh again and then a small, muffled voice came on the line. "Gary?" Darla sounded so afraid and helpless.

"Sweetheart, be brave. Keep her busy until I—"

"Until you what, asshole?" Patti's strident shriek was back on the line. "I told you! The bitch is history. Your only hope is for the kid now, understand? Do you fucking understand me?"

"Yes," he said, swallowing hard. "Yes, Patti, I do."

*****

When the attendants came by with plastic bags to collect their cups, Maggie felt a rush of energy fill her chest. She'd had plenty of time to plan exactly what she would do when they finally landed.

What she would *not* do was waste another moment calling the police. She would grab a taxi and go straight to Gary and Darla's in Midtown. At this time in the evening, she could probably make it there in under thirty minutes. If she was lucky—if they were all very very lucky—she would grab Darla and they would...well, she hadn't completely figured that part out. The last place she could go was her own apartment. Not with Laurent there. And she couldn't go to her folks' place because that would be the first place he would look for her.

Her seatmate gave his seatbelt a tug and she looked at him.

"Sorry I was such a basket case. You'll be rid of me soon."

He smiled at her. "I hope everything works out for you."

She turned away and thought of Patti and Elise and Darla and Laurent and Nicole. And with a growing feeling of dread, she wondered how likely that was.

*****

Burton hung up the phone and turned back to the blackboard.

"No answer?" Dave asked. He sat, lounging at his desk eating a piece of cold takeout pizza.

"It went straight to voicemail."

"Call the art director. What was his name?"

"Poke-along or something. Bizarre business, advertising. They're all basically freaks."

"Call him and ask if Parker was sleeping with anyone in the office. Ask about Maggie Newberry and Deirdre Potts specifically."

"Will do. What are you going to do?"

"I'm supposed to be home tonight at a reasonable hour. If you can handle this on your own, I'm going to head out."

"No prob. Which, by the way, is one of the many copious reasons why you won't find me slipping my neck in the old matrimonial noose."

"Yeah, right. *That's* why you're single. Just make the call. I'll follow up tomorrow on the driver of the truck."

*****

Patti sat at the table in the cluttered kitchen, boxes stacked on counters and kitchen chairs. "We'll go away, just the two of us, Gary and I. Perhaps Columbia, or maybe Mexico."

Afraid to speak, but convinced her fate was decided whether she did or not, Darla cleared her throat. "Why...why not just let him divorce me?" she asked in a whispery croak.

"*Divorce* you?" Patti's face contorted into a sneer. "You must think I'm a moron. Is that what you think, Darla? Do you think Patricia Stump is stupid?"

She slammed her hand down hard on the table beside the gun. She snatched it up and pointed it at Darla's head.

"Go into divorce court with that mewling brat of yours and stick us with alimony and child support while you take the house and the car and the agency? And then you would always be popping up in our lives. 'Haley needs shoes, Haley needs money for college, Haley needs, Haley needs." Stump put the gun to Darla's head and stroked her cheek with the barrel. "The only way Gary and I can begin our new life together is for me to erase his old one."

Darla was surprised she wasn't crying. The bitch was pointing a gun ten inches from the bridge of her nose, and she was just sitting there, continent and calm. *So this is what true fear does to you,* she thought numbly. *This is what facing your own death feels like.* Perhaps it was the realization that she was totally helpless that made her calm. There was no sense in trying to come up with a plan. Whatever was going to happen, was going to happen.

The sound of the doorbell made them both jump. Stump's finger twitched against the trigger. She lowered the weapon and looked suspiciously at Darla.

"I don't know who it is," Darla said, her eyes suddenly hopeful and desperate.

"Stay here and keep your mouth shut. I'll kill whoever it is if you so much as fart in here." Darla couldn't help but think the woman's mouth was a tight, nasty little slit that spewed her words like the snakes and toads from one of Haley's book of fairy tales. But she nodded.

Stump took the gun and walked to the front door.

Maggie stood on the porch and rang the doorbell a second time. Gary and Darla lived in an in-town tract subdivision with double and triple story elevations of stucco and brick. A typical bedroom community, it was virtually deserted by day.

She noticed it looked pretty deserted right now, too.

The house was quiet, but she knew Darla was home because she could see lights on upstairs and in the back of the house. She practically vibrated with excitement and anticipation. Just to see Darla's face was going to feel like such a relief after that agonizing trip from hell, where she went through every imaginable possible scenario—and all of them bad. In one nightmarish image, she discovered Darla's body hanging from her favorite apple tree out back. She shook the image out of her mind. In less than an hour, the two of them would be comfortably holed up in a luxury room at the Buckhead Ritz with room service.

She heard footsteps coming to the front door and shifted her purse onto her shoulder, ready to embrace her friend and feel the titanic relief of their escape.

The door swung open to reveal Patti Stump in a purple pantsuit, grinning at her from behind a large ugly handgun that was pointed right at her.

"This is Christmas morning, you showing up here, Maggie. That's all I can say. You're dead. You know that, right?" Stump grabbed Maggie by her jacket and jerked her into the house.

Chapter Thirty-Two

She lay on the large, queen-size bed. The house was quiet now. No more screaming or phones ringing. Patti rolled over and buried her face in one of the cotton floral pillowcases. Her heart quickened as Gary's distinct scent filled her nostrils. *This must be the side he sleeps on.* Here's where he dreams and reads and makes love. A jarring thought pierced her when she called an image to mind of her beloved locked in a passionate embrace with either of the creatures downstairs. She replaced the picture with a more vivid one of herself and Gary, together finally, in this bed.

A thought came to her and she got up and walked to the closet. On the floor amongst his shoes was the laundry basket. She pulled out a man's blue and white striped dress shirt. She held it to her face and breathed deeply.

She peeled off her violet-colored pullover and tossed it onto the bed. She slipped the soiled button-down over her shoulders and fastened it up to her neck. Raising an arm to her face, she smelled the fabric. Now, whenever she wanted to, she could access him.

Patti moved to an old maple dresser standing against one wall of the bedroom. She pulled open the drawers one by one. Underwear, undershirts, socks, his passport, bowties, cufflinks, a Father's Day card, a packet of condoms.

Patti held the condoms in her hand and reflected on how she felt about finding them. Deciding that they were his commitment not to have any more children by the bitch downstairs, she replaced them in the drawer. Her fingers touched a greeting card in the drawer. *To the man I married on our anniversary.*

Feeling instantly annoyed and agitated, she turned and left the room, scooping up the Glock from the bed as she did.

Time to do it, she thought. *Time to finish it.*

Darla sat next to Maggie, who was now also bound in one of the kitchen chairs. Stump had pressed packing tape to their mouths, and so the two sat mutely watching each other, as if willing the other to be either solution or solace.

Darla knew it was all over. She knew it was going to end right here at her own kitchen table, her own macaroni-and-cheese-hot-soup-and-tea kitchen table. A bizarre thought came to her. *She and Gary had made love on this table once.* She wished she was ungagged just long enough to tell the crazy bitch *that*. She looked at Maggie. She looked dazed and scared. Darla felt a rush of guilt.

"Botched it with you once, Maggie," Stump said as she entered the kitchen, wagging the gun at her. "Remember all that great advice you gave me? About how to make a man run for his life from you? Remember that? You bitch. I'm going to enjoy killing you more than wifey here." Without another word, she placed the barrel of the Glock to Darla's temple, her finger quivering on the trigger.

"Bye, wifey. Time to become the ex-wifey."

*****

"What are you doing still here? Thought you were heading out."

"Got cornered by Jamisons downstairs and then realized I left my jacket and cell phone up here. Any luck on that phone call?"

"The art director said Parker was scheduled to be out of town tonight."

"Okay. So?"

"He also said it was commonly known that the media director, Patricia Stump, was infatuated with him. He made it sound like maybe it wasn't...healthy."

A silence mushroomed between the two of them and they stood looking at the blackboard. Burton grabbed his jacket from the back of his desk chair and strode to the door.

"Bring the address," he said over his shoulder.

*****

Maggie saw Darla squeeze her eyes shut and the movie of exactly what was going to happen in front of her played out in her head. She screamed behind her gag as loudly as she could and was rewarded with Stump snapping her head around to look at her.

"Got something to say, Maggie? Oh, this I gotta hear. If you scream, though, I shoot you both and no more fucking around." Stump tucked the gun under her arm and grabbed the tape on Maggie's mouth. When she ripped it off, Maggie felt a layer of skin go with it and she couldn't help her cry of pain.

Stump pointed the gun at Maggie and grinned. "You could beg for your life. I'd listen to that."

"You can't seriously think you'll get away with this," Maggie said, her lips on fire from the removal of the packing tape.

"Why not? No one talked to me about either your sister's death or Deirdre's. Isn't that wild? The cops interviewed *Pokey* but not me! Did you know that eighty-two percent of all non domestic murders in this country go unsolved?"

"You killed Elise instead of me. Why?"

"That is a very good question, Maggie. Why, indeed?"

"It couldn't be a case of mistaken identity. You knew I wouldn't be home from the office in the middle of the day."

"That's true. But the idiot I sent to do the job didn't know that."

"You...you hired a guy?"

"And learned once and for all that if you want something done right, etc."

"Okay, so he killed Elise thinking she was me. Then what were *you* doing there?"

"How do you know I was there?"

"I found something you dropped."

"Yes, well, when the moron called to say he'd finished the job and I knew for a fact that you had just left the office to go shopping at Lenox Square, I then also knew he'd screwed up. So I went to see for myself."

"And you were in the crowd of gawkers in my apartment building."

"Everyone was buzzing everyone else in. A very friendly bunch in your building. When I saw the cops taking names and statements, I left."

"This is different, Patti. You can't just execute us tied to kitchen chairs. The cops will pick you up before you've driven a hundred miles."

"Well, first off, Maggie, I'm not going anywhere. I'm waiting here for Gary to come home. And second of all, I've done my research. You don't think I've seen CSI? Every piece of evidence in this house will point to the inevitable conclusion that you and wifey here duked it out over who gets Gary. Sadly, you killed each other in the process. I'm not stupid you know. I've given this at least as much thought as the average crime show scriptwriter."

The arrogance of the woman was as unnerving as the gun she kept waving at Maggie. *Patti really thinks she can outmaneuver the police because she's become a forensic expert through watching television.*

"But this time, Gary knows," Maggie said.

"Gary loves me. He's upset right now, but he'll be fine in time."

"You're crazy." It had just slipped out, but from the expression on Patti's face it had hit home, too.

"And you're minutes from being dead, Maggie. I'm actually doing you a favor," she said, turning to Darla. "Gary's practically in love with her as it is. You should see the two of them together in the office."

Maggie knew their only hope was to stall long enough that something might happen. A miracle might happen. Anything. Just something besides their deaths. She looked at Darla and saw that tears were streaming down her face. Stump noticed them too.

"Aw, don't fret. We'll raise little...what's her name? Doesn't matter. I'll change it anyway, if I don't kill her. I know Gary wants to emigrate and that fits perfectly for us starting over together."

She put the gun barrel to Darla's head. "Time to finish this ladies. I got a date with a widower."

Burton stepped across the front lawn and sidled around to the back of the house. These new housing designs made his job easier, since they eliminated all side windows. A beam of light at the back of the house pushed through the row of oleander bushes crowding the kitchen door. The light illuminated the back yard and the trunks of the trees in the woods behind.

Moving as quietly as he could, while still being mindful that Kazmaroff's watch was usually fast when timing ten-minute rear entries, Burton heard the first sound of voices coming from inside the house. His heart beat quicker. He crouched on the small deck under the large kitchen window. Through it, he could see two women tied to chairs, their backs to him, and another—dressed like some kind of homeless person—waving the familiar, angular shape of a Glock semi-automatic pistol. In the instant it took Burton to process the scene, the armed woman brought the gun to the head of one of the seated women.

And then the front doorbell rang.

No! Too soon!

The gunwoman froze. She looked over her shoulder toward the front door, then scanned the kitchen frantically, as though looking for an intruder to suddenly materialize. The expression on her face reminded Burton of a cornered, wild animal, but her gun hand never wavered from the woman's head.

Would she try to answer the door? Would she make a run for it? *Jesus, would she kill her hostages first?* He aimed his Smith & Wesson pistol but one of the hostages was in the way.

Think, man, think! She's not gonna wait forever.

The impact of the brick as it hit the seven-foot expanse of window in the breakfast nook felt like a nuclear explosion to Maggie. She screamed and forced her chair to fall over on its side, crashing into Darla and knocking hers down too. She could hear Stump screaming and shooting out the back window.

"I'll kill you, you bastard! Is that you, Gary? She's dead, you bastard! I killed her! I killed her! I killed her!"

Maggie squeezed her eyes shut against the bedlam and heard what sounded like a tank coming through the front of the house as Kazmaroff smashed his way in. He barreled down the hallway to the kitchen, knocking over packing boxes as he went.

From where she lay on the floor, Maggie saw him appear in the doorway to the kitchen, window blinds still attached to him from his entrance through the front window.

He held his gun in front of him. "Police! Drop your weapon!"

Maggie could tell that Stump had frozen, and that she was still facing the back yard, where the brick had come from.

"Police!" he shouted again. "Drop it!"

Without moving, Patti lifted her arm as if she were going to drop the gun, then casually straightened her arm to let it hang by her side——pointing downward at Darla's head.

Kazmaroff shot her three times in a tight cluster in the back of Gary's pinstriped shirt.

Murder in the South of France

Chapter Thirty-Three

Maggie sat with Darla in the back of the police cruiser, each with a blanket around their shoulders. They didn't speak. They didn't need to. They were safe now and there were no more monsters in the night.

Burton and Kazmaroff were too engaged with the clean up of the aftermath of the night to do much beyond take basic statements from them, but she knew they felt as if they had redeemed themselves.

Who knows? Maybe they had.

When Burton handed her his cellphone to call someone to come get her, she didn't have the energy or the emotional strength to think very hard. She knew she needed to be home and protected and loved and cared for.

She'd called Laurent.

She closed her eyes and felt the exhaustion of two long, sleepless days of anxiety and terror.

"When did you know it was her?" Darla whispered to her.

Maggie shook her head. "Way too late," was all she said.

Darla took her hand and squeezed it. "We're alive, Maggie. It was just in time."

Gary arrived in a whirl of tears and hugs, having made the trip from Savannah in under three hours—the last forty minutes with a police escort. Maggie watched him and Darla cling to each other for dear life. She closed her eyes again and imagined she was back on the airplane, or maybe back in Paris. When she opened them again, Laurent was there. He knelt by her where she sat in the police car and took her hand.

He knew she knew. His eyes said as much. And it was all too much tonight.

Without a word, he picked her up and carried her back to their car, and their apartment in Buckhead.

Maggie slept for the entire weekend.

She was vaguely aware that Laurent was bringing her food, tucking her in, watching her. But for the most part, she just let the week she had endured fall over her and through her, and when she awoke on Sunday she knew she had come out on the other side.

That morning, she sat in the living room of her apartment and waited for Laurent to bring in their coffees. While he hadn't made an overture to her beyond that of a friend, neither had he moved to the couch at night.

She took her first lucid look at the world around her since she had emerged from her sleep, and her nightmare. For the first time in six months, she realized she didn't care if Burton and Kazmaroff ever called her again. She registered that she didn't need to know one thing more than she already did about Elise or Deirdre's last hours.

Ever.

It was over and done. Except for Laurent. She watched him as he moved into the living room. It always amazed her to see the way he moved, so graceful and silent for someone of his size. She dropped the afghan that had been on her lap and stood. She moved, with her hands on her hips, to put the couch between them.

She had things to say to him.

"You lied."

Laurent watched her move behind the couch, but he would have none of that. Too many things had come between them, beginning with the way they'd met. He wouldn't allow it now, of all times. Her took her by the arm and gently moved her back to sit next to him on the couch.

"*And* you let me believe what we did was a one-night stand. No contact from you for nearly six months!"

He widened his eyes, and it was all he could do not to smile at the absurdity of this complaint leading the pack of all the much, much worse ones. "You are only bringing this up now?"

"It's been on my mind, believe me!"

He could see she was becoming more upset the more she talked. "I perhaps should have called," Laurent conceded. "But I couldn't come right away because I had to wrap up some business."

"Skulduggery business? Monkey business?"

"Business that could not be left undone."

"You were only in it for the money." She crossed her arms in front of her chest, as if to guard her body against him or to protect herself from his gaze.

"How much melodrama do you think I should allow?" he asked, smiling drily. "Is this the price I must pay for a few lies?"

"Lying is bad, Laurent! I know there's a culture difference here, but I would've thought even the French were on board with that. You lied. To me."

"*Je suis desolee.*" *I'm sorry.*

"Which reminds me, your English has improved remarkably."

He shrugged. "I am on trial for my language proficiency now? If it consoles you, I always had trouble understanding you." He smiled.

"Everything between us was a lie."

"Surely not everything, *chèrie*. Are your reactions to my caresses a lie? Are your whimpers when you are under me a lie?"

"Stop saying things like that! Why is it you think you're in control, Laurent? You bilked my family out of thirty thousand *euros*! You pawned off a street urchin as a member of my family. You took advantage of us when we were at our most fragile—when Elise died!"

"Did you remember that when Nicole died, I too lost a niece?"

Maggie sucked in a breath. He could see her mind working. *He was Gerard's brother. Nicole's uncle.* "I had forgotten that," she admitted. "But that just means you were in a good position to take advantage of the situation."

"I won't apologize for who I am."

"I don't know which is worse—being a criminal or being proud of it."

He shrugged, and he could see that she was interpreting it as a gesture of nonchalance. The way she sat watching him, her face flushed, her eyes flashing, he realized he desired her strongly at this moment.

"I can't bear to think of how you were involved with the whole Elise and Nicole thing. I can't bear to look at you when I think of it."

Laurent sighed. "Your sister's story is not our story." He pointed to the two of them on the couch. "*Nicole's* story is not our story either. Neither of those sad stories has to do with you and me, together. Only you and I can write our story."

She made a face. "Then our story is built on lies."

"Am I the only one who lied? Did you not attempt to see Gerard, *twice,* after I told you not to?" He saw her hesitate, unsure. Guilty.

"You can't tell me what to do."

"That's not the point. The point is you said you would not see him. You promised me."

"It's not the same."

"I am eager to hear how it is not. Yours was a lie by omission."

"And yours was a deliberate con. In fact, you were conning me all along."

"If that is so then answer this: what is it I wanted from you?"

Maggie frowned at him, but he could see she was processing the question.

"What do you mean?"

"It is not a difficult question, *chèrie.* What do I want from you?" He could see her mind visiting all the possible ways he could be taking advantage of her. In truth, she had probably visited those possibilities many times since she'd found out who he really was.

He would not allow her any more self-indulgent complaints. If she had discovered even *one* thing that he had taken from her—and he knew she must have searched desperately to find it—she would be able to answer him now.

"I know what you want," she said, the anger draining from her face. He thought she had never looked more beautiful. Her eyes were large and trusting—*ahhhh, my Maggie*—her lips were full and quivered ever so slightly.

"What is it, *mon ange?*" he asked softly, touching her arm with his fingers, a moment away from bringing her to him. "What is it I want?"

"My heart." She spoke the words as if she didn't realize she was saying them out loud, as if she hadn't realized she'd known all along.

He nodded and his fingers wrapped around her arm. "Your heart."

He pulled her into his arms and her hands went to his face as he nuzzled her neck, her long hair hiding them both. "You had mine from that first week in Cannes. You cannot doubt that, *chèrie*."

He felt her soften in his arms. "No more lies, Laurent.

"There will be lies, *chèrie*. Man is imperfect."

She stiffened again. "Laurent, for us to continue, you must promise never to lie to me again."

"I cannot promise that, *chèrie*. I may need to lie to you in order to protect you or to do something that I believe is important. You see that, yes?"

She gave a gasp of frustration and incredulity.

"But while I cannot promise I won't lie to you, I can promise to always protect you and to love you."

Maggie looked at him, her eyes wide with longing. "But if we throw out all the rules touted in every women's magazine in practically every nail salon in the world, how will I know if we're going to be okay?"

Laurent ran his hand down her shoulder and smiled. "Don't worry, *chèrie*. You will know." Then he lowered her onto the couch and proceeded to end the discussion once and for all.

*****

Gary walked away from the gate and patted down his jacket pockets. He kept his wife and daughter in view at all times. In time, I'll calm down, he thought. After a while, I'll be able to relax again.

He watched Darla sitting in one of the long lines of plastic airport chairs, a roll of magazines in one hand and little Haley's mittened hand in the other. She seemed very animated as she talked to Laurent. Only the clutching hand holding her daughter told a different story.

"I guess you got everything?" Maggie stood next to Gary in the airport gift shop and watched him anxiously.

He tapped his inside coat pocket. "Passports, visas, *beaucoups* American dollars, and a representative sampling of Kiwi dollars. Want to see them? They're very pretty." He stuck his hand in his jacket and pulled out a few pastel money notes in purple and pink.

"Very nice."

"I was tempted to bring Monopoly money, but Darla assured me the vendors Down Under would be too sophisticated for that."

Maggie shook her head. "I just don't know what to say."

"You act like you're at a funeral."

"I'm losing a dear friend."

"There are daily flights to Auckland."

"And applications for the next space shuttle, too. Excuse me for thinking neither is a very viable possibility for me."

"You choose your own limitations."

"Oh, thank you, Dale Carnegie. And I want to officially apologize for that crack I made in the car."

"You mean the one about Kiwi fruit causing cancer? Forget it. Darla will explain Auntie Maggie's sense of humor to Haley, and I'm sure we'll get her to eat fruit again."

"I'm going to miss you."

"I'll miss you too, Maggie. But you'll visit. We'll come back here for visits."

"Won't you be afraid of being gunned down in the concourse if you come back to the U.S.?" Maggie instantly regretted saying it.

"Well, no," Gary said slowly. "Not being a fanatic or obsessive or anything. I think I can handle bringing my family back for a visit from time to time."

They were both quiet a moment. Gary smiled at Darla and waved to his daughter where they sat with Laurent.

"I forgot to ask you how you knew that it was Patti," he said, quietly.

"It was her scarf ring that made it all click for me."

"Her what?"

"It's something women use sometimes as an accessory with scarves. Patti lived by them. Brownie found it in the hallway the afternoon Elise was killed and he'd pocketed it. Anyway, he gave it to me thinking it might be important, only he didn't know what it was. I knew it was a scarf ring, but it wasn't until I was sitting in the cemetery at Montmartre that it finally came to me where I'd seen it."

Gary shook his head.

"Yeah, only about a million times stuck on Patti's graceful bosom. And that's when I knew." Maggie rubbed her arms as if a terrible chill had come into the room. "She'd been there that day. When her hired killer called to say the job was done, she knew it couldn't be me since I'd just left the office to go shopping." She shivered. "Anyway, as soon as I made the office connection—Deirdre and all that—well, the rest of it fell into place."

"You said on the phone that the cops got the hit man who killed your sister?"

"They did. With help from the private detective my father hired to track him down."

Gary nodded, then turned to throw a pack of gum on the counter at the newspaper kiosk. "How about Laurent? You got that sorted out yet?"

"He's told so many lies about so many things...it's hard for me to get past that. He's got a lot of good reasons for much of it, and some very lame reasons for other stuff." She made a helpless gesture with her hand. "My Dad likes him."

"I suppose that's good."

"He's not what I thought he was. Not as wonderful, but not as awful." She ran a hand through her combed hair, knocking loose a restraining barrette. "Of all the things he's lied about," Maggie said, watching Laurent as he stood talking with Darla, "I do believe he loves me."

"*Quelle surprise, mon amie,*" Gary said, smiling.

Maggie gave him a long hug. "Good-bye, boss. Show 'em how to do real American retail advertising down there."

"I fully intend to," Gary said, wiping a quick tear away. "The starburst price-point and the use of oversized type is about to arrive in the land of sheep and honey. Antipodal advertising will never be quite the same again."

"Nor on this side of the world either, dear friend."

*****

The little dog cocked its head, causing a small scruffy ear to flop into one of its eyes. It sat, attentive and enduring, in Nicole's lap. The little girl's small fingers pressed into the animal's fur.

"*Grandmère* says he's got fleas," Nicole said, her face screwed into a mask of serious concern.

Maggie stood by the fireplace in the library of her parents' home and watched the flames. Christmas was a week away and she never remembered their home looking or feeling more enchanting. The whole mansion smelled of fir boughs and toasted cinnamon sticks, with the scent of even greater, impending wonders wafting in the air.

Maggie moved from her position by the fireplace and sat down next to Nicole on the overstuffed settee. She could hear the low rumble of male voices as Laurent and her father conversed in the den down the hall. The puppy looked at her with solemn, large brown eyes. She touched its soft fur.

"I have a *cadeau* for you, Nicole. An early present."

Nicole looked up questioningly into Maggie's eyes, her little hands momentarily stopped in their incessant searching of the dog's coat.

"Is it from *Maman?*"

Maggie bit her lip. "In a way," she said, placing the glittering bracelet of charms in Nicole's lap of swans' down and cashmere. "It belonged to your mother when she was a little girl."

Nicole touched the tiny charms with her fingers, lifting the bracelet up to watch the tinkling figurines. An ice skater, a ballerina, a miniature horse and rider, a typewriter, a Cocker Spaniel dog.

An easel.

Nicole looked into Maggie's eyes and smiled.

"*Merci,* Aunt Maggie."

Maggie's story continues in *Murder à la Carte* where she agrees to move to France temporarily with Laurent who has just inherited a vineyard. While the two move into the ancient stone farmhouse to ready it and the surrounding land to be sold, it does appear to Maggie that Laurent is settling in rather too comfortably for her taste.

In the meantime, Maggie combats expatriate boredom by trying to solve her village's oldest mystery–and its newest murder–both at the same time. Along the way she meets two new sets of friends–both American–and both destined to change her life forever.

Murder in the South of France

ABOUT THE AUTHOR

Susan Kiernan-Lewis lives in Nocatee, Florida and writes about France, mysteries and romance. Like many authors, Susan depends on reviews and word of mouth referrals by her readers. If you enjoyed *Murder in the South of France*, please consider leaving a review saying so on Amazon.com, Barnesandnoble.com or Goodreads.com. And *merci* in advance. And finally, don't forget that there are four more books in the Maggie Newberry Mystery Series: *Murder à la Carte, Murder in Provence, Murder in Paris* and *Murder in Aix.* Visit Susan's website at susankiernanlewis.com and feel free to contact her at sanmarcopress@me.com.

Murder in the South of France

30262171R00219

Made in the USA
Lexington, KY
24 February 2014